LUSH

LUSH

LAUREN DANE

HEAT | NEW YORK

THE BERKLEY PUBLISHING GROUP
Published by the Penguin Group
Penguin Group (USA) Inc.
375 Hudson Street, New York, New York 10014, USA

USA / Canada / UK / Ireland / Australia / New Zealand / India / South Africa / China

Penguin Books Ltd., Registered Offices: 80 Strand, London WC2R 0RL, England
For more information about the Penguin Group, visit penguin.com.

This book is an original publication of The Berkley Publishing Group.

ISBN 978-1-62490-362-5

PRINTED IN THE UNITED STATES OF AMERICA

Cover art by Tony Mauro.
Cover design by Rita Frangie.

This one is for Ray.

ACKNOWLEDGMENTS

A special thank-you to all the musicians whose art kept me company and on track throughout the writing of *Lush*: Lykke Li, Kings of Leon, Garbage, Neko Case, Foo Fighters and many more.

Mary, Fatin and Renee—thank you three for being the best beta readers anyone could ask for.

Leis Pederson, my wonderful editor—thank you for all your hard work to make me better at this.

Thanks, as always, go to my agent and friend Laura Bradford.

Friends—Megan Hart, who always appreciates a good beefcake link. To my Secret Author Illuminati Ninjas at the List That Shall Not Be Named—thank you all so much for your support, for the laughs, the indignation and the endless information and education on all things writing, publishing and other important stuff like hot dudes.

But let there be spaces in your togetherness and let the winds of the heavens dance between you. Love one another but make not a bond of love: let it rather be a moving sea between the shores of your souls.

—KHALIL GIBRAN

1
....

Damien clapped his buddy Adrian on the back. "Thanks for the invite."

Adrian Brown tipped his chin. "Glad you were in town to come. Least I could do after you've been in the studio with me so much."

Adrian had needed a drummer. Damien was a drummer. End of story. Plus it had been awesome to work with someone he respected as much as he did Adrian and his sister Erin.

He'd been in a band with his brothers since they were nineteen, twenty and twenty-two. They'd made a lot of music together, they knew each other well, worked magic most of the time. But it did something good for his soul to work with other people.

He'd met Adrian several years ago and they'd clicked. Hell, they even shared a manager and a record label.

Plus, he liked Bainbridge with its small-town appeal, though it was just across the water from Seattle.

Tonight was Adrian's engagement party. He was set to marry the lovely Gillian in one month, something else Damien would be back for.

"Come on through. I'm looking for Gillian and I'll bet you she's in the kitchen trying to dislodge Jules or Mary."

The gorgeous old farmhouse the party was being held at was the backdrop to the yard, which was dotted with tables and conversation areas. There were little tented areas in case of rain, which thankfully had missed them that day. Pretty lights in the trees and candles flickering all over the place.

It was pretty. Simple. Full of friends and laughter. It reminded him an awful lot of the ranch his family lived on.

"I go to parties like this one very rarely. I wish it was more often."

Adrian gave him a lopsided grin as they moved through the front room toward the kitchen. Damien heard feminine voices and laughter and quickened his step.

"The road has its charms. Nice hotels—well, a lot nicer than in the old days anyway. Travel to lots of places. Swanky parties. But this life?" Adrian waved as they came around the corner into a kitchen filled with activity. "With my friends and my family. No paparazzi. No drama. Just great food and drink. That keeps me grounded and sane. Makes me happy."

Damien tended to agree. Though he did like fast cars, parties and fast women, he appreciated the slower pace on the ranch his entire family lived on. There would be no games here tonight. No label people to impress or to try to impress you. It was real people, and god knew he needed that.

A pretty blonde scooted out the back door and he was disappointed, as he loved a pretty blonde. But then he saw *her*. Dark hair held back from her face though acres of curls strained at their confinement.

She was bent over a counter, slicing a tomato. Her hands glistened against the red flesh. He'd seen women cut up tomatoes hundreds of times over his life and had never actually gotten wood. Until that moment.

And when she looked up, it was on a full-throated laugh as Gillian put her head on Curly's shoulder, also laughing. Gillian was friendly and sweet, but this woman was clearly comfortable with her friend, totally open.

"English, there you are." Adrian stepped to his fiancée to give her a kiss.

Gillian smiled up at him. "I was trying to shoo Mary out of here. I already got Jules gone. Thank goodness for Cal, who was more than willing to help with that. But Mary is being difficult."

Mary. Ah, a name then.

Mary gave Gillian a somber look. "I have problems with authority."

Damien laughed.

Curly glanced up to catch his eye. "Hey there. Damien Hurley is standing in Gideon's kitchen."

And then . . . he blushed. Damien couldn't recall the last time he'd blushed, but it had been a while.

"Mary Whaley, this is Damien Hurley. Damien, this is Mary;

she's responsible for the food you *will* gorge yourself on. Trust me on this. Once you start, you can't stop. She's also our very dear friend."

Gillian wrapped an arm around Mary's shoulder, beaming. Clearly so very proud. Damien couldn't help but respond in kind.

"I'd shake your hand, but mine are covered in tomato." She held them up. "Hang on, let me wash up."

He watched as she moved to the sink. As she washed her hands with precision she spoke over her shoulder to one of the servers. She dried off and then removed the apron.

Wow.

Underneath the apron she wore a dress that hugged her curves. And she had them.

"I'm so glad you went with that color." Gillian beamed and Damien agreed.

"Raspberry sorbet." Damien hadn't meant to say that out loud.

Mary looked to him, holding her hand out. He took it in both of his, bending to kiss her knuckles instead.

"Pleasure to meet you."

"Please tell your mother I said she raised you right."

"You smell like vanilla and cinnamon." Why he kept blurting stupid shit, he had no idea. He was normally far more finessed at this. "That's a compliment, by the way."

She laughed. "I made some coffee for my brother, Cal. He likes vanilla and cinnamon in it."

He liked the sound of her laugh.

"Mary, out of the kitchen now. I know you've pestered your

staff more than enough. Everything is wonderful. I want you to enjoy this party and I forbid you to do any more work." Gillian snatched something off a tray and popped it in Adrian's mouth.

"Okay, okay. I just want everything to be perfect."

Damien bent his arm and held it in her direction. "Shall we go outside then?"

"All right."

So, yeah, she knew Gillian would only tolerate her fussing with the food for so long before she nagged her to stop and come enjoy the party. But to up her game with this?

Damien Hurley sat across the table from her, drinking champagne and laughing with Miles, Adrian and Gillian's son, before Miles grabbed his plate and ambled off with his friends.

He was a thousand times more arresting in person than he was on the television screen. Long and tall—and she had a weakness for long and lanky—he seemed to take up the air in the room when she'd looked up to find him standing in the kitchen with Adrian.

He had dark hair, a bit too long, so it flopped down over his eye every once in a while so he'd have to push it back. A casual gesture that worked wonders with the muscles in his biceps. Drumming muscles.

A rogue's eyes, her mother would say. Big, fringed with lashes as dark as the hair on his head. Intelligent with the light of humor in them. His lips were framed by a neatly trimmed mustache and beard. She knew too that he had lots of great ink on his body, though most of it was hidden by the clothes he wore.

He had energy. Even as he relaxed he seemed to hum with it. She tended to like that, as she was the same sort. And he kissed her knuckles. Who kissed knuckles?

"Are you thinking dirty things?" Daisy slid into the chair next to Mary. "And if so, fess up."

Daisy was Mary's closest, dearest friend. She had few filters, a heart bigger than Texas, was an incredibly talented artist and dancer and was absolutely gorgeous. If it weren't for all the other stuff, it would be easy not to like her at all.

Damien swiveled to catch her eye. "Dirty, huh? We all need to hear."

Mary, admittedly, was surprised he didn't seem to give Daisy a second glance. Daisy was, well, the aforementioned gorgeous.

"Pay no attention to her. She's trying to start trouble." Mary waved a hand in Daisy's direction.

Daisy laughed. "True. But that doesn't mean I don't know that look on your face."

"Don't you have a handsome man to poke at?" Mary looked around for Levi, Daisy's boyfriend. Man friend. Lover. Whatever. They'd found something powerful together and Mary liked Levi a great deal. Very few people would be good enough for her friend. He managed to be.

"He's off with Brody talking tattoos. And who are you then?" Daisy smiled up at Damien.

"This is Damien, he's a friend of Adrian's. Damien, this is Daisy." Gillian made the introductions.

"Nice to meet you." Daisy grabbed a server as he passed with a tray. "What's this? I haven't had this one yet."

"Figs with cheese and prosciutto. You had these just a few days ago."

"Oh, yes. Then I need several because they are fabulous." True to her word, Mary watched as Daisy grabbed three little plates and put them down on the table. "I got one for you, Damien, because you didn't have any and you should." She pushed one his way and then dug into hers.

Damien obediently took a bite and Mary got sort of sweaty when he closed his eyes for a moment and sighed happily. Normally she liked it when people enjoyed her food, but this, well, he was delicious.

"This." He nodded solemnly.

Warmth flooded her. "Thank you. People often miss how good simple food can be. Fresh makes a difference too."

Mary tried to rein it in because she loved talking about food and ingredients and she could go on and on.

"She's an artist. You have music, she's got food."

Mary blushed. "Thank you, Adrian."

"She's doing the food for the wedding too. Next time you're in town we'll have to be sure to go to her supper club. Insanely good food."

"I'll be back for the wedding next month."

Her heart sped for a few moments. It would be fun to flirt with him again.

Adrian looked back and forth between them and leaned to say something to Gillian, who nodded. Mary knew that look on Gillian's face.

"Damien and his brothers are going on tour with us."

"Really? Awesome. I saw you guys. Twice, actually. Once at Lollapalooza over at the Gorge. Another time Daisy and I drove down to see you in San Francisco."

Daisy mock-slapped her forehead. "I knew you looked familiar! Sweet Hollow Ranch, right?"

"That's us."

"We sat so freaking far back for both those shows. Up on the grass at the Gorge. Though when you go places with Mary she brings treats. So everyone else will be eating crappy eight-dollar nachos and she'll whip out fresh mozzarella and tomatoes. Tailgating is swankified with Mary on your side."

Damien wanted to reach over and kiss that mouth. Every time Mary spoke, her bottom lip was so juicy and shiny it began to make his cock throb in time with his pulse.

She seemed to gleam in the starlight and the glow of the fairy lights in the trees. He liked the way she lit up when she spoke with her friends. He liked the way she talked about food too.

"You'll have to come see us when we're touring then. I promise to get you better seats than up in the rafters if you'll bring me something tasty." Like that mouth.

One corner of said mouth tipped up and he had to strangle back a moan.

"All right. I'm getting pretty good at traveling with food."

"She can whip up a freaking gourmet meal from a convenience store on the dashboard of a car. She's amazing."

Damien also dug the way her friends spoke about her. Adrian had mentioned to him that Gillian had a very close group of friends there on the island. Clearly their love for one another was genuine and deep. It said a lot about a person—who loved them best.

"Who's that guy who keeps staring over here?" Damien asked Adrian in an undertone. The way the guy stared, he began to wonder if it was the boyfriend of one of the women at the table. Of Mary, which would totally bum him out.

"That's Cal. He's Mary's older brother. He's with the pretty blonde sitting across from him with the other blond guy. He's with her too. And with Cal."

This was the second triad he'd learned of in this group. Was it something in the water?

Big brother stares . . . Ah well, he'd had more than one in his lifetime. And this woman was clearly capable of handling herself anyway.

"Would you like a drink, Mary?" He stood.

"Yes, I would, thanks." She stood as well and he couldn't resist a leisurely tour from the toes of her shoes, up a pair of shapely legs over the breasts—good god, the breasts—the long neck and to her face. Gracious.

"The bar is over there." Mary indicated the opposite side of the yard before she took his arm.

"Did you always know you wanted to be a musician like Adrian and his sister?"

"My eldest brother Ezra works the ranch with my father. He'd bribe me and my brothers to do chores with the promise of being able to use the barn to practice music in. 'Course he was a wild one too, Ezra." He'd been in the band for a few years. But the road, the life wasn't meant for everyone. Ezra's demons had been rehab sized and he'd retired from the band to save his life.

Last year they'd renovated that barn and made it into a home studio.

"My parents are musical. They sang in the choir. My dad plays piano and guitar. They got me drums. Well, actually, my uncle got me drums to punish my dad." He laughed, pausing as they got to the bar.

She ordered a beer and he wasn't sure why, but he was charmed by that. He especially liked that she left a tip. He'd worked as a server and at parties like this one and had people treat him like crap. From then on, he'd always tipped generously.

"Anyway, so we lived in the country so it wasn't like we could get up to trouble anywhere else. So we rode horses and motor-cycles and then when I was nineteen, Paddy—that's my next eldest brother—and Ezra started a band for real. Vaughan and me, well we just went along because why not? Once we were all of age, we played shitty clubs and couch surfed and then my mother showed up and would spend a few months at a time with us. She'd rent a house and feed us, take care of stuff for us while we tried to hit it big. And then we did."

"I like your mom already."

"She's pretty impossible not to like. She'd pester you until you at least faked it. We wanted her to manage us but she refused. But she helped us find someone. That's how we met Adrian and Erin, actually; we share a manager. To this day our mom keeps an eye on our manager and the money people. She's smart about making sure we save for retirement and all that too."

Mary had to admit she liked that he seemed close with his

family. Her perception of musicians, especially at his and Adrian's level, used to be that of spoiled, self-centered jerks, but all the ones she'd actually met had been lovely and warm. Centered, even.

"What about you? Has this been a lifelong thing? Cooking?"

"I've always liked to cook. When I was little I used to make snacks for my brothers to get them to let me play with them. Of course later I figured out they got into a lot more trouble than I did, so playing with them involved punishment and/or injuries. My god. The stuff they used to do." She rolled her eyes.

"Anyway, it became a way for me to pay for things I wanted. Then I started these dinners at my house. One day a month. People kept saying they thought I should go into business. I started to believe it. First I had a food truck, which taught me a lot about business and dealing with regulations and all that. The dinner club grew more and more popular. I started getting a few catering jobs, which began to multiply. So I quit the truck and put down roots in a shop I share with my friend Jules. It's her shop actually and, oh my god, you just asked a simple question and here I go. Sorry, I talk a lot."

"I like to hear you talk, so that's a win. How about we sit over here and look out over the party and you can tell me more. Jules is the blonde with your brother, who was staring daggers at me earlier, right?"

She laughed. "He was? Oh, he's so silly. But he's my brother. My other one probably did too, but he's wilier than Cal."

He pulled a chair out for her and she sat, happy to be off her feet 'cause the heels she had on were pretty and all, but they hurt like hell.

"So hang on one sec." He dashed off, returning with a tray filled with all sorts of small plates. "I'm starving so I figured we could eat your food while you tell me the rest."

She sipped her beer. "I warned you. By the way, that sauce there"—she pointed—"is perfect to put on top of the strawberries."

He tried it and nodded. "What is this deliciousness?"

"Roasted strawberries with balsamic reduction. You like?"

"Hell yes, I like. Now, you started working from a shop. Continue. I'll be eating and listening."

"She runs a bakery called Tart. Probably, as you can figure out, the best tarts you've ever tasted, along with a variety of other awesome baked goods. So I put out some stuff from that evening's catering gigs if I have extra so people can buy it along with her pastry. I also moved my supper club to that space twice a week and we're fully booked for the next five months. So suddenly I'm very busy, but really excited about the prospects. It doesn't hurt that my friend is marrying a rock star who gives my card to all sorts of people who like to throw catered dinners."

"Wow. That's amazing. Congratulations."

"Thank you. To you as well."

Music started up in the background and he shoved a few mushrooms into his mouth. "I've got to run. We're doing a little something for Miles. He wanted to do a warm-up. You know, before the wedding. Which is a secret, so, god, don't tell Gillian."

"I can't wait to hear it. And, of course, your secret is safe. Gillian will be so pleased."

It wasn't something she'd really shared with Gillian, but she did love to watch a man at his art. Be it painting, dance, food

or music. The sight of Damien up there as he got behind his
drum kit made her tingly and a little wet.

He rolled his sleeves up before picking up the sticks, waiting
for Adrian as he spoke and addressed the crowd and his fiancée.

Gillian, Daisy and Jules stood to her left as they all watched.
She was glad she wore the waterproof mascara too, because
Adrian and Miles pulled out all the stops, showering Gillian with
love. What they had planned for the wedding would be even
more sniffle-worthy. Mary knew it would be a two-hanky day.

"You're so lucky." Mary leaned in to kiss Gillian's cheek.

"I am, yes." Gillian sniffed, dabbing her eyes with a handkerchief. "Thank you for being here to share it with me."

"Where else on Earth would I be?"

It wasn't his party. But he liked playing with Mary watching
anyway. He liked the way she cocked her head, the sway of her
hips. Sensual. Playing music always made him think of sex, and
while he did, he watched her watch him.

And imagined fucking the hell out of Ms. Mary Whaley.

Sadly, they hadn't any more time to really chat as the party
went on but they were never alone after that.

He kissed her cheek as he left, liking the way she blushed.
"See you next month at the wedding?"

"Definitely. I'm in it and you'll be eating my food too."

"Two great reasons to come back to Bainbridge then."

2

"That dress makes you look so sexy." Daisy winked as she gave Mary an up-and-down look.

Mary laughed, giving herself one last glance in the mirror. They were getting dressed for the wedding, which would start in an hour. Gillian was getting her makeup done and the rest of the bridal party sat around talking and laughing.

"Yeah?"

"Double yeah. The drummer's gonna love it."

"I didn't choose this dress for him." This was technically true because the dress was one they all wore as bridesmaids in the wedding. Daisy had one on too. As did Jules and Erin, Adrian's sister.

"Gurl, I saw him looking at you. He wants to take a bite. And you should let him."

"Daisy, I think you should take a class on how to say what you really feel. You're so shy."

Daisy laughed. "I'd try to fix you up with Levi's older brother Jonah, but I think he's an even bigger handful than Levi and you already have a full-time job. But a little rock-star action sure has done wonders for Gillian. Why not you?"

Mary shook her head, trying not to laugh. "You have a one-track mind."

"Because I'm getting some on the regular-like."

"As it happens"—Mary looked around—"he's pretty smoking hot."

Daisy clapped her hands, her eyes lit with mischief. "I knew it!"

"'Course you did. I told you."

"Well, you said he was cute and you two had sparks. You gonna get some today?"

"I'm a little busy today, it being my friend's wedding and all."

"So I guess you don't need to know he was asking about you earlier."

Mary narrowed her eyes. "He was?"

"I was in the kitchen grabbing some coffee when he came through with Adrian. Asked all casual and stuff, *'Hey, anyone seen Mary around?'* I told you were obsessively scaring your staff most likely but would be around later today."

"I do not scare my staff."

Daisy waved it away with a perfectly manicured hand. Which was unusual, as she usually had paint and other stuff in her cuticles. "I'm not playing make-believe with you. I know exactly where you've been because that's also where Jules was. Anyway, it was nice that you weren't here when he asked. Gives you some mystery."

"Mystery? Yes, nothing more mysterious than a caterer making sure the basil is nice and fresh."

"And it was, wasn't it?"

Mary scoffed at the very question. Of course it was. As if she'd serve anything else.

Raven turned from where she'd been working on Gillian. "You two. Ready for your makeup?"

"Ready as I'll ever be."

"You sit there and I'll just do you both at once. No, you don't get any say in what colors I use. I know what's best and I don't work with others well unless I'm in charge."

"That sounded totally dirty and bossy." Daisy beamed.

Raven paused and then laughed. "It did. Wouldn't be the first time I've done two at once."

"You really need to share those details. Keep us entertained while you work."

"A lady doesn't kiss and tell. So I guess it's good I'm not a lady."

"Do tell." Daisy leaned forward and Mary held still while Raven put a drape over her dress so no makeup got on it.

"I'm positively boring compared to Jules and Erin."

Mary laughed at that as Jules and Erin both snorted. "You're many things. Boring isn't one."

Raven was . . . well, not boring, that was true. She lacked filters, which made her hard to deal with in more than small doses. She was defended, closed off. But at the same time, she went out of her way to help Gillian. Even though Raven and Adrian did not like one another at all. And Erin, Adrian's sister and someone Mary liked a great deal, adored Raven.

There was more beneath the surface to this woman. Though Mary wasn't sure she'd ever know just exactly what. Or even that she wanted to know. But one thing was certain: Raven was compelling.

Especially as she told them randy details of a threesome she had some years before. Then again, it left Mary feeling a little itchy without anyone to scratch it for her.

She thought about asking for a different color lipstick, but Raven would have ignored her anyway. Tattoos, piercings and makeup were Raven's art and she seemingly had all the confidence in the world over her choices.

And little tolerance for other opinions once she made up her mind. Mary wasn't entirely sure if she admired it or was annoyed by it. Probably a bit of both.

"I see you sneaking looks at that pink gloss. You don't need pink. Not with this dress and your hair. You're all dark and doe-eyed. Work it."

"You're scary."

Raven snorted. "I'm right."

She stepped back, handing Mary a mirror. She had to admit, Raven had indeed been correct. "You were right about the lipstick."

"Didn't I just say exactly that? Of course I was. I've been doing makeup since I was nine years old."

"Really? That's got to be some story." Daisy grinned. "I love the thing you did with my eyes."

Raven neatly dodged the reference to her story. "I like it too. You have the perfect face for it. The vintage thing works on you." She packed up her stuff. "Erin Brown, you are next. Get over there." She sent a look back over her shoulder to Mary and Daisy. "I'll see you both downstairs later. I hope Adrian realizes Gillian is way too good for him." She sniffed and gave her attention to Erin.

"She's like a hurricane," Daisy said under her breath.

Mary looked to Daisy. "Yeah. But she loves our Gillian, so that means she's got some sense."

Daisy hugged Mary. "Totally. Also? You look gorgeous. My god."

Mary blushed but sneaked a peek in the mirror. She sort of did. If she saw Damien Hurley, and if he made the right move at the right time, she might just, you know, let him get on it.

"You're totally thinking about boning Damien Hurley." Jules came up behind them, putting an arm around each one of their waists.

"Jeez, you know, you ladies get boyfriends and suddenly everything is about sex."

Jules rolled her eyes. "I suppose it's probably true that when you have someone who makes your life really nice, you want that for your friends. Also, it means we want every last dirty detail afterward."

Mary snickered. "Look, this is all conjecture. He's hot, and if the tabloids are telling any truth at all, he's a legend with the sexytimes and all. But this is *not* what you have with Gideon and Cal, not what Gillian has with Adrian, or what Daisy has with Levi. If it happens, it'll be hot sex and then it'll be over. I'm not looking for a relationship and you know he sure isn't."

She had a career that was finally taking off. A business to run. Family and friends to be with. She had no time, and really no real desire for a romance. Hot sex? Sure. Forever? Too busy.

Damien milled around the yard, trying, not so sneakily, to locate Mary. He'd heard her voice a few times. Heard people talking about her. Had even asked her friend Daisy about her earlier when he'd bumped into her in the kitchen of Adrian and Gillian's house.

He supposed he'd see her when she came down the aisle in any case.

She'd been on his mind a lot in the month since he'd first met her. Had found himself looking forward to the wedding because he knew he'd be seeing her again. He'd even talked to his mom about her. Just a mention, but enough that she'd given him a narrow-eyed once-over and said that if Mary was as nice as he'd said, and if she wasn't like one of those *floozies* he'd been taking up with, that it might be a good thing if he pursued it and found himself a woman worthy of him and his family.

He wasn't sure it was that big a deal. She was a pretty woman he liked. Different from those aforementioned floozies. Someone not from that lifestyle, but a woman a lot like him in many ways. A woman he seriously wanted to get horizontal with.

The music changed and he meandered to find a place to sit.

That's when he saw Mary's brother Cal and figured he may as well introduce himself. He sat next to Cal and held his hand out. "I'm Damien. You're with Gillian's friend Jules, right?"

The brother looked dubious but not entirely unreasonable or without manners. He shook Damien's hand. "Cal Whaley. And yes, Jules is with me." Cal looked around and waved at the blond guy from the engagement party. "Him too."

"You too, huh?" He did actually know, but he didn't want to seem like he'd gossiped about them. "I knew about Erin. Well, more power to you. Oh, and you're Mary's brother, aren't you?" Ha! So smooth. He wanted to groan at what a dumbass he sounded like.

The blond came over to sit on Cal's other side so Damien held a hand out. "I'm Damien."

"Gideon." He shook it.

Before they could say anything further, the music started and everyone turned to watch the procession.

And there she was. Holy shit, she looked fine in that dress. Her hair was up in some pretty bun thing but he bet it would start coming undone before the ceremony had finished.

That made him smile, as did the way her ass was so beguiling as she walked. Side to side. Side to side. Damn, he wanted to dig his fingers into that luscious flesh and take a bite.

The ceremony was nice, as wedding ceremonies went. He liked Gillian a great deal. Really liked how happy she made Adrian, who'd been a bit restless and bitter the last few years. That kid of theirs was fabulous too.

He'd spoken to Adrian about it, but Damien really felt like the boy had so much talent it would serve him to either go to an arts-based school or get him in the studio and out on the road when he could.

The kid's mom wanted a normal life for him. And Damien respected that more than Gillian could know. His parents had made all the brothers finish school and he was glad of it. But Miles was Adrian Brown's son. Normal was relative at that point. And talent like his wasn't common.

But right then, Damien had other things in mind. He moved through the crowd of well-wishers, heading in her direction. When she turned and he caught her eye, she smiled and it zinged through him.

Chemistry. They had it. It made him sort of nervous and excited. Like a teenager.

"Hey there, Mary Whaley. You're looking mighty fine today."

As he'd thought, a curl had already won free from the pretty updo. He tugged on it and she sighed.

"It never behaves. Once, I had it blown out all straight and sleek. It was so pretty and within half an hour it was already curly again."

He leaned in close. "I kinda dig it that your hair is so naughty."

She laughed, but it was lower than it had been moments before. Husky, full of promise.

"What sort of deliciousness did you prepare today? I'm really hungry because I skipped breakfast to have room for your feast."

She blushed and took the elbow he held out for her.

"Your brother is really suspicious."

Mary looked up to catch sight of Cal giving them the stink eye. She sent him a raised brow. The man was there with his boyfriend and his girlfriend! He was going to give *them* a look? Puh. Leeze.

"Don't mind him. He's a dork."

Damien laughed. "He's your big brother. It's his job to scare men away from his sister."

Especially ones who looked like this one, Mary wagered. Then again, she bet Cal thought Damien was hot, even if he didn't like that Damien was lusting after his sister. Cal had good taste.

The reception tent was so pretty inside. She headed for the table she'd been told to sit at, not at all surprised to find he'd been placed right next to her. That Gillian totally kicked butt.

He pulled her chair out.

"Like I said, your mother did a good job with you."

He ducked his head a moment. "What do you mean?"

"You put your arm out for a woman to hold. You pull chairs out. Your compliments are genuine. Manners are something so many people take for granted or don't think are important."

He laughed. "Would you like a drink?"

"Yes. Sit. There'll be people by with champagne and other drinks in a moment."

He obeyed, scooting his chair closer to hers.

"What have you been up to this month?"

"Catering jobs. Prepping recipes for this and for the reception the label is doing for Adrian. What about you?"

"Oh! Food on the way." He brightened and it flattered her to see the genuine interest he had.

The server saw her and made a beeline. She'd spent a great deal of time training her staff to be sure they served in the way she thought best, so Mary approved when they did it right.

He bent perfectly and she waited for Damien to peruse and then grab what he wanted. Mary nodded when they were finished and the server melted away.

The champagne hadn't begun to flow yet, though. Hm. She looked around, waiting, and began to get antsy.

"Would you hate me if I disappeared for a bit to check on a few things?"

He grinned, putting his boot on her chair. "Yes."

Surprised, she paused and then laughed. "Did Adrian or Gillian talk to you?"

He finished off a Thai chicken slider and rubbed his belly. "About what? Also, my god, I want to keep you in my pocket and hoard all your talent to make me food like this every day."

Oh. My.

Some men complimented her looks. Or her hair, whatever. But to compliment her food? Well, that was the way to her . . . um, parts.

"So"—he paused to hold up the shot glass—"this is . . . ?"

"Sweet potato bisque. I should really get to the kitchen to check on something."

"Are you fucking kidding?" He drank it down. "This is . . . If I come back, will you make me a whole pot of this?"

Her anxiety lessened again at his praise. "Yes, of course. It's pretty easy to make. It's one of Gillian's favorites."

Finally, several servers came through with trays of champagne and the sangria she'd made the day before.

He noted her attention on the servers with the drink trays. "Ah, you were anxious about the drinks?"

"They should have been out ten minutes ago. Before the food.

Two people just got married. Everyone needs a glass of champagne."

"It looks like they're catching up now and everything is fine." He paused to get them each a glass of champagne.

The server spoke quietly. "Had a mishap in the kitchen. Everything is back on track now."

"What sort of mishap?" She stood.

"We couldn't find the right glasses. But then we remembered you'd set them aside so we could find them easier. I've been told to promise you all is well."

"Can I help?" Damien looked up at her as he sat and a shiver made her knees weak. What would he look like on his knees on front of her naked?

"I just need to be sure everything is all right. I'll be back in a bit."

He smiled, unfurling himself to stand very slowly, very close to her. "You like things your own way, don't you?"

"I . . ." She gulped. "This is for Gillian. It needs to be perfect." She hoped she didn't get too breathy on that one, but holy cow. She could scent his cologne, feel the heat of his body. See the beat of his pulse at his throat. Her mouth watered to taste his skin right there.

Speaking of Gillian, her friend made her way over, hugging Mary tight as the server escaped, most likely to warn the kitchen she was on her way.

"You have that look, Mary Whaley. Who got in your kitchen and mixed up the flatware?" Gillian's tease referred to a dinner incident and some salad forks. That's when the no-one-in-my-kitchen-but-my-chosen-assistant rule came about.

"I'm so sorry. The champagne is late."

Gillian smiled, taking Mary's hands, squeezing. "Are you apologizing for something so silly? I see it's all out now. Adrian and I just got in here. So I'd say it was perfect timing. Now we can all toast."

"I want it to be perfect. You deserve it."

Gillian paused, blinking away tears before leaning in to hug her friend. "*You* are perfect. You and Jules, Daisy, all of you have been so good to me. I'm so happy right now and you're the reason. This is amazing. I already had one of those salmon things. Okay, so I had three, but that'll be our secret."

Adrian, Gillian's brand-spanking-new husband, showed up, putting an arm around Gillian's waist and hugging her to his side. Any time Gillian came into his view, his entire focus changed and there was nothing else in the world but her. Mary thought that was an entirely appropriate way to look at her friend, as Gillian happened to be awesome, gorgeous, smart, talented and absolutely perfect in every way. Like Mary Poppins. Only, you know, with a rock-star husband.

"Mary is trying to escape to go prod the kitchen staff." Damien had a drawl when he spoke to Adrian. Hm. It wasn't fake. Maybe just something he did around those he was totally comfortable with?

"And I was telling her everything was totally perfect and to have a lovely evening."

Adrian kissed his wife's temple. "I'm with Gillian on this. Sit. We're joining you." He held a chair out for Gillian and their friends also made it into the tent.

Soon the table was full of their close friends and family and she'd been urged to leave the kitchen to the staff and enjoy herself.

"A whole table of Delicious!" Jules grinned and held her glass high.

"Delicious?" Damien looked to Adrian.

"It's what these gorgeous women refer to themselves as. It's also the name of Mary's supper club." Adrian sipped the sangria and nodded. "And I should add, what this sangria is."

"Jules needs to make a toast. Now that we all have champagne and everything." Cal winked at Mary and she rolled her eyes.

"Me? Why not Brody? Brody is best man, that's his job."

Brody snorted and grabbed some of the stuffed dates. "I've got some for later."

Jules stood and there was tapping and clapping and whistling until the room quieted down. "I'm told since I'm the maid of honor I'm supposed to do a toast."

Mary knew that Jules had not only prepared a toast, she most likely prepared five or seven and practiced them all. Mary was organized. Jules was compulsively so. And this was about Gillian, so it would have been incredibly important to Jules to get every last detail totally correct and perfect.

"Fourteen years ago, this woman moved into our neighborhood with her infant son. We went to check her out, as you do. And it turns out that while she was totally beautiful and had a great accent, she was sort of wary. Which would not do. At all. I wanted her to be my friend because she was awesome. So I just sort of . . . um, bugged her relentlessly until she finally just gave in and even better, shared that sweet baby with our group of friends. I've been fortunate enough to count Gillian as my best friend ever since. And that sweet baby is now a fourteen-year-old boy who is taller than his godmother.

"It makes me incredibly happy to see Gillian with someone who deserves her the way Adrian does. Though he had his moments and I wasn't so sure we should let him have our lovely Gillian." Jules winked and Adrian blushed at the memory to his not-so-stellar entrance into Gillian and Miles's life. "But in the end, he proved himself to be the man Miles could be proud to call Dad and Gillian could call her partner in life. So let's lift a glass to Gillian, Adrian and Miles—the Brown family."

Mary held her glass aloft and took a drink, believing every word to be true.

"Stop now or I'll start crying again." Gillian took the handkerchief Brody handed her way, dabbing her eyes.

"It's your wedding day, English. You're supposed to cry." Though Adrian's eyes were pretty glossy too.

There was cake and laughter. Drinking and music.

Damien couldn't stop looking at the back of Mary's neck where the little curls had won free from the bun. He wanted to press kisses right there. Wondered if she was ticklish. Wondered what she tasted like.

They'd performed a few songs, from Adrian's new CD, one he'd written for Gillian. Miles had played with them, and then did a song of his own for his parents. Damien liked these people and their strong sense of love and family a great deal.

When he'd finished up, they'd sat together again and he'd

wanted her even more. She'd disappeared; he figured she'd gone to hound her staff again.

He and Miles had discussed music for a bit and finally, Damien had gotten an itch only she could scratch and he excused himself to find her.

3

The night had been full of magic. Mary hadn't felt so light and carefree in ages. Things had been great with work and for her friends and this wedding felt like the capper on all that wonderful.

After the emotion of the music Adrian and Miles had dedicated to Gillian and the success of the food, she'd paused just at the large back porch to grab some alone time.

The air carried the scent of all the peonies decorating the entire space. Heady and sensual, it made her tip her head back to breathe deep.

"Well, lookie here."

She opened her eyes slowly to take in the sight of Damien walking toward her. A slow, sexy lope, his features intent on her. It sent a shiver through her because, goddamn, he was delicious.

She smiled. "Hello there."

He kept walking until he was just a breath away. "What are you doing over here all by yourself?"

"I snuck in to check on the food. Don't tell Gillian or she'll have my ass."

He sucked in a breath that made her hold her own. He was going to say something, she could feel it. Something that would change everything.

"Your ass? Hm. Well, I'd rather have it than let anyone else get to it."

A burst of heat flashed over her.

He got even closer, his hand at her waist. "I'd really like to get up in what you've got, Mary Whaley."

She was absolutely sure he'd used that line before. She was, after all, not stupid and she'd seen him on the celebrity news dozens of times.

Didn't matter. It worked. She liked him. And she liked what he said and how he said it. And she wanted to fuck him. Men got to do this stuff, why shouldn't she?

She licked her lips as she thought about it.

And then he bent a little and brushed his lips over hers in a surprisingly sweet kiss. A kiss that deepened, hinted at what else he could do with that mouth of his.

She was slightly tipsy. Very happy. In a great mood. A hot dude just laid a smooch on her and he wanted to get down. As it happened, she liked getting down. He wouldn't want to marry her the next day so he wouldn't be underfoot as she got her business off the ground. It would be totally about fun and pleasure. No fuss, no muss.

Well, maybe some muss would be all right.

"All right. Make it worth my while, then."

His grin made her tingle and she knew everything else he had was going to equally please her system. She'd totally have to confess this to Gillian when they returned from the honeymoon.

"Inside?"

Mary jerked her head toward the house. "Follow me."

Like he'd do anything else? He walked behind her, taking in the sway, the pretty heels, the way her rebellious escaped curls brushed the back of her neck. Her neck, where he'd have his lips as soon as he could make it a reality.

He wanted her more than he'd wanted something in a long time. "I'm staying here. Just upstairs."

Luckily, most everyone was still outside so it wasn't so very hard to get up the stairs quickly and into his room, which thankfully had a lock on the door.

She turned and smiled, rooting him to the spot. Moonlight from the nearby window bathed her in silver. Music wafted from the party below. But it was just the two of them in this moment in time.

"I don't even know where to start." He suddenly felt shy.

"Well, let's see." She reached up to unpin her hair. It was longer than he'd remembered. "I seem to recall a few things about this sex stuff." She stepped to him and took his arm, turning the wrist to undo his buttons there, and then the same with the other.

Then she loosened his tie, tossed it over her head and went back to the buttons on his shirt until she was able to push it off his body.

"Now then."

He had to have her mouth right that very moment, so with one hand he cupped the back of her neck and with the other he pulled her against him. Her lips parted on a little gasp of surprise and he took advantage of that moment to lick that bottom lip and then slide into the kiss fully.

She tasted better than he'd imagined from that brief brush of lips outside. She was cherries and champagne. So fucking delicious and lush he wanted to roll around in her.

Mary nipped his bottom lip as her hands slid all over his upper body. Her touch was soft and smooth, even as she lit him up.

"Goddamn, baby. I want to lick every single inch of you." And that wasn't a lie. At all.

She unzipped her dress, letting it fall from her body, and he nearly swallowed his tongue at how perfect she was. Small. She couldn't have been more than five feet and an inch, maybe two. Curves that made his mouth water. Gorgeous tits and a high, round ass.

He shook his head as he took a long look. "Today is clearly my lucky day."

"You're about to get luckier, so get those clothes off."

He was beginning to get the feeling Mary Whaley was all kinds of dirty up under her pretty dress. "My day keeps getting better."

He pulled his shirt off the rest of the way and couldn't deny how awesome it was that her eyes widened and then went half-lidded. She took a few steps closer, reaching out to grab the waist of his pants and haul him the last little bit until they were skin to skin.

He closed his eyes briefly, bending to bury his face in that glorious mass of curls.

Until she flicked the button of his pants open and unzipped, pushing the material down, along with his boxers.

"Impatient." Not that he was complaining or anything.

"Mmm hmm."

He reached around her body to unhook her bra and trace over the ribbons crisscrossing the top of her panties. "These are . . . It's like opening a present on my birthday." But he forgot whatever else he was going to say when he caught sight of them in the mirror. Hooking his fingers on the sides of her underpants, he pulled them down and she stepped from them.

But his face was level with her pussy and he thought that was a fairly good place to start.

She looked down, watching him on his knees. "Like déjà vu."

He pressed kisses from one hip to the other before focusing on her. "How so? 'Cause I'd remember being here before. I'm certainly never going to forget it."

She sucked in a breath as he licked across her belly button. "Earlier. You were sitting. I was s-standing." Mary lost her train of thought for long moments as he drew his hands up the backs of her legs, stopping to tickle the backs of her knees.

"Hmm. I think I found a spot I'll have to investigate." He did it again and her legs nearly buckled. "Well now. Yes indeed. After. Or again. Whatever."

He was beyond her imaginings. His upper body was banded

by flat, hard muscles. Probably from the brutal workout of drumming the way he did. Tattoos covered his skin and she noted one of his nipples was pierced as well. She'd investigate in detail. After.

She nearly fell over when he breathed against her labia. Hot. So hot it sent shivers through her as she grabbed his shoulder to keep from dissolving into a puddle on the floor.

Then he picked her up like she was nothing, turning to place her on the edge of the bed. "This way I can still be on my knees when I eat this pretty, pretty pussy."

Like she'd complain.

He turned his head to lick the side of her knee, wrenching a gasp from her lips. Then, just behind, which made her hot and wet, aching. Until that moment she hadn't even really known it was one of her sweet spots. Not many men paid any attention to that spot, but hot damn, he did. Thank God for it.

Kisses up the inside of her thigh. The barest contact against her pussy and then kisses and licks down the inside of her other thigh until he got to the other knee.

"Goddamn. You're easy for some back-of-the-knee action. I like that."

She gulped, enjoying what he was doing to her. Each kiss and lick devastating her a little more and he hadn't even really made contact with any of her best parts yet.

He tossed one of her legs up on his shoulder and sent her a look that would have rendered her jelly if she wasn't already lying down. Hooo, he knew this sex stuff.

"Now then." He spread her open and sucked in a breath. "You have one seriously gorgeous cunt."

She started at the word.

"You don't like that word?" He drew the tip of his tongue over her clit, teasing.

"I— Oh god. I never really thought about it."

He sucked her clit between his lips several times before backing up. "I know it's got negative history. But it's not an insult when it's used properly. This is a *beautiful* cunt. Slick. Dark with desire. Sometimes it's a pussy. Sometimes it's a vagina. But when it's spread open to me like this, when I want to shove my face into you and lick every part? Then it's a cunt. In the best way."

That made sense. And it did make her tingly when he said it.

She nodded and he bent again, this time circling her gate with a fingertip while he went back to licking her clit. Slowly. Surely. The pressure just a breath more each moment. She wanted to lay back. Wanted to close her eyes and luxuriate in the way he made her feel. But she couldn't. Couldn't tear her eyes from the picture he made there on his knees between her thighs. His hair had fallen forward so she only got a glimpse of his face here and there.

He paid homage to her pussy, his big, strong hands, palms flat against her inner thighs, holding her wide as he devoured her. She'd never quite had sex like this before. He so clearly enjoyed what he was doing, so clearly had no shame or hesitation about having sex. It was raw and hot and taboo all at once.

And she loved it.

Down his kisses went until he slid his tongue deep, bringing a shiver and a gasp of delight from her. And then he moved back up to her clit again.

Mind-blowing pleasure started at her scalp and moved down, started at her toes and flowed up. She hung there, suspended, just before climax for several long minutes. Drowning in it. Drowning and letting go until it crashed through her entire body and she closed her eyes against bursts of color as she shook.

His kisses slowed. Gentled as she got her breath back.

"You come so prettily."

She opened her eyes to catch sight of him as he stood. To catch sight of his . . . rather impressive attributes.

She grabbed his cock as she sat up. "Let's see what *you* look like when you come."

He made a choked sound but no move to stop her so she continued. "First, can I look at you?"

His cocky grin was back as he stood. "Look your fill, darlin'."

She hadn't been able to really concentrate on the tattoo on his back, but now that she got close, she could see it wasn't abstract lines at all, but that those lines made a tiger that took up his entire back. She brushed her thumbs over it, amazed at the work. Amazed at the muscled, broad shoulders that tapered down to a narrow waist. She moved back to his front, her gaze snagged on his cock for long moments. She wasn't a size queen by any stretch of the imagination, but Damien might convert her. It wasn't so huge she cringed, but he'd definitely fill her up. Not a bad thing at all.

On his inner forearm was the word *Hurley*. His family name so that made sense. His nipple was pierced. More tats on his belly and one that curled from his wrist up to his shoulder.

"Wow."

He raised a brow at her. "That's my line."

"I hope you have a condom."

"I have several in my toiletries bag."

"Good." She pressed a kiss over his heart, down to his nipple where she dragged her teeth, rewarded by a hiss of pleasure and his fingers tangling in her hair.

"Yes."

She moved across his chest to the pierced nipple. Good gracious, he was . . . wow. It wasn't that she didn't possess a good vocabulary. She did. But there weren't any really good words to describe how hot this man was. She tugged the bar with her teeth and he nearly growled, his hands at her hips, pulling her snug against his body.

Mary brushed her body from side to side against his. Against his cock. Her desire, momentarily sated, began to bloom back into life as she took a deep breath and fell to her knees. "My turn to be on my knees."

"You'll hear no arguments from me."

She grabbed him at the root and angled him so she could lick around the head, learning him, learning what he liked and responded to. He liked the way she dug the tip of her tongue under the head. Made a desperate sort of gasp when she sucked him in, just the head, keeping her mouth wet and very tight around him. His fingers tightened when she palmed his balls and then dragged her nails gently over his sac.

She loved this moment. Loved being on her knees before a man, controlling his every response with her actions. She brought him pleasure. He arched into her and she breathed through her nose to keep from gagging. He backed off, more gentle this time.

Over and over she took him as deep as she could, the surface of his cock changing the closer he got to climax. When she slowly brushed her fingertip over his asshole, he whimpered and widened his stance until he finally pulled her to her feet with a snarl.

"I need in you right now."

She licked her lips and he gulped. She felt like a goddess.

"I wasn't done."

"You can suck my cock again any time you like. I want to fuck you. Right now."

He pressed a hard kiss to her lips and dashed to the bathroom, returning with several foil packets, which he put under the pillow.

"Now." He picked her up, tossing her to the mattress, and she had to struggle not to laugh.

The moment was surreal as she attempted to process it all.

Music floated up from the reception still in swing in the yard below. She felt reckless in the best sort of way. Their chemistry rendered her sort of sex drunk. He moved like no one else she'd been with. Sure of himself. Charming. Certainly he knew what he was about. But more than anything else, what hit her the hardest was that she *knew* he wanted her.

Knew he wanted to fuck her. That he dug her chemicals and found her totally hot. That sort of focus from a man like this one was dizzying.

And, he liked the dirty talk.

So. Very. Dirty.

Covered in tattoos. Pierced nipple. A drummer whose hair was too long and who grinned at her like a pirate about to plunder. It was like her fervent tenth-grade fantasy fuck had manifested itself in the room.

Only back then she hadn't even known how to begin to fantasize about a man who clearly loved eating pussy like this one.

Still standing, he broke into her little fantasy objectification of him as he took her foot and began to knead his way up her calf.

She knew he was headed for . . . holy shit. She sucked in a breath and arched on a moan when his thumbs brushed over the dimples at the back of her knee.

Pleasure coursed through her, warm and sticky. The back of her knee! Who'd have thought?

He hummed his pleasure and she didn't miss the slight note of amusement at her reaction to what had been until that moment, just the back of her knee that had never made her doorbell ring this way.

"I want you from behind."

Fancy that, she wanted the same thing!

She got to her hands and knees quickly. His hands stroked over her skin. Down her spine. Over the curve of her waist, the swell of her ass. He paused at the space just below the cheek, at the beginning of the thigh, he slid his fingertip back and forth. Just a few times until gooseflesh broke over her and she arched back toward him.

Damien snarled a curse because he couldn't wait another moment. He'd wanted to draw it out before he fucked her but she made it too hard to resist. That little thrust with the bossy little growl had been the last straw.

Reaching around, he tested her. Her pussy was soft and warm. Ready. He licked his lips, tasting her again. Quickly he got the condom on and lined himself up, slowly sliding into her.

So. Fucking. Good. This sweet, good-girl-on-the-outside, hot-as-hell-in-bed thing was hotter than anything he'd had in a very long time. There was real heat between them.

He'd taken a taste of Mary Whaley and he liked what he found. Spicy sweet. Bountiful curves. Hair that spread out around her face and shoulders. Bold and unashamed about her sexuality. Which was so hot. This woman liked to come. She liked to fuck and if she didn't get what she wanted, she'd demand it.

She pushed back, taking him inside with one movement. He ground his teeth together as that tight heat surrounded him.

"*Fuck.* That's so good."

He slid his hands around her torso, taking her tits into his hands. Her nipples pressed against his palms. He stroked slow and deep, not in any hurry to leave.

She squirmed against him when he squeezed her nipples and then tugged. "God, yes."

Smiling, he kissed her shoulder blade, wondering how many other little pleasure spots he could find in unexpected places. She sighed softly when he kissed her spine at the center of her back. She fluttered around his cock and moaned when he found the perfect spot between her ribs on her left side. He dragged his beard against her skin and she shivered and squeezed him.

"You're full of delightful secrets."

She laughed. "Me?"

He sped up just a little and she lost some of the rigidity in her back. "Gonna take me a while to find all your best spots. Just sayin." He moved a hand down her belly to her pussy. Her clit was swollen and hard when he pressed the pad of his finger there. Side to side. Side to side until her breathy moans got a little more bossy.

Damien thought he'd tease her. Drive her over the edge into climax and then maybe the next one after that he'd come with her. Except as she came all around him, it was too much.

She met his thrust, taking him deep. Her hips rocked from side to side, even as she tilted to grind herself against his fingers. Too much indeed and he came hard and fast. Back from his teeth.

And when he pulled out slowly, she flopped, face-first, to the mattress with a happy sigh.

4

M ary pulled a tray of empanadas from the oven, humming at how they'd turned out.

"I have such great timing," Daisy sang as she entered the kitchen. "Don't know what it is, but I can smell that I'll be having at least four."

Daisy was not only Mary's best friend on the planet, she also served as a manager for Mary's catering business. Oh, they both told one another she'd only do it until things evened out and Mary could find a replacement, but for the time being, both women liked it that way and that was what counted.

When Daisy's art career fully took off, Mary would hire a manager behind Daisy's back so she wouldn't feel guilty. But until then Mary knew it would keep Daisy working only one job other than her art instead of four.

"You're my best taste tester anyway. Everyone else just says things are yummy. You'll tell me if something is greasy or needs something."

Daisy rolled her eyes as she grabbed a shrimp puff from a platter, popping it in her mouth. "First of all, you've never made anything your whole life that could be described as greasy. I bet if you made a bowl of grease as an entrée, it wouldn't taste greasy."

Mary smiled, satisfied and proud. She worked hard at what she did, but most of it her mother liked to say was Mary's natural talent with food. It was her art. She just instinctively knew how to make things people loved to eat and drink.

Not that it wasn't nice to hear that reinforced by her friends though.

"There's a second thing. Lay it on me." Mary began to core the green peppers and get rid of the seeds. The kitchen filled with the scent.

"This shrimp thing is awesome. I'd totally let this shrimp thing feel me up. Levi and I are hosting his parents. At his house of course."

"Yes."

Daisy's grin was quick. "Like that? I haven't even said what I needed yet."

"You want me to make dinner for them. Something elegant and classic without being too heavy. Something with a twist because you are not classic, but exotic and delicious. You want them to know this but not in a negative sense. I'll get you a few menu ideas. When is it?"

Daisy hugged her. "You're awesome. How do you always know?"

"Because I love you, silly."

"I'm so lucky."

Mary grinned back. "We both are. Now you have Levi too, and that makes you even more lucky. His mother likes you already, which we both know was the biggest hurdle. No one cares what his dumb bitch sister-in-law thinks anyway. We'll get Jules to make you a dessert that knocks their socks off."

"I've never had a boyfriend like this."

"That's because he's not your boyfriend." Mary tipped the green pepper into the bowl with the cilantro, tomato and diced onion. "He's your significant other in the best sense. He'll be your husband one day. The daddy to your kids. My god, they're going to be ridiculously beautiful kids I'll spoil rotten."

"Marriage?"

"Take that shock out of your voice. I know you too well. Of course, marriage. He lets you continue to live in your little house because it makes you happy and you can both pretend things aren't totally serious yet. But they are."

"Whoa now. Marriage is a ways off. Yes, we love each other. But he's got issues and I'm still young. We have time."

Mary used the hand blender to quickly pulse together the ingredients for the salsa-style dipping sauce.

"Sure you have time. But he's not some guy who'll be content to date you forever. He knows your value. Knows you're amazing and he will want you under his roof. He'll want you to marry him and have his babies. He's traditional that way. And you want that too, even if you try to tell me you don't." She put some of the sauce into a little bowl, pushing it and an empanada to Daisy. "Taste."

"More cilantro. You should open up like a counseling business you run while you prepare food. What about you? When do you find your forever?"

Mary shrugged. "I will when I'm supposed to. Right now, I have Luxe up and running. I've got jobs lined up for months. I've got the supper club booked for nearly a year. Profits are up. My friends are getting married. My brother has finally admitted he's in love with Jules. I'm not opposed to forever. I want it and all. Just not right now. I feel like I'd shortchange a relationship in favor of my business. I want all my energy on that and I don't want to have to feel guilty about it."

Daisy nodded. "Fair enough. The dinner is in two weeks. There'll be six. Well, I guess eight if you count me and Levi. His brother Jonah and Jonah's daughter will be there as well as two of his other brothers. Mal and his *wife* are conveniently unavailable."

Mal Warner's wife had been atrociously rude to Daisy and thus was on Mary's we-hate-you-forever list.

"It's unavoidable that we'll come into contact. Levi loves his brother. And I do too. Mal is a sweet guy. With horrible taste in women, obviously. But I don't ever want Levi to feel like he has to choose me over his family. I won't be that."

"You aren't that. People need to be responsible for what they do or say and to stop hiding behind the excuse that because it's family no one should ever say anything."

"Says the gal with the perfect family."

Mary laughed. "Not perfect, but we do love each other. You were right about the sauce." She poured it into a container so it could travel safely and tucked it into one of the big fridges.

"You're still going to New York next month, right?"

Adrian was on a summer and early fall tour that had started just a few days after the wedding. For most of it, Gillian and Miles would travel with him. And then Gillian would bring Miles back so he could start school.

Next month they had a date at Madison Square Garden and as a big thank-you for all the wedding help, Adrian was flying out all their friends to see his shows there. Backstage passes. Swank boutique hotel. He'd even pulled some strings and gotten Mary reservations at a few restaurants she'd been dreaming about.

"Hell yes. I wouldn't miss it."

"Damien's band opens for them. That'll be interesting." Daisy's attempt at innocence made Mary laugh.

"Don't make me sorry I told you."

Daisy grinned, delighted. "It is your duty as my best friend to tell me about hot one-night stands with rock stars."

"It certainly was hot. He texts me sometimes. Just little things here and there. Sometimes pictures from venues, that sort of thing. Oh and he asks for my opinion on where he should eat in whatever city they're in."

He could have never said another word. She wouldn't have been offended. She understood the rules. Knew what he was.

But the little texts were . . . well, she felt like they had the beginnings of an actual friendship. Which she liked. He didn't send her pictures of his dick. Didn't sext her or anything like that. He asked her about her business and sent her pictures of food and landscapes.

Yes, she was looking forward to seeing him next month and would have been lying if she'd said she wasn't hoping for a repeat of their scorching night—and the following morning—between the sheets.

"I think he's sweet on you."

Mary julienned the carrots for her veggie sushi. "I think he's a drummer in a rock band who drinks a lot, parties a lot, has a lot of women and shows up in the tabloids on a regular basis. I don't even really follow the celebrity news and I know these things. I just have no desire for that. At all."

"Well, that's just one side to him. He could be more."

"Daze, we had hot sex. He knows where all a lady's parts are and what to do with them. But I'm not one of those women who thinks she's the one who can finally tame that bad boy. That way lies madness. I'm a lot of things, but I am not dumb. I don't want that. I don't want to be in the paper. I don't want to have to worry about my picture online being picked apart by his fangirls. I see what it does to Gillian and Adrian didn't even have that sort of reputation with women and partying. Anyway, it was fun. I know what it was. He knows what it was. That's all. Don't go trying to make it something it can never be."

Daisy shrugged and Mary rolled her eyes, knowing that Daisy wouldn't let it go until she was good and ready.

"Don't eat those. That's for an event later today. I made you extra. There's a tray in the walk-in that has your name on it and a bag in the pantry for you as well."

Mary took care of the people she loved. It made her happy

to cook for them. Made her satisfied to know they got sustenance from what she prepared. Knowing she did it for them.

"What would I do without you?"

"Eat takeout a lot more. But you have no such worries because you're stuck with me."

"Thank God for it."

She needed to run by her parents' place to check in and take over some food. Her dad met her at the door, taking the bags from her.

"What'd you bring me, Bess?" No one else called her Bess but her dad. Her given name was Mary-Elizabeth. When she was little, her father had said Mary seemed such a serious name for a girl like her and he'd taken to calling her Bess. It had stuck.

"Gazpacho. Goat cheese tarts. Well, Jules made those. Roasted beet salad. Don't make a face. Beets are full of wonderful stuff and I made them so you should give them a try." She thrust the totes at him and moved past, toward the kitchen where her mother would be. "There's salmon patties in the bag as well. Don't eat them all at once."

"Bless you."

She shook her head, still smiling when she entered the room. "Hello, you."

Her mother turned her face up to receive Mary's kiss.

"Hey." The huge puzzle on the table was nearly finished. She'd taken up puzzles back when they were kids. Their dad had told them she needed it to calm her nerves after parenting them all day. Which was probably true.

"He's probably already eaten four of those salmon patties."

Her mother spoke absently, her glasses perched on her nose as she looked over the remaining puzzle pieces.

"Probably. But they're good for him. I made a batch for Ryan too, but took them to his house first. I know they'd never get out of here."

Her mother laughed. "You've got your dad's number. How's business?" She looked up, taking a sip of her tea. "There's tea. Freshly brewed."

Mary got up to get herself a glass and to top off her mother's. Her father wandered into the room and began putting things in the fridge.

"Good. I've got jobs for the next several months. I can pay my staff without stress. An agent called me three days ago. Said she thought I should put a cookbook together."

"That'd be something now, wouldn't it? Our Bess being a published author? And why shouldn't people want to buy a cookbook with her recipes in it?"

She loved her parents more than anything. They were kooky, no doubt. But they were good, solid people who'd raised her and her siblings well. Always proud and supportive of them.

"I'm working up a proposal. We'll see. I need to talk to Daisy about doing the photography for it."

"You have your own talent with a camera. You might be stretched too thin though, so I'm sure Daisy would be a huge help. How's that boyfriend of hers?" Her mother shot a glance in her dad's direction as he opened up the second container of the salmon patties. "At least use a fork."

"He digs her. She's not quite sure what to do with him." Mary snorted. "He's big and bossy and handsome and sort of overwhelming. But he adores her. He buys her things. Takes her places."

"She'd be bored shitless with a man who wasn't like that. Girl'd run right over a lesser man." Her mother had a way about her. Always seeing to the heart of things. It was sort of scary, and yet Mary admired it all the same and hoped the best parts rubbed off on her.

"Probably."

"And why shouldn't he buy her things? It's not like she expects it. But he's got the money and wants to treat her. I hope I raised you well enough not to turn down gifts from people when they want to do for you."

"I don't know. I guess I'll have to land a rich older boyfriend to know for sure." She winked at her dad, who glowered for a moment.

"Jeanne, you stop it now. Bess makes her own way."

Her mother sighed. "Of course she does. She's not a whore. I'm saying that people should be able to do for others. Mary brings us food how many days a week? We never pay her for it because it's her way of taking care of us. She does it for everyone. Levi does for Daisy because he can. I bet you the girl makes amazing art for him and gives it to him as a gift. Given her talent, that's sort of the equivalent of jewelry or a trip. Generosity is important."

She was tucked into bed with a book hours later when her phone buzzed with an incoming text.

Damien.

Sitting here drinking an excellent glass of red wine after an awesome steak. Was thinking you'd probably have something far more tasty to accompany it than the plain old potato they served.

She picked her phone up and started to type.

Probably. But I'm gifted that way. What city are you in?

Her phone rang.

"I'm in St. Louis."

There was a lot of noise in the background.

"Sounds like it's busy where you are."

"I'm in my hotel room. Well, actually, Paddy's room. They're blowing off steam. Big show tonight."

She blew off steam in really different ways, apparently. It sounded loud and wild and she was glad she wasn't there. Well, mostly, though she wouldn't mind jumping on Damien if she had him in the flesh.

"Ah."

"Little word for all you're feeling."

She laughed. "Just thinking that my blowing off steam usually means I make ice cream or go for a bike ride or hike. But I remember the last story I saw about you guys, so . . . ."

"Don't believe everything you read."

He didn't sound amused.

"I didn't mean to offend you."

"I'm sorry. You didn't. It's just . . . it gets old having the tabloids follow you around and make stuff up. You never know who's gonna say what."

She got that part. Knew Gillian had to deal with it now. But at the same time, what she heard in the background didn't sound like they were playing backgammon.

"Adrian said you guys were coming out to MSG next month."

He wished he hadn't snapped at her. Their ease had stiffened up a little. And god knew she was mainly right.

She answered, not sounding angry or hurt at least. "Yeah. Looking forward to it. Adrian even managed to get me some really wonderful reservations at my coveted restaurants. Be nice to me and I might let you be my plus one."

He realized he wanted to see her enjoying food from the standpoint of the consumer, not the producer. What would she be like in a restaurant? He knew she wholeheartedly embraced enjoying sex; he bet she was like that when she ate out too.

He found himself smiling, really smiling, for the first time in a few days. "Yeah?"

"Yeah. If you're not busy you can come along. That way I can try more things off the menu and no one will think I'm a hog."

She made him smile. A lot. "You have an ulterior motive? I'm scandalized." He had no plans. Once he heard from Adrian that she'd be there, he'd kept his schedule clear during non-show hours so he could be with her.

"I do. I'm sneaky that way."

He grinned, though she couldn't see it. "Okay then. Good

to know that in addition to all your other . . . talents, you're also sneaky. It's a good quality."

They spoke for a little while longer before he hung up and went back into the main room where his brothers drank, smoked and shot the shit about the day's events. A few women lounged around and he couldn't find it in him to invite anyone back to his room.

He told himself it was that he was tired. But really, he knew on some level that Mary would disapprove if he was fucking other women right before he fucked her when she visited New York in a few weeks. And to be truthful, he wanted her to think well of him.

The specter of his past rose. He wasn't ashamed of his hard living. But because he'd been that way and openly so, it had played in the media. He wasn't just the drummer of Sweet Hollow Ranch. He was the party-boy, sex-hungry, hard-drinking drummer.

From the outside, he could see it all bringing pause to Mary. He liked her. He wanted to know her better. And he wanted very much for that reputation to not get in the way.

5

"Jeez, a private plane too?" Jules waggled her brows as they got settled in for their flight to New York.

"Erin, I wager. She loves to give presents," Daisy said. Levi sat next to her, his hand in hers.

"I bet you Levi is no stranger to private planes. Look at him." Mary winked at him and he snorted. They had a good back and forth. Once she accepted that he was good for Daisy and would continue to be so. She also liked that Levi had wanted her to approve. Some guys wouldn't have cared.

"I did my time in coach."

"You make it sound like prison," Daisy scoffed.

Mary laughed. "It is! If I could do this every time you'd never see me in coach ever again jammed in the center seat for seven hours while I begged for peanuts after having to take my shoes off in an airport." She shuddered.

"Jules says you're doing a food-truck tour tomorrow. Is there room for me?" Gideon Carter, Jules's other man, looked at her hopefully.

"Definitely."

"Is the rock star coming?" Cal asked, trying to be casual.

Ryan, their brother, groaned. "You have no finesse at all."

"And you do?" Cal tossed back. The two of them bickered a lot, but it was a front. They were, as her mother often said, thick as thieves. But they did love to poke each other.

"I could have found out if Damien Hurley was coming along way smoother than you. And I wouldn't have agitated her in finding out." Ryan shrugged.

She snorted. "Boys, please. Yes, he's coming along. I think he is, anyway. I think one of his other brothers is coming too."

She was admittedly a little nervous about that. Sure, they were just having fun and all, but she knew he was tight with his family. Didn't want them to think ill of her.

"So what do you envision this thing between you being anyway?" They took off easily as she sat back and let Ryan pepper her with questions. She'd probably want to know if their situations were reversed so she'd answer until she thought he went too far.

"Look. He's an adult male with a busy schedule. I'm an adult female with a busy schedule. Occasionally, for however long this works, we meet up and hang out awhile and then go back to our busy schedules. I like him. He's sexy and funny and talented." She shrugged.

"I've seen the celebrity news." Ryan was calmer than Cal, but no less intense. Maybe more once you scratched the surface. She heard the warning and wanted him to know she understood.

"So have I. I know what he is. But I think he's more than the shorthand we know from the Internet. Anyway, I'm not going to marry him, for heaven's sake. I'm going to fuck him and let him make me laugh and enjoy his company. I'm not stupid."

Ryan closed his eyes and she winked at Daisy, who tried very hard not to laugh.

"Surely you didn't think we were playing Yahtzee and making s'mores."

"I try very hard not to think about whatever you get up to with your boyfriends. You're our baby sister, we worry."

She squeezed her brother's hand. "Thank you. I appreciate it. But I'm good."

"If he hurts you, I'm going to crush his nuts."

That made her laugh. "Deal."

Amazing how fast a flight went when you were on a private plane. Mary made a note to herself to make Adrian something yummy in thanks.

There'd been a limo waiting for them at the airport as well. It took them straight into the city to the hotel Adrian had arranged for them. She loved New York City. Loved the lights. Loved the way the city simply never stopped. She loved the restaurants, the clubs, loved the museums and the shopping. The next few days would be so much fun.

She'd barely gotten her toiletries out and on the counter in the bathroom before people were at her door. She smiled as she opened up to admit them.

Levi and Daisy stood with Jules, Gideon, Cal and Ryan.

"We want to see your view." Ryan came in and everyone followed. The view was pretty spectacular, she had to admit.

"One, I'm starving and two, it's not that late, especially on West Coast time. I want to go the Empire State Building. I hear it's open late."

Jules nodded. "I looked it up. It is. I want to go." She pulled her phone out. "I want to check in with Gillian first."

Of course she'd looked it up. "Good idea." Mary's phone rang at that moment and she saw that it was Damien.

"Hello." She knew she grinned, but he made her giddy, so why not.

"I hear your plane arrived. We're making our way back to the city. Do you have plans yet?"

"We were just talking about dinner and the Empire State Building. Jules is checking in with Gillian to see what's up with them."

"Will you call me and let me know where you're having dinner? I'll come down and meet you."

"Sure. We're doing the touristy thing first, I imagine. Then dinner." She wanted to see him. Felt that little zing his presence had brought with it. And then she was so getting naked with him.

"I'll see you in a bit, then."

She hung up to find everyone staring. "No." She sent Cal a warning glance.

"No what, Tiny?"

"Tiny, my patootie. You hush. You have a boyfriend *and* a girlfriend. You don't get to be judgy about my life. I support your choices, butthead."

Cal stepped closer, kissing her cheek. "Aw now, I'm not being judgy. I just want him to be perfect. He's got a reputation. I don't want you to get hurt."

Big brothers. Even when they were all adults they wanted to protect her. Which she usually thought was sweet. "We went over this on the plane. I'm not getting hurt. I know what he is. This is fun. This is sex and hanging out with someone I enjoy. I have a life. I'm not giving that up to hitch my wagon to some hot-stuff bachelor. When I settle down, I know the difference between right now and Mr. Right. I'm not stupid. We have good chemistry. That's all. And that's all it needs to be."

"Leave her be, Calvin. Your sister is a smart one. She's perfectly capable of managing her life." Jules sent him a look and he rolled his eyes before giving Ryan a different sort of look. They'd keep an eye on things, she knew.

Which was fine as long as they didn't act like jerks.

"Gillian says they'll meet us in the lobby in fifteen minutes. Miles is all over the Empire State Building idea." Jules nodded toward Daisy. "Did you bring your camera?"

Daisy, who loved to take pictures, held up her bag. "Brought the little one for tonight."

Mary had left hers at home, sitting on her dining room table. Damn.

"Let's get moving. I'll treat you to a drink before everyone meets us down there." Cal linked his arm through hers.

"Hurry the fuck up." Paddy's driving left something to be desired. He drove like an old woman, not in any great rush to get back to Manhattan. They'd been out at the Hamptons looking at a place they were thinking of buying and giving to their parents.

"You got a date or something? What's the hurry?"

"As it happens, Mary just arrived and I want to have dinner with her."

"Oooh, the famous Mary. Can't wait to finally see this chick you've been mooning over."

Vaughan shifted his legs. "Ignore him. He's just jealous. She sounds pretty fabulous. Gillian was talking about her last week. Saw some pictures. Hot."

"She is. Hot, that is. Smart too. Talented. Don't tell Mom but she's the most amazing cook. Anyway, I like spending time with her. Is that a crime?"

"No. Can we come to dinner too? I'm starving." Vaughan rubbed his belly.

"You're always starving. But yes, you can come. I think Adrian and their friends will be there too. I'll get her alone later."

They dropped the car off twenty minutes later and he called to see where they were.

"We're in the lobby still. Trying to get all these people moving is like herding cats. Poor Jules doesn't deal with chaos well. She's the organizer of the group."

He walked around the corner and saw her there, smiling at her friends as she spoke to him.

"That works." He hung up and tapped her on the shoulder. "Hey there."

Her confusion melted into a smile and he leaned down to kiss her.

"Welcome to Manhattan."

"Are you the official welcome wagon? I can't imagine the budget for such a thing."

He kissed her once more quickly because he had to taste a little more.

"Just for you."

"Aw, does that mean we don't get to kiss her?"

He looked over his shoulder. "Don't think so. Mary Whaley, this is my older brother, Patrick, but everyone calls him Paddy, and my younger brother, Vaughan. Guys, this is Mary."

She shook their hands and made introductions as well.

"I'm so hungry. We need to go now. Take pity on me, please." She headed toward the doors and everyone followed. He took her hand and she smiled up at him.

"Have you eaten at the Gramercy Tavern yet?" They'd eaten there the last time he and his brothers had been in Manhattan. He figured she'd love it.

Her face lit and he was glad he'd suggested it. "I've wanted to but didn't have time the last visit."

"Since you're so hungry would you like to eat first? Then we can head to the Empire State Building."

Adrian nodded. "Good idea. Let's get a cab over and I'll see if we can't get a big table or one of their private rooms. Short notice I know, but it's a weeknight."

And he had the juice to make it happen. Damien bet tables opened up for Adrian on short notice all the time.

The doorman grabbed them two cabs and they headed over. Mary ended up between him and his brothers in their cab.

"So, Mary, we hear you're amazing in the kitchen." Paddy gave her a Hurley grin and she grinned back.

"I do okay in the kitchen, I'm told." She paused and then snorted. "That's bull crap. Yes, I am amazing in the kitchen."

Paddy laughed and Damien squeezed the hand he was holding.

"I like to cook so I'm lucky I'm good at it and that I can make a living from it."

Vaughan nodded. "I hear that."

"What were you all up to today?"

"We went out to the Hamptons to look at a house for my parents. Running a ranch is a huge job and my dad loves it. But he and my mom need some time away from it. We can run it while he's on vacation. But they'd never go if we didn't do this."

"Well, by 'we can run it,' what Damien really means is that Ezra, our oldest brother, can run it and tell us what to do and we'll do it. We can shovel and lift things and put out fencing and that sort of thing. But Ez, well, he's the brains at the ranch. He'll take over from our dad when it's time."

"What do you all, um, produce? Ranch?"

"Pears, alfalfa and hay. The hay is new. My brother thought it would be good to diversify and when we bought some extra acreage five years ago, he started then."

"I love pears. What kind?"

"Anjou."

Her eyes lit and he really, really liked it. "I have a recipe for pear and gorgonzola soup that I make with red Anjous. So good."

Their mother would adore her.

"Ah, here we are."

He got out first, helping her from the back, sliding an arm around her shoulders as she leaned into him.

Paddy raised a brow at him but a hint of a smile lived on his mouth.

Cal's gaze moved over them and Damien read the concern on her brother's features. But his girlfriend tipped his chin in her direction and kissed him quickly.

They were met and led to a table in a lovely private room.

"Damn, remind me to travel with you more often." Vaughan tipped his water glass in Adrian's direction.

"I think Mary should order for us." Jules looked over the menu in their direction.

"You do just fine without me, Juliet." Mary blushed and he pulled one of her curls straight only to have it spring back into place quickly.

"You're blushing, Curly."

Paddy snorted. "Leave the woman be, Damien. Will you at least tell me what you think would be best right now? You can give me several recommendations maybe?"

"If we all get different things we can share. That's always my favorite way to do this. Though I don't usually share dessert. Just so you know in advance. I cannot be relied upon to share sweet things. Ask Jules."

"That's a good idea. How about we do a selection of the first and second courses? Does that work?"

They ordered, and wine was brought out along with something nonalcoholic for Miles.

Damien couldn't seem to stop touching her. Which interested him. Damien wasn't one for PDA like that. But she smelled really damned good. Her voice seemed to burrow under his skin. It made him truly happy to be there with her.

The chef came out with the first course and Mary's gaze lit up.

She chatted with him, asking about this and that. For his part, the chef seemed to be excited right back to be talking with someone who knew her stuff and clearly loved the food.

Mary paused as they all filed outside to head to the Empire State Building.

"So, Gillian." She put her arm through Gillian's and her head on Gillian's' shoulder. They were alone, the others clustered a few feet away.

"Whatever you need, darlin', it's all yours." Gillian smiled.

"I did notice you didn't have a glass of wine. Any reason you're not drinking alcohol?"

Gillian blushed wildly and Mary grinned so hard her face hurt. "Really?" She did a little dance but then everyone looked and she stopped.

"That made me feel so much better." Gillian hugged her. "I feel old and sort of sick all the time and it's new so I'm worried and Adrian follows me around offering me things. Miles is over the moon. I'm excited and worried all at once. It's not like I'm new to the mum business."

"What are you two on about?" Cal called out.

Jules and Daisy trailed back, bending their heads and giggling.

"I've only just told Jules a few hours ago, before you left Seattle. I was going to tell everyone but Jules bet me you'd notice before I told anyone."

Jules grinned. "Thank God. I was dying. I wanted to announce it over the intercom."

"We're not telling anyone for a few more months. It's early days. I only told you because you're my family and you'd notice anyway."

If the news got hold of this they'd splash it all over the place. And Mary knew she and the rest of Delicious would pull together to protect their friend as long as they could.

"Of course. Your secret is safe with us."

"We're coming!" Jules waved at Cal. "Lady stuff."

The men had all stood there on the sidewalk, just staring at the women as they giggled and hugged. Most of them were befuddled and affectionate. Paddy and Vaughan shook their heads.

Miles appeared confused and a little embarrassed. "They always do that sort of stuff, then? Even when they're old?"

Adrian laughed, putting an arm around his son's shoulders. "Don't let them hear you say that. They're nowhere near old. But yes, they do. Wait till Elise gets in and she and Erin are part of the group."

"Aunt Erin doesn't really count. She's sort of . . . well, a thing unto herself."

Adrian snorted. "That, kid, is what you call an understatement. Your aunt Erin defies definition."

"It's cool. I want to be like that."

Damien saw Adrian's face soften, washed by pride and love.

"You already are, Miles. There's no one else on Earth like you."

"Let's go to the Empire State Building." Mary joined them, taking the hand Damien held out.

"Clear night. We'll see everything from up there."

He headed right when everyone else headed left once they got out onto the observation deck. In the dark, with the world lit up and spread out in all directions he spun her and pulled her tight to his body.

"Alone at last. For two minutes anyway." He bent his knees to kiss her and she tiptoed up to meet him halfway. Need, which had been simmering all day long, exploded through him, pushing at his control.

Her taste settled in and he savored it. Savored the soft, lush lips, the feel of her curves against his body.

She hummed as he ended the kiss, licking her lips.

"I'm coming to your room tonight."

"Bring clothes so you won't have to do the walk of shame tomorrow."

He laughed, turning her to walk so they could catch up to everyone. "Thanks for protecting my honor."

"Least I can do. Because I plan to ride you like a pony when we get alone. I hope you took your vitamins." She murmured this last as she waved at everyone.

That Curly was trouble. He grinned. The best kind.

6

There were photographers on the sidewalk outside the hotel. Adrian cursed and looked to Gillian. "English, you're going to have to run the gauntlet. I'm sorry."

She sighed. "Comes with the territory now."

Mary watched, worried, though sure he'd protect her. Damien had ended up in the other cab with his brothers and they'd been a light ahead so they'd most likely gone through the mess already.

Admittedly she was glad. The last thing she wanted was to be photographed with him going into a hotel.

Levi and Daisy got out first and he glared at them, holding Daisy to his side. Mary took Miles and dared anyone to do anything. They pushed, taking pictures, but she held her bag in front of his face so they couldn't get any good shots.

But it was nothing compared to the furor when Adrian got out with Gillian.

They shouted his name, shouted questions at them. Shouted Gillian's name. The doorman held the door open for them and hotel security made sure no one got in, though the flashes kept on even after they got inside.

"You okay?" she asked Miles.

"Mum's going to be upset. I hate that."

Mary kissed his cheek. "You're such a sweet boy. Your dad made sure no one got near her. She knows his life comes with this. She chose it to be with him. It's okay."

They headed to the elevators and Mary overheard Adrian speaking with Gillian about bodyguards. "English, you know I have to. Erin is arriving soon with the guys and Alexander. That scene out there . . . well, she won't handle it well. And I don't want you to get hurt or jostled."

The baby. Mary knew he was thinking of Gillian's pregnancy. Knew he was worried about her emotional and physical state. Erin, his sister and the bass player in his band for these shows, had been involved in a horrific stalking and kidnapping years before that had ended with her daughter murdered and her life shattered. Crowds and paparazzi were one of the reasons she didn't tour with him and had semiretired from music. She still wrote with him and did his studio work, but aside from special shows like this short tour she didn't go on the road.

"I know. Stop worrying. I'll get used to bodyguards someday, I suppose."

He kissed the top of her head and looked to Miles. "You okay?"

"Yeah. I don't like seeing Mum upset though."

"Me either. We'll make it better for her. Maybe with ice cream."

Gillian snorted but smiled. "Oh, my men."

"This is my floor. I'll see you in the morning. Call me when you wake up."

She hugged Adrian quickly and Gillian, kissing her cheeks. "Love you."

"Love you too. I'm so glad you're here, Mary. Makes everything better."

Mary whispered in Gillian's ear. "You're having a baby."

Gillian squeezed her tight. "I'm so glad I could share that with you. See you in the morning."

She headed to her room. She figured Damien would call her or show up at some point. He knew the number.

It was Daisy waiting at her door though, with Levi. "Are you all right?"

"Um? What do you mean?" She slid the card into the slot and invited them inside.

"The crazy media outside. You were with Adrian and Damien too right?"

"Ah. Not with Damien. They got into a different cab. But with Adrian, Gillian and Miles, yes. She wasn't pleased. But she's all right. This is her life."

"Could be yours too."

Daisy was her friend and so she understood the concern. But she didn't want to discuss this yet again and she sure didn't want to discuss this in front of Levi.

"Thanks for coming by." She went to the door. "I'll see you guys in the morning."

"Oh. You're mad." Daisy looked back over her shoulder to Levi. "This rarely happens."

"I really can't tell the difference. She's still smiling."

"*She's* right here."

Daisy paused to hug her. "I'm sorry. I worry."

"I left you alone. For the most part. When this one was making you crazy." She gave the eye to Levi, who had the good sense to cringe a little. "I already said all I want to say this trip about Damien."

Daisy grinned. "All right. Fair enough."

"Love you."

"Love you too. I was just worried."

"I know. Don't give me puppy eyes, they don't work on me."

Daisy laughed as they left the room. "Yes, they do, you big softie."

She managed to get back inside and lock up before her phone started buzzing again.

"You amenable to a visit?"

She grinned. "Is this how you open all your phone calls?"

"Only to hot brunettes with curls for miles and a mouth made for sin."

"You're so good at this."

"Does that mean I'm invited?"

"Are you a vampire then? I need to invite you in?"

There was a tap at her door and she looked through the peep-hole to find him standing out there in a hoodie with a baseball cap on.

She opened up. "You look like the Unabomber."

"Paps out front." He shut the door after putting out the DO NOT DISTURB sign. "Don't want that headline tomorrow."

"Yeah, I saw. I don't know how you deal with it, to be honest."

He tossed the hoodie and cap aside before drawing the drapes. "You deal with it." He shrugged. "It's part of the gig. I don't like it, but over time you adjust your life around it. Learn ways to cope. Let's speak of it no more because I'm here to fuck you."

"Well, I certainly approve of that topic change."

"I'm a little dirty." He waggled his brows.

"You're a lot dirty. It's one of your best qualities."

He laughed, prowling her way, pulling his T-shirt off as he did. "That was my not-very-subtle way to suggest a shower. I like you wet."

"You don't need a shower for that."

Damn, she made him laugh.

"However." She turned and walked toward the bathroom, tossing her shirt and bra in a nearby chair. "I think shower sex is pretty nice, so I won't argue."

He loved to look at her naked body. He hadn't realized it so much while he had it to look on three weeks ago after Adrian and Gillian's wedding. But in the time since he'd thought about it a lot.

She stepped into the huge shower enclosure and he followed, tossing his clothes to the side when he did.

"I wish my shower was this big," she murmured as she stepped under one of the many showerheads.

"Mine is. You can come use it after the tour ends." Even if he didn't have a huge bathroom at his home, that she wanted one would have him making calls back home to have one put in.

She smiled, her eyes closed, head tipped back. Water rushed over her curves as her nipples tightened, darkening.

"You have freckles." He stepped to her, banding an arm around her waist to haul her closer. He kissed her shoulder, over the freckles he'd just noticed.

"I do. I used to worry about it. Of course Cal has nothing like a single freckle. So much pretty on a man seems unfair."

"Oh, Curly, your freckles make my mouth water."

"Mmm. Thank you." She reached around his body, grabbing two handfuls of his ass, and pulled him even closer.

"I've thought of pretty much nothing but seeing you naked for the last three weeks. Now that you're here, naked and slippery, I'm so stunned I'm not sure where to start."

Her eyes opened as a smile curved her lips. "I'm sure I have a few suggestions if you're really at a loss." She let go and squeezed some soap into her palm and the scent of oranges hit his nose.

"That's what I've been smelling!" He copied her, sliding his palms over her breasts and down her belly as she found his cock, wrapping her fist around it, sliding up and down until he made a sound he hadn't intended to make.

"There's a bench in here, Handy. I think you should fuck me."

"I plan to. But I want to taste you first. Make you come a few times. Then."

She frowned a moment and he laughed.

"Turn around. Hands on the tile. Stick your ass out."

She did and he looked his fill at the bounty of her back and that ass of hers. Mmm.

He slid soap-slick hands all over her until she'd relaxed. She was greedy. Wanted it all and right then. But he liked long, slow fucks. So he'd tire her a little with some orgasms and then they'd get to the fucking portion of the program.

Her breasts fit in his palms perfectly and she arched into him when he rolled and tugged her nipples.

"Sensitive nipples." He kissed her shoulder, sliding his teeth over that sensitive skin until gooseflesh broke over her. He wanted to learn her. Their coupling back in Washington had been fast and furious. Intense. Now he had the time and he planned to take it. Every last moment he could.

He sent his free hand down her belly, between her legs. All while he crowded her from behind. It was enough to slide his cock against the lush flesh of her ass, slick from soap as he found her clit hard and ready.

He teased her until she thought she would lose her damned mind. Slowly ramping her up and then backing off a few beats. And then starting over. She lost track of time as the water beat at them, as he slowly stroked her clit, brushing his cock against her butt. One hand still pinching her nipple.

He was so very good at this.

And finally, he pinched her clit between his thumb and middle finger and there was no holding back. She leapt into climax as it swallowed her up, holding her under. She hadn't even noticed that he'd rinsed her off and turned her.

"Now then. I need you in that bed in there so I can eat your cunt."

Whoo.

Funny how easy she went from discomfort at the word to the sound of it from his mouth sending a wildfire of heat through her system. Like Pavlov's dog. Only for sex.

She dried off, tossing the towel over the rack, and headed to the bedroom. She'd been sort of shocked at the size of the bed. It dominated the room, which wasn't overly large. But it worked, gave the bedroom a very cozy feel.

The bedding was soft and very fluffy, which was good because he bent to pick her up and toss her on it.

"You like to do that."

He grinned, looking like a rock-star pirate. "You're small enough to make me feel like the Hulk or something. Plus, you jiggle in all the best parts. What's not to like?"

Holding up some foil packets, he placed them on the nightstand and joined her on the bed. "Now then."

She wanted to kiss him awhile. So she moved close, leaning in to get one eyelid and then the other. Across his brow line. Down his jaw. Over his chin and up again. Against the blade of each cheekbone and over the bridge of his nose. He relaxed into her touch, accepting her kisses easily. His fingertips traced each bump of her spine.

He opened to her immediately, his taste rushing back through her as if it hadn't been absent for those weeks. He was a bold kisser. He knew what he was about. He used his lips, his tongue, his teeth. He didn't just kiss, he tasted. He seduced and then he feasted. By the time she realized it, he'd already taken over the kiss and made it his. She had no complaints about that part. Not at all.

She found herself on her back as he kissed over her eyes. Each step was an echo of what she'd done. The tickle of his beard added extra sensation against the skin of her neck.

He found his way to her nipples. Those kisses and licks took on an edge as he bit. Just barely shy of pain. Shivers exploded through her. He nibbled, licked and bit over each breast until she writhed into his touch. Needing more.

Damn, she was responsive. Beautiful in the way she arched, demanding more. Each place he kissed told him more about her. She sucked in a breath when he kissed the hollow at her hip. Made a weepy sort of gasp when he'd bitten her nipples. The spot beyond her jaw had made her moan. She liked having her belly kissed, especially around her belly button. He filed it all away for next time.

And there *would* be a next time.

He licked down the seam where her leg met her thigh, spreading her wide open so he could get at her pussy.

He hummed his delight as he took a long look. So pretty. Slick. Ready for him.

He took a lick and she shivered.

Responsive here too. Ready to come again after the short recess from that orgasm in the shower. He liked that too.

She tasted so fucking good. And the noises she made shot straight to his cock. He tried not to think of it, but it was difficult when she punched the mattress, digging her heels into the bed on either side of his body.

Demanding more.

So he gave it to her.

Gave it to her hard and fast, glorying in the way she came

so hard against his lips and tongue. In the way she tasted and felt beneath him.

He kissed her gently as she recovered, trying to get his control back into place before he got inside her again.

He flopped to his back and she got to her elbow, looking down at him. "You should get a platinum record for that."

He grinned, his eyes still closed.

"Glad to be of service."

"Now it's my turn."

She kissed his belly and he stopped her. "Curly, I'm very, very close. If you put those lips anywhere near my cock, it'll be over. I very much want into your pussy. I want to fuck you until your tits jiggle."

"Oh. Well then."

He opened up to find her grabbing the condom, holding still as she rolled it on.

And then she straddled his thighs and he nearly blacked out.

But he managed to keep his cool as she got into place, angling him to slowly sink back, taking him deep.

"Mmm."

She wore that smile he'd been thinking of. She smiled a lot in general, but this was a sex smile. A private Mary smile she only gave him while they were like this. He didn't care if anyone else had seen it before. It only mattered that he saw it then. That this Mary was his delicious secret.

And she began to ride.

Slowly, she rose to her knees, nearly coming all the way off, and then she reversed course, sliding back down to take him in fully.

Over and over until beads of sweat popped out on his brow. He knew he had a thin sliver of control left.

"You're killing me."

Again her smile. "Nuh-uh."

She felt so good. Her body right around his cock. The heat of her burning against his skin, even through the latex. Her hair had begun to dry and curl up again. It flowed around her face and down her shoulders like a wild river.

Her skin gleamed with the sweat of a good, hard fuck. Her breasts swayed just so. Her expression was open, candid. A woman who liked to come. Who liked sex and wasn't afraid for him to know it.

For some reason this got to him in ways no other woman had.

She swiveled when she came back down on him and the last threads of his control wisped away. He was so close he could already feel climax sliding through his system.

His fingers dug into the muscle at her hips, holding her in place as he rolled his hips to thrust up as he came.

She fell to the bed beside him as he managed to roll out. "Be right back. Don't go anywhere."

When he returned she snorted. "Where would I go? I'm naked, pretty boneless and I have an equally naked man in my room. I have everything I need right here."

"Want a beer? I didn't order one at dinner, but after the day with my brothers looking at houses, my god."

"I haven't even looked in the mini fridge but you're welcome to whatever is in there. Or we can order some. Was it awful, then? I thought you got on with your brothers."

He laughed as he padded from the room to poke around in

the mini fridge. As he suspected, Adrian had taken care to stock it well.

"Adrian is a good host," he called out, but she moved out to join him, now wearing a bright yellow short robe thing that showcased her tits.

"Wow, that's my favorite robe ever."

"Daisy gave it to me. She does that."

He cracked open the beers, handed her one and clinked his to it. "Cheers. Welcome to New York City, Mary Whaley. I'm sure glad you're here."

They settled on the couch. He pulled her legs up over his. "I am close with my brothers. But the process of looking for a house is stressful enough. Paddy kept getting calls and Vaughan chatted up the real estate agent and I just wanted to look at the one house and come back. But of course Vaughan wants to nail her so we had to look at other houses and really, a few we saw were also pretty awesome and great options, so that meant calls back to Ezra. Herding cats. That's what our mom says we're like. She's right."

"I can't even imagine being a real estate agent and having you three show up. My lord. All that charm in one place. It's lucky she didn't pass out. Did you choose one?"

"I think so. I sent pictures to Ezra. He's going to look them over and get back to me in the morning."

"Ezra is the oldest, right? He runs the ranch with your dad, you said?"

He nodded, wondering if she knew the story.

"He's the stable one? Ryan is the stable one in our family. Cal is a hothead, though not at work. I'm the artsy one. My dad—who is a retired ironworker, by the way—says I'm flighty. But he smiles so it's not an insult. Ryan is a schoolteacher. Math and biology. At a middle school. I don't know how he does it. But the kids love him. He never loses it with them. He's the one I talk to about my business stuff. Cal sets up my business paperwork, but Ryan gives the best advice."

Being with her was . . . surprisingly normal. He didn't sit around after sex, drinking beer and talking real estate with other women. He couldn't have told anyone about their backgrounds or what their families were like.

"Ezra used to be in the band. He started it actually. But it was not easy for him. He decided to leave and focus on the ranch. It was his idea to start the hay crop. He and my dad are a lot alike. He's a hell-raiser. Or he was, he's mellowed." Since he got out of rehab and worked all day long on horseback or in a truck. The physical nature of the job seemed to fill a need in him.

"It's nice you guys can do this for your parents."

"It's one of my favorite things about fame. Having the money to do things for my parents like this. They've done so much for us. It's a good thing to take care of them."

Later that night, as she fell asleep against him, he realized he'd gotten used to her awfully fast.

7

"Can I just tell you you clean up well?" Damien looked her up and down. She wore a smart navy-blue dress with towering heels. Truly she was absolutely gorgeous and elegant and he was very glad he was with her that evening.

"As many times as you like."

Her smile was saucy. She was saucy. He liked it. Liked her.

"I've got a cab ordered for us downstairs. We have some time first. Would you like a drink?"

"That's nice of you. Yes. I'd love one. Here or . . . ?"

They were set to head off to some swank restaurant that was ridiculously hard to get a table at. Adrian had buttered some people up and scored a reservation for two and she'd chosen him as her plus one.

"They have a bar at the restaurant. I looked it up. Not that I needed the bar. I mean I wanted to see what I was getting into." God, he was fucking this up. She made him nervous. Not because she was judgy or snooty. But he wanted her to like him. Wanted to be sure he could handle himself at this place. He liked to know things. Being prepared was his measure of control.

Her laugh calmed him a little. "It's fine. Yes, let's go there. I like to check out bar food too. I haven't eaten all day just to be ready."

She took his arm. "Also, you really do look amazing in a suit. It works on you."

He'd dressed up for her and he was glad he had.

"Come then, lady. Let's get our grub on."

When they arrived at the restaurant, her eyes glittered. He squeezed her to his side, loving that she was so happy and that he could share that with her. In the bar, she ordered a very dry vodka martini with an olive and a few items from the menu.

Plenty of people recognized him, but none approached, which he was thankful for. Maybe they forgot when they got a load of Mary's legs in those damned heels. He knew he'd nearly stumbled twice because he'd been staring as they walked.

By the time their reservation came up, he was ready to have her to himself in a more intimate situation. Bars were fun and all, but at their table it was intimate. He sat close enough to speak quietly with her, close enough that he could smell her perfume.

She chatted with the server, asking a million questions. So much so that the chef-owner came out and her eyes widened, though she managed to keep it together. He asked about her catering, her food, and invited her to come back again the next time she was in the city.

"If you'll permit me, I have a menu in mind."

Jean Louis Valpar was her idol. And he stood right there, gray-haired, French and impeccable. Oh and charming. And he had a menu planned? As if she'd say no?

"We would be most appreciative. I've been an admirer of your food for some time. I can't wait to taste what you've got in store for us."

He took her hand, kissing her knuckles. "It will be my pleasure."

He spoke to the server in rapid-fire French and the server disappeared to procure whatever he'd told her to.

"She'll be back momentarily." Jean Louis bowed. "It was wonderful to meet you, Mary and Damien."

Once he'd gone, Mary turned to Damien. "Oh. My. God."

Damien smiled, taking her hand. "I sensed you might admire him a little."

"He's like . . . my idol. The first real cookbook I ever had was *Jean Louis's Kitchen*. When people say they wanted to go to Disneyworld or whatever, I always said I wanted to come here."

"That's awesome."

The server returned with several appetizers, and the sommelier came by with wine.

"Chef Valpar suggests these wines to go with each course."

She looked over the list and handed it Damien's way.

"That's a lot of courses."

Mary grinned at him. "I know. I'm so glad I have an empty stomach. Though the martini has hit."

Wine was poured and she dug in, sharing with Damien.

"I wish you were with me every time I went out to eat. I'd never have chosen any of this stuff. And yet, each forkful you create is perfect."

She blushed. "Thank you."

"So what ignited this love of food?"

"I don't know. I just have always loved it. My grandmother took me to a swanky restaurant in Portland for my eighth birthday. It doesn't exist anymore. But it was old-school French. I was astounded by all the silverware, by the menu, which had been in French as well. My grandmother told me, after I had made a very safe choice, that I'd never ever look back at my life when I was her age and say I wished I'd made safe menu choices. She said life was about taking chances and trying new things. So I did. And I never really stopped."

"I like that story. When I was growing up— Oh my god, what is that?"

"Abalone."

"Wow. Love it." He finished chewing and went in for a few more bites. She loved to watch people eat. Especially Damien. He had started off wary but had taken up the challenge.

He sipped his wine. "This is also awesome. Anyway, we rarely went out to dinner when I was growing up. We didn't often have much extra money. My mom's a great cook, but we're a meat-and-potatoes family. I never really went to fancy places, not until we hit it big and label people started to take us to lunch."

"I love meat and potatoes. My favorite meal of my mom's is meatloaf. Also, small hole-in-the-wall places can really be great finds. Some of the best food I've ever eaten has been from some three-table place in a strip mall."

Another course arrived and she had to clasp her hands on her lap to keep from rubbing them together with glee.

"You're really happy right now, aren't you?"

"I am. This is . . . it's special. I'm blown away. Taste this." She held her fork out and he leaned in to take a bite. "I hope you're not weirded out that I like to share." She really did hope not, because she wanted to grab some of what was on his plate.

"Hell no. I like it." He indicated his plate and she hoped she didn't look like a hungry animal when she forked up some of his food.

It was hours later when they walked outside. He hailed a cab and she leaned into his side, despite the August heat.

"It's a beautiful thing to watch you around food."

She tipped her head back. "Yeah?"

He nodded. "Oh yeah. You enjoy it like nothing I've ever seen. You get this light in your eyes. Pure joy. Sensual. Really, really hot. Thanks for sharing this with me."

"Thank you for coming with me. And for not complaining when I ate off your plate."

He kissed the top of her head. "Anytime."

Two women approached. "Oh my god, you're Damien Hurley!" They giggled and he smiled at them.

"I am. How are you two ladies this fine evening?"

"You're so hot. Would you sign an autograph?" She started digging in her purse, unsteady on her feet.

"So are you staying in town? We have tickets to see you tomorrow night. Can we come backstage? We'd totally make it worth your while, if you know what I mean."

He chuckled.

They ignored Mary totally. One of them even sort of edged in front of her. She stepped back, shocked at the behavior.

He looked back to her. "Hey, don't go anywhere."

Damien saw the look on her face, knew she was pissed. He felt bad—it had been a pretty fucking stellar night up until that point.

A cab rolled up and the doorman opened the door. She shot him a look over her shoulder and got in. "Looks like you're busy. I can go back on my own if you'd like."

"Gotta run. Have a good night, ladies, and enjoy the show." He hurried, disentangling himself from their grabbing hands and slid into the cab.

Mary stared straight ahead as they pulled away from the curb.

"I'm sorry about that."

"Yeah, I could tell." There was enough ice in her voice to make him shiver.

"Look, it happens. What am I supposed to do? Be rude?"

"Um, in case it's escaped your notice, you *were* rude. To me. I don't give one tiny drop of fuck about two drunken skanks offering you a three-way for a backstage pass. You gotta do what you gotta do, but don't cry to me about being rude when you were to me."

The cabbie met his eyes in the rearview for a moment, sharing one of those sympathetic guy glances.

Damien had considered her pretty easygoing, but Mary Whaley had a temper on her. He should have guessed given the way she was in bed, but wow, she was pissed and he was probably going to hell because it made him hot for her to see it.

He took a deep breath. "You're right. It happens so often I guess I just sort of get immune to how it affects everyone around me. Don't let this ruin what has been one of the best nights of the entire year. Please?"

He took her hand and she gave him one slowly raised brow.

"How do you do that? I can manage a single brow raise, but the slow draw up, I can't do it." He managed to give her his most charming smile.

"It *was* a lovely evening. Until that. Look, I get it. We aren't married or anything, but we were on a date. I don't own you. I just expect to not have some floozy push me out of the way while she offers up her sexual services."

He nodded. "You're totally right. Can I tell you that the overwhelming majority of my fans are awesome and respectful? And I was raised right, I'll have you know. We're on a date and you deserve respect."

"Hm."

He knew she'd forgiven him, thank goodness. But the way she'd so casually tossed out that they were just on a date and nothing more rattled around at the back of his mind. She was so much more than just some woman he had fun with.

"How about we go up on the roof and look at the stars? There's a pretty garden and places to lounge around."

She finally smiled. "All right then."

On the roof it was quieter, but the sounds of the city still rose to greet them. The air was warm, the sky was clear and even the lights from all around them couldn't totally kill the stars high above.

He got them both drinks and steered her to a padded chaise he'd sighted as they got outside. It was in a quiet little corner so he could have her all to himself.

She sat, taking her shoes off and tucking her legs up under her body.

"What is this again?" he asked her. She'd been the one to tell him what to order back at the bar.

"They call it the Skyline. When I make them I just call them ginger lime fizzes. It's fizzy water with ginger and lime juice. I steep my ginger in the fizzy water in a little muslin bag. Don't know how they do it here. But it's quite tasty."

He clinked his glass to hers and they settled back.

"I'm so full. Like to-the-brim, I-need-to-unbutton-my-jeans-and-take-a-nap full."

He laughed. "Exactly. Or as my dad calls it, Thanksgiving full." He put an arm around her shoulders and she leaned in to his body.

"Are you ready for tomorrow's show?"

"I am. This is a special venue for us. We played here the first time our CD hit Billboard at number one. The crowds are always good to us, always rambunctious and noisy. It feeds your energy."

"Is it as amazing as it seems to have them sing the words to the song? I go to see Pearl Jam at least twice every tour and from the audience perspective, it gives me chills to be singing along and have Ed get quiet and let the crowd finish the words."

"I don't even know if I could do justice to what it's like. You're flattered that they like you enough to pay to come to a show. They gotta deal with traffic and parking and then everything costs so much. But they come. They spend their hard-earned money and time and they come to the show. And then they sing along. It's . . . I don't even know. Astonishing. Humbling. Our fans kick ass. They've been so loyal from day one. We meet our fan club folks in every city when we roll through and love 'em."

He liked that her questions showed how much she really thought about things. She was insightful as well as beautiful.

"It's a slog sometimes. The road I mean. You're in a different hotel every night, or the bus. And the toilet is always breaking down and you don't have much privacy. You get sick of everyone. The food is utter shit most of the time. So you roll into the next town and you set up and then you walk out on that stage and it all comes back to me. When I sit behind my kit and I look out over that audience and they're cheering and they've made signs and they throw stuff on stage and yell out their favorites and yeah, sing along and it's the most powerful reminder of just how lucky I am. The exhaustion fades and the joy of making music with my brothers comes back and I remember I'm so fortunate to have this life."

"That's lovely. I'm so glad you have that. I can't imagine the pressure you must be under sometimes. I know some of it through Gillian about Adrian and this chance he took making this double album and all that. But it's got to be so much more than what she can tell me. I admire that you do what you do."

"Thank you. Thank you for coming out here. And for dinner and for being you. I'm really glad to be here with you right now." In fact, he couldn't think of a single place he'd rather be than right there with her at his side as they stared up at the stars.

He was, indeed, a really lucky man.

8

S he had her special access badge on and stood just left of the stage, watching Damien play drums. The crowd screamed so loud she wasn't sure how Adrian avoided losing his hearing.

Sweet Hollow Ranch was up first, opening for Adrian. They were pretty damned successful in their own right, so she knew this mini tour was more because they all liked each other and had fun playing together.

And it showed.

From where she stood she could see the container of extra drumsticks affixed to the stand to Damien's right. He wore black fingerless gloves and no shirt. Sweaty. He sang along on the chorus and occasionally took a line or two on his own. He had a good voice. Slow and a little whiskey and smoke. Like he was.

Paddy had a knockout stage presence. He was every inch the frontman. He cocked his head, letting his hair fall forward over one eye. He crooned, the gravel in his voice bringing sighs and hoots from the women in the audience.

Vaughan had his own way. No less sexy than the others, but with a sort of laid-back ease the other two didn't have. He grinned when the women threw their panties on stage.

"Who does that?" Jules's lip curled.

Mary tended to agree that it was gross and lacking self-respect. But she was also lucky enough to have spent many hours naked and sweaty with one of the Hurley brothers. She didn't blame other women for wanting a slice.

"Doesn't look like they find it to be a hardship." Cal shrugged, kissing Jules's temple as she sniffed her annoyance.

"Is he, like . . . that energetic in bed?" Daisy asked, watching Damien play the drums like a madman.

"He's certainly that creative." Mary knew she was grinning but she couldn't help it. "He's really good with his hands."

And other parts. All his parts really.

"*Damn.*"

"Yeah. Usually I'm the one that sweaty when he's finished. If I had any muscle control left I'd totally use my lighter."

Daisy laughed, her arm linked with Mary's. "We need to have a long, graphic discussion when we get back home. Levi is, um, enthusiastic about hotel sex. Who knew? His house is way nicer than our hotel room, for goodness sake. But he's keeping me nice and relaxed. I figure it'll be a chore to get you away from sex dude over there so you can tell me when we get back. Then I want every single detail."

"I'd say something like how it wasn't as exciting as you made it out to be. But I'd be lying."

"Gurl."

She nodded at Daisy. "I am *not* exaggerating. Anyway." Her gaze went back to him. He was so sexy she could barely stand it. She wondered if he'd feel odd if she wanted to lick him. He was sweaty and it should have been gross. But it so was *not*.

Probably not. He liked sex. He hadn't shown anything less than total enthusiasm for it in whatever manner it came.

He was sort of feral up there. So much energy. Legs moving. Arms moving. His biceps actually rippled as he played. His tattoos glistened under the lights.

Something south of her belly button might have actually pulsed. Good gracious.

She was going to have to jump him the first opportunity she got and that was all there was to it.

And when the audience sang along with "Lay Back," one of their biggest hits, it was different for her. After their conversation the night before she watched them from a totally new perspective.

He turned to catch her eye as she sang along too. He grinned and she grinned back. Their connection surprised her because it was so unexpected. He got to her without even trying.

They finished their set and exited on the side where she waited. He tossed his sticks out into the audience and then headed right to her, kissing her hard and fast, leaving her even more breathless.

"You were on fire out there."

He tried to step back, but she kept her arms around his waist to hold him in place. "I'm getting you sweaty. Sorry."

She gave him a smile, sending one brow up. "Don't be sorry. I've been sweaty ever since you started playing."

He laughed. "Oh, so it's that way?"

She shrugged. "Does that make me a deviant?"

"Whatever it makes you, I'm glad of it. I do need to clean up. Just for like ten minutes. I'm playing Adrian's set too."

"I'll be here."

He leaned in close. "I'd invite you back. You know how much I like you wet. But my brothers are around."

"You can get me wet later."

"That's a promise I'm going to make you keep."

She watched him retreat. He had a really nice back. Damn.

It was fascinating to watch them take down Sweet Hollow Ranch's gear and put Adrian's out. People were everywhere seemingly all at once. Techs brought out and tested various guitars. Microphones were being checked.

She'd seen it before when she'd been in the audience. But it was different here. So close she could see it better. See the hive of activity in the wings and back behind curtains. She'd had no idea that there were things beneath the stage as well.

Like a whole secret world she now had access to. Crazy and awesome.

Brody had Rennie on one side and Elise on the other. Rennie had cool headphones on to protect her hearing. Miles had them too. Todd and Ben were on the other side of the stage, keeping an eye on Erin in their way. The area was positively awash with friends and family and it made Mary so happy for Gillian and Miles. So much love and support. They both deserved it so much.

Adrian's CD had dropped just two weeks before—much to Adrian's relief, Mary knew—and had skyrocketed up the charts, dominating everything in its path. The double CD was full of material about the change in Adrian's life. About finding love both with Gillian and his son. About bitterness and finding salvation in those you loved.

Mary adored that CD and not just because it was about people she cared for. There was an energy in the music that she'd connected with. A joy in creation. She was thrilled to be part of it.

Damien avoided the women who always seemed to make their way backstage no matter how much security was in place. He smiled at them, nodded but kept walking.

He had company for that night, thank you very much, and no plans to fuck that up. Especially after that scene the night before with the two chicks outside the restaurant.

Mary was a classy woman. She'd take one look at this insanity and run. So he went straight to the dressing room, showered, chugged a protein shake to get his system back on track and headed back up to where she was.

"Hey, Damien."

Shit. What was her name? Lisa? Sandy? He smiled at a woman he partially remembered having given him a blow job last tour. Maybe. She looked familiar enough. A little bit of guilt lay in his belly. It wasn't much fair to her either.

"Hey." He nodded with a smile and kept walking. She caught up and he slowed down, not wanting to come up the stairs and have Mary see.

"What are you up to?"

"Gotta run, back on stage for Adrian's set in two minutes. Have a good one."

She got it, he could tell. It made him feel like an asshole, which his mother had been saying for a while. But now he knew Mary and she'd given him some perspective.

Sure, it was early with her and all. But not so early he couldn't tell it was different than all the women before. And not so different he didn't know instinctively that Mary would hate this part of his world. He never wanted to hurt her.

He waved and kept walking. She peeled off and headed back down to the hallway they'd come from and he moved toward the best part of the tour.

He put an arm around her waist when he got back and she smiled up at him, leaning into his body.

"I'm disappointed you're not sweaty anymore."

"You are? God, why? I'm a beast when we get off stage. You don't want any of it, I promise."

She tiptoed up and he bent to hear.

"It was hot. Really, really hot to see you so sweaty from playing drums. I wanted to take a long lick."

A shiver went through him. "Ah. Well, next time then. Or you can watch me practice and in private you can lick me. Long as I can lick you right back."

Her laugh was low and sultry and she made him happy.

He stepped away, needing to get back into the right head space.

Damien put his rock star back on and Mary gave him the room to do it, fascinated as she watched. Adrian approached. He was . . . different. Wearing a different face. His performance face maybe, but damn, he was sexy. He moved to Gillian, taking her into a big hug. He spoke quietly in her ear and she blushed.

Erin didn't look a whole lot different than she normally did. She tended to wear that otherness more boldly.

She nodded at Damien and grinned over at Adrian and Gillian. "You all ready?"

Across the stage Brody had come out with Martine and Ben held Alexander. Both little ones wore big headphones as well.

Erin waved at them all. "Swiss Family Rock Star. We're like the Waltons of rock and roll."

Mary laughed. "Totally."

The lights went down and the excitement and tension back-stage ramped up. Erin had her eyes closed, her head was down and she patted a little pattern on the thigh of her jeans.

Damien rolled his head on his shoulders and Adrian bounced up and down a few times.

"Ladies and gentlemen, Adrian Brown."

The crowd roared and the lights flashed as he jogged out, waving. Erin followed and then Damien got behind his drum set testing them, delighting the fans.

They launched into an old Mud Bay song, the band Erin and Adrian started many years ago when they were little more than kids.

One of Mary's favorites, too.

She danced around, waving her arms, clapping and having a great time. Vaughan and Paddy joined them, bracketing her sides. She liked Damien's brothers, really liked that they'd come to watch him play.

Several songs in and they finally took a break. Adrian gulped down some water as he handed off one guitar for another.

"Hey, folks, so I know this young musician and I convinced him to play a song or two with us tonight."

"Oh my god! They're calling Miles out!"

Miles took a deep breath, handed the big headphones off to his mother and put in an earbud-type thing in one ear as he headed out.

She took Gillian's hand, squeezing.

And Miles walked on stage like he'd always been there. That shy, sweet toddler was something far more as the lights hit him.

He blushed though, when the tech handed him his bass. Erin leaned in to kiss his cheek as he got plugged in.

Adrian hugged him, one armed. "This is my son, Miles. You can hear him a little on the new record. He helped out in the studio. We're going to do a cover. One of his favorites."

The chords sounded for Radiohead's "Creep."

Mary moved to Gillian's side, Jules on the other. Gillian cried, but they were good tears. Mary had her own, as did Jules.

"Creep" had been the first song Miles had learned the bass line for right after Adrian had come into his life. It was a special song between the two of them. And for Gillian as well.

Miles had been part of Mary's life since he'd been an infant. To see him out there on stage, acting very much like his father, totally blew her away. Tears came and she made no move to stop them. This was her Miles. She'd changed his diapers. Had cooked French toast for him when he'd slept over at her house. He'd ridden his bike in her long driveway. Had cleaned out her pantry on more than one occasion. He was like a son and she really couldn't be prouder of him.

"That's our boy." Jules gave a whistle as the song ended and everyone applauded. Miles nodded his head, tipping his chin in a way she'd seen Adrian do dozens of times. In fact, the way Erin did. Those Browns.

Gillian had found her special someone. Miles had the father he'd always deserved. What a beautiful time in Mary's life to see her friends so happy.

Until this tour, Damien and his brothers had tended toward some hard-ass partying after a show ended. But with Adrian, things had changed, and Damien hadn't minded. If he wanted to party, there was always one to be had if they wished it.

There was power in that. Seductive to have so many people at your beck and call willing and able to make your every desire a reality. But he'd done plenty of shots. Had banged plenty of women whose names he couldn't recall. He'd done more things than he'd ever dreamed of back home on the ranch.

And yet, he thought as he watched Mary hug Miles and compliment him about his performance that night, the simple things still made him happiest. And that was a powerful lesson.

"Kinda fast, isn't it?" Vaughan sidled up next to him.

"Hm?"

Vaughan laughed. "Her. You. You and her. It's clear just by

watching the way you are with Mary that she's different. You're different. But you don't really know her."

"I know her. But I want to know more. Over the last few months I've shared more with her on the phone or via text than I think I have with any woman ever."

"I like her." His brother shrugged.

"Me too. A lot."

"Yeah, kind of obvious, that."

He grinned. "I know. I can't help it. It seems silly to pretend I don't dig her."

"She digs you too. But this life . . ."

Damien nodded. "I know." It was hard to have a relationship in the industry. So much temptation. And he knew without a doubt that Mary Whaley would not tolerate any nonsense with other women or with wild partying.

"Dude, can you give her that?"

"You think I'm so weak I can't?" Damien paused. "I'm not asking her to marry me or anything. I like her. I want to like her more. I want to know her. I want a real relationship with her. I know it'll be hard. But I'm not an idiot."

"I don't think you're weak. I think you love women. A lot. But I can see this one is different and that's good. At the same time I want you to be careful with her. She's a . . . well, she's not what we're used to seeing out here."

"All I can do is take it slow and step by step." He could actually stop seeing her now. End it nicely. It would probably save heartbreak. Maybe. But he wanted her. Wanted more.

A year ago he'd have been so freaked out by the very idea he'd have never even looked her way again. But he'd already begun to get tired of that life. Of fast women—though not of fast cars.

He couldn't help but think Mary Whaley was meant to cross his path exactly when she did. He was ready for her.

He caught up with her once things had calmed down and they'd gotten back to the hotel. Adrian, Miles and Gillian had gone to bed, as had Erin and her family.

He tapped on her door and she opened with a smile.

"Wanna come take a walk with me. See New York this late?"

She smiled. "All right."

He liked that she wasn't afraid. New York City was, in his opinion, the most exciting city on the planet. He loved it there and he dug that she didn't hesitate to jump in and enjoy it with him.

Though it was late, the path down by the river wasn't deserted at all. Couples walked, people jogged, dogs walked their owners. He and Mary strolled, hand-in-hand, and he relaxed a little bit more as each minute passed.

"I like being with you." He sighed happily.

"Thank you. I like being with you too."

"How'd you like the show tonight? Is this your first time backstage?"

"It was. I have to say it's pretty amazing. I figured it'd be cool and all. I love live music so much. I've seen many, many shows from out front. But so close, with all the activity that goes on behind the scenes? Amazing. I have so much more appreciation and respect for what you all do now. Plus, no tall guys blocking my view or spilling beer on my feet. That's a win too."

He laughed. "Ah yes. Or the narrowly avoided puke incident that leaves you twitchy and nervous any time anyone else leans forward."

"Scars you forever."

"I'm thinking of buying a place here."

"Really? To live in New York full time? I mean, around touring and all?"

"No. I have a place in Oregon and that's my home. But to retreat. Like after a tour when I want to stab my brothers in the face because I've been on a bus with them for months at a time."

"I totally get that. I mean, not that I've been on a bus with my brothers for months. I'd be in prison right now if I had. But sometimes you need a place to escape to for a while."

"Will you come out to our last show? I'll send you tickets." He hadn't planned on asking, but now that he had, he was glad.

"When is it?"

"Little over two weeks from now. At the Gorge."

"I'll have to look at my schedule. The end of summer has turned out to be pretty busy for me so I might have a job. But if I don't, yeah, I'd love to. But you don't need to fly me anywhere. I can drive to that. It's only three hours. And, if you like and you have the time, you can stay at my house for a night or two after. Or whatever. I know you have other things to do."

She flustered him. On one hand she'd invited him to stay with her. On the other she seemed so casual about his invitation. He didn't know what he expected. But being off balance wasn't something he was used to. Or confident about.

He'd have to let it play out the way it was supposed to, he guessed.

He squeezed the hand he'd been holding. "No. I'd like that. You can make me that soup. You did promise."

She laughed. "I did. And I will. For now, I'm so hungry."

"Do you like tacos? I know this place that's open late."

"Who doesn't like tacos?'

9

oney, I promise I will not break your business." Jules patted her shoulder. "It's one day. You're finishing up the job before you leave, for goodness' sake."

Mary knew all this. But leaving to go to the Gorge to see Damien had come so fast, and she worried.

"If anyone calls, I'll have my cell."

"No one is going to call because Daisy is handling everything should there be an emergency. Which there won't be because, hello, one night. You'll be back and everything will be fine. Go on and have a good time."

"*You're* not going." This was the first time she'd ever put someone before her business when they weren't sick or in dire straits. It made her nervous.

"No. But my boyfriend isn't in the band. And my business is different than yours anyway."

"He's not my boyfriend."

Jules rolled her eyes. "Puh. Leeze. You turned away a job for tonight to do this instead. You never do that. He's obviously someone to you. Plus, he's sending a fucking helicopter to pick you up to fly you to the Gorge. Guys like him don't do that for casual flings."

The helicopter thing was pretty freaking awesome, she had to admit.

But she didn't miss the concern on Jules's face and it agitated her.

"Look. He's a nice guy. We have smoking sexual chemistry. I enjoy him. But he's a rock star. His life is on the road and mine isn't. I can't even imagine living like that. It's fun to visit. I'll have a great time while we're together. But this thing isn't permanent and you know it."

"You're not the fling type. If he's not your boyfriend, what is he then? What does he expect from you, and can you give it and walk away unscathed?"

Mary made a face at her friend. It shouldn't have pushed her buttons. She knew they all cared about her and said this stuff out of concern. But it pissed her off that they assumed she was fragile.

"How do you know what type I am? Also, this is more than a fling. Less than a relationship. I'm getting really, really tired of people telling me what I am and am not capable of."

"I'm just saying . . . his life is not yours. He's not in a different lane, he's in a different hemisphere. I love you. I don't want you to get hurt."

"Who wants to see a friend get hurt? My assumption is that all of us would prefer that none of the rest get hurt. But back when you were trying to work this thing out with Gideon and Cal, I supported you. I trusted your ability to make it work, or to deal with the outcome if it didn't."

"Cal and Gideon live here. They wanted to make something with me that was permanent. It's different with Damien. We don't even know him that well. A one-night stand is one thing. But this is uncharted territory for you. He's an expert here. You're not. This isn't the same as what I have."

"Didn't I just say that? Like three minutes ago? We're not moving in together! And I'm saying this because I love you, but if anyone else spoke to me the way you all seem to have been lately, I'd punch them in the throat. Stop assuming I'm a moron."

Jules blushed, speechless for long moments. "I don't assume any such thing. But you're not their type of people."

"Their type? This again? Like Adrian isn't Gillian's type? Better hop on over there and tell her. Or is it only me? Only now that you're in a relationship that you feel so free to hand out advice based on what you think I am? And you admitted you didn't know him, so how do you fucking know what his type of people is anyway? When did you become so judgy?"

"Is that what you think this is?"

"I think you and Daisy like to believe this is about protecting me. But in the end, it makes me feel like you find me incapable of being a big girl and having a nice fun thing with this guy until it loses steam. I'm not stupid. I'm not a virgin. And you're not Dr. Ruth because you're in a relationship." It hurt that they didn't believe in her. That they didn't trust her damned judgment.

"You're being a bitch."

"Maybe. I'm also right. You don't like it. I'm leaving now because I do love you and I don't want to fight with you. I know you care about me. I'm asking you to back the fuck off right now because despite what you may think, I know what I'm doing."

Jules sighed. "Don't leave with this mad between us."

Mary stepped to Jules, giving her a hug. "Tell Cal I said to get his nose out of my business. I know where this is coming from. He's worried. But I have *always* supported his life and his choices, and it's supremely messed up that he can't find it in himself to do the same for me."

She walked out, frustrated.

The truck was prepped and loaded for the breakfast she was catering. Her assistant would handle the cleanup so she could get to the helicopter-pad thingy in time.

Her annoyance faded as she thought about that part. A helicopter.

She knew they worried. But Mary was having the time of her life. They both had a good time. She wasn't in love. She was in like. He was in like. He wanted to shower some rock star in her life; who was she to turn it away?

He met her at the helipad, helping her out with a big grin.

"Girl could get used to this stuff. Hope you don't mind, but I brought my camera." She held it up after taking shots as they flew over the venue. Over the river and then as they landed.

He kissed her once they got away from the helicopter. "Hello there. Long time no see."

"Hello right back."

"Take whatever pictures you want. We don't mind. I doubt Adrian will either."

"Thank you."

She wasn't an artist like Daisy was. But she liked taking pictures, and while they were in New York she realized there was so much to the backstage world at a show that she thought would be beautiful to photograph, so she remembered to bring her camera this time.

"Wow. You know I've been here to at least ten different shows. But seeing it from this perspective is pretty amazing."

The Gorge Amphitheatre was in the middle of nowhere. A hot, dusty parking lot. A venue with no real shade. And yet people came out because of the amazing acoustics and the view. The stage sat between the audience and the Columbia River just beyond. Totally stunning, and once the sun went down the heat was a memory. The breeze came up, the sky turned purple and you were suddenly all right with the fact that it had taken you nearly an hour to get the few miles from the freeway exit to the parking lot.

She'd seen the tents and outbuildings she figured were for the artists performing, but wow, they got a view too. A view not only of the river but of the bowl the venue sat in. Up the sloping hillside from the seats to the lawn, already dotted with blankets and early arrivals.

"Last time I was here I sat way back there." She pointed and he laughed.

"Funny how short a distance it is, but how long the trip can be to get here."

"You're very down-to-earth about your success."

"What else can I be? I could let it go to my head, but fame is fleeting. I want to appreciate every moment I have it, but be grateful for it and know it could just as easily go away. We can't all be Adrian." He snorted.

"He says pretty much the same thing. Not that everyone can't be him." She quickly amended. "But that he wants to be grateful and never take it for granted."

"When you have people like him around you, it's not quite as hard to stay grounded." He tugged on her hand. "Come on. Let me take you back to where Gillian is. I promised her I'd bring you when you got here." He stopped and she nearly bumped into him. "Though I would love to hog you all to myself."

"We have a few days. You can hog me all you want when we get to Bainbridge."

He smiled. "Yeah. I'm counting on that."

There was a labyrinth to get through, crammed with activity. He put a set of badges around her neck. "This will get you everywhere you need to go. If you get lost or whatever, the number for our guy is on the back there. Call him and he'll come get you. He knows you're here."

It was . . . nice that he wanted to take care of her. Truthfully, the whole thing was sort of overwhelming, even as it was exciting. She wasn't going anywhere anyway.

Vaughan strolled out and when he saw them he raised a hand in greeting. But when she got close, he bent to hug her. "It's Mary. Nice to see you."

"Thanks. Excited to see the show tonight."

"Tour closers are always the best. Paddy had a cold, but he's doing much better. Adrian is in high spirits. You just missed Ezra and my parents. They came to see us last night in Portland."

She wondered what, if anything, Damien had told his family about her. Probably nothing. Maybe.

"Too bad. Did you guys get to visit a little at least?"

"Yeah. But we'll be back home soon enough. Gonna be nice to sleep in my own bed for a change."

"Amen to that." Damien waved and Mary turned to see Gillian coming over.

She hugged Gillian tight.

"So glad to see you. I'm happy you were able to come."

"We need to do sound check. I'm going to leave you with Gillian, but I'll come find you once we're done." He gave her a kiss, one that surprised her, but she liked it anyway.

"Okay."

"Well now." Gillian smiled. "I do believe our Damien is sweet on you."

"Speaking of sweet on, where are your men?"

"Nice way to change the subject. We'll be back to that momentarily. Adrian is off with Erin doing heaven knows what. Probably plotting on how to buy Miles more guitars. As if he has a shortage."

Mary linked her arm through Gillian's. "He's one of them now."

"A Brown you mean? Or a musician?"

"Both."

"This is true. He decided in New York that he wants to go to the arts high school now. So I told Adrian he has to drive the boy to Seattle every morning and pick him up every day."

"He'll benefit from it, you know he will."

They went to sit in the shade cast by a fabric overhang. Some-one brought them cold drinks and said food would be arriving shortly. Gillian seemed to have adjusted to it, but Mary was a little starstruck by it all.

"I know. I'm trying. He's losing his anonymity. I'd hoped to protect him better but once he got up on stage the pictures came out and people recognize him now. He'll be safer most likely at the new school. But he'll have to make new friends and spend time commuting. But he's quite good, isn't he?"

Mary nodded. "He has a gift. It would be a crime not to nurture it."

"Which is why I agreed." Gillian sighed, looking out over the area. "He'll thrive, like he should."

Knowing Gillian had a lot to process, Mary left it alone for the moment. Instead she indicated the drinks they'd been handed and the way people stopped to check on them. "Wow, this stuff is . . ."

"It's odd. But then you just sort of, I don't know, deal with it I suppose. I have a handler. The one who gave us the drinks just now. He's a lovely man, makes sure I keep hydrated, that I get fed and don't get left on the outside of all this security. Miles and Adrian have one too. It's . . . well, I'm not used to it, but it's the way this world goes. I'm trying." Gillian sighed. "I seem to be saying that a lot. It makes Adrian happy to be out here. He'd be miserable if we weren't with him. So we're here. It's good for Miles. And it's good for me to have this understanding of what Adrian does. Of how much goes into his career. Plus, it's rather fun. Most of the time. The groupies are not fun, though."

Groupies. She cringed.

"There's a lot of security. Adrian's quite cross when they get in to where his dressing room is, so it's a rarity. But they seem to always be at the periphery. And they have absolutely no qualms about coming on to him right in front of me, or in front of Miles."

"Ew."

Gillian laughed. "Succinctly put. Those Hurley boys do love the ladies. Not Damien though," Gillian added.

"In New York, outside a restaurant, two of them approached him. Just sort of stepped in front of me, edging me out. Like I wasn't even there. I was pretty astonished."

"People are usually nice. They get so excited to see Adrian, and who am I to get mad when they're such big fans. He's flattered. They're the reason he's out here. But those few . . . well, it makes it tough sometimes."

"Everyone at home is on my case because they think I'm blinded to this world by stars in my eyes. Like I'm so naive I can't be with him without falling in love and getting crushed because he's not a forever type of guy."

Gillian sighed. "I've spoken to Jules a little about it. I've gotten to know him. Damien, I mean. He's a good lad. Parties a little hard at times, but not so much that he can't stand. He loves his family. He's quite talented. And he *is* truly sweet on you."

"I'm not expecting anything long term out of this. I wish they'd believe me and realize I'm not a moron."

"You know they don't think that. This is not your world. Or mine, for that matter. It's fast and brutal, and if you scratch the surface there's loads of heartbreak. They see the bad and worry that it'll affect you. You're ours, part of Delicious; we adore you and would neuter anyone who harmed you. But at this point I have a unique perspective, I think. Being back here, watching this world from this side of the stage gives me insight I didn't have before. Yes, it can be wild and crazy. But at the same time, you get to know these boys and how they are. Being on the road means they're in hotel after hotel, plane after plane, or on the bus. They're close, the Hurleys. He's not a rogue or a rake or anything like that. Though he was before. He's intelligent. Well spoken. Respectful of what Adrian and I have. He's good with Miles. I met his parents yesterday, and his oldest brother. They're lovely people. His mother"—Gillian paused to laugh—"is quite a bit like yours. She's bossy and irreverent and totally capable of managing four boys who you know must have been frightfully wild as children. You've spent your life taking care of us. Being a shoulder and a sounding board. Delicious wants you to be happy, and they worry about this life. But I'm living this life right now and it's not as bad as one might believe." She squeezed Mary's hands.

Some food arrived and in her head, Mary thought she could do better, though it was tasty. Gillian's support was important and it made her feel a lot better to know that at least someone understood.

It was enough for the time being.

10

H e woke her gently once he turned the engine off. "We're at your place, Curly. Wake up."

She'd talked and talked on the drive back but once they got to North Bend she'd begun to slow down. He knew she'd been up since four the previous morning to do a job before she'd come to the Gorge, so he was fine to let her sleep.

In lieu of taking a helicopter back, he'd had his car brought out to the Gorge and they'd driven back after the show had ended. The rest of his gear would go back to his house, but he had a suitcase and his wheels and Mary Whaley in the passenger seat, and all felt right with the world.

She stretched, opening her eyes. "Oh man. I've been asleep awhile. I'm sorry."

He came around to open her door. "You needed it."

He grabbed his bag and followed her to the door and then inside. It smelled like her and he paused. He'd only been there briefly, once before when he'd given her a ride home the morning after the wedding.

Pictures took up most of the wall space. He wandered, looking. Her as a child with her brothers. "Is this you and Jules?"

She came over, smiling. "Yes. From fifth grade. She still looks pretty much exactly like that."

"Is it weird that she ended up with your brother?"

"They've been meant for each other for a very long time. I'm thrilled for them both. He needed her. She's ruthlessly organized, a calming element in his chaos."

"I like the way you talk about your friends."

"I'm extremely fortunate to have the people in my life that I do. Are you hungry?"

"Do you have any work today?"

"Nope. I'm off all day long."

"Mmm. Good. So yes to breakfast, because you need to be fueled up for what I'm going to do to you. Twice. Maybe even three times. Then a nap and we can start over."

"My bedroom is around the corner and to the left. You can put your things in there."

He left her bustling around her kitchen, curious about her room.

A big bed. Wrought iron. Bright blue bedspread with orange sheets his mother would call tangerine. It was crisp and fresh and bright. It smelled like vanilla and citrus. More pictures on the wall in here. Some art he wagered came from Daisy, her friend the artist. Books on shelves with cracked spines so he knew she'd read them all.

A robe hung on a hook on the back of her door. The yellow one she'd worn in New York. A mirrored tray on her dresser had a few simple pieces of jewelry on it. He noted she didn't wear much dangly stuff, opting for simple hoops in her ears. She wore her nails short with clear polish. He figured with her job, her hands in other people's food all day, she wouldn't risk a ring that got gunk stuck in it or nails she'd only mess up. Mary was practical that way.

When he came out, it was to the scent of ham and strawberries.

"Wow." He went into her kitchen and noted that she kept an eye on him. "You don't like people in your kitchen, do you?"

She laughed. "It's sort of a joke among my friends. But people have a tendency to touch and adjust, even when they don't mean to. I like things just so. When people mess with *my* just-so it makes me cranky and messes with my food mojo."

He backed off, sitting at a stool at the nearby island. "I totally understand. I have an office at my house. Well, an office and a practice space. When I practice I want to be alone sometimes. They know that if I'm in there they'd better leave me alone. We have a larger space in a studio, a renovated barn actually, where we practice and record together. But my space is about my art. I like it how I like it. Tell me if I can help. Otherwise I'll be right here watching you cook. Because frankly I've never seen anything sexier than you making food."

She blushed. "Flatterer."

"Maybe so. But it's true just the same. Whatcha making?"

"Fried ham, some gravy and toast. Oh and some strawberries, blueberries and mint. Sorry it's nothing fancy."

He laughed. "Nothing fancy? Curly, toast is nothing fancy. Ham, gravy, toast and fruit with mint is so fancy."

"Should have asked if you were like low carb or anything."

"When I come off tour I let myself go for a few weeks. I get up when I want. Eat what I want. Do what I want. Then I get back to working out and being on a schedule. We'll be starting a new record later in the fall. But for now, I will not only eat gravy, I will eat lots of it."

"That's what a girl like me likes to hear."

They ate their breakfast at her large farmhouse table, taking one end. She poured coffee and fresh juice and he just let himself be.

"This is the best thing I've eaten since the last time you cooked for me. Do you ever get tired of it? Want to have others cook instead?"

"I love to go out to eat. Love to taste other people's food. But I'm horribly judgmental. If it tastes like someone phoned it in, or worse, got it out of a vat and made it in the microwave, I get vexed. I don't mind simple food. I love pizza and hot dogs. I just don't like those places with menus that come in three-ring binders and you know that to have a twenty-eight-page menu everything is from a vat, a freezer or a can. I can do that at home; why go out for that?"

"Good question. What is your position on diner food?"

"I love diner food. Next question."

He grinned.

"Microwave popcorn?"

"Love it. Eat it for dinner sometimes, though I do have a few different mixes I shake in for extra flavor. And I do make a homemade version of Cracker Jack."

"Of course you do, Curly."

"Cooking makes me feel better. It relaxes me to create things. I'm not Eric Ripert or Jean Louis Valpar, but making food, sharing it with people pleases me. I feel like I was supposed to do this."

He remembered something. "Wait here."

He jogged to her room, digging through his bag until he found what he was looking for and returned to the table.

"What is it?" She examined the little box.

"A present. Open it."

Inside was a little silver container and a bag.

"A salt cellar!" And not just any old salt cellar, but one that would last forever and take a beating. The bag was—she paused to open it and sniff. Sassafras hit her nose first.

"We were in New Orleans and went to this place that had the best gumbo I've ever eaten. The owner swore it was because of their filé powder they made right there, specifically for the restaurant. I convinced her that I knew someone who would do justice to her filé if she'd sell me some. The cellar I saw at a shop in Portland yesterday. My mom actually saw it first. Just little somethings. Not a big deal."

He blushed and she felt herself fall for him a little bit. Which she knew was a bad idea, but he'd clearly done this thinking of her. Not jewelry. Not a fur coat or something like that. But a salt cellar and some filé powder. It was like the best gift ever.

"It's hard to find the right filé so I can't wait to try it. In fact,

I'll make some gumbo for dinner to give it a test run. As for the cellar, I love it. This is so thoughtful."

He drained his coffee and stood. "I want to see you naked."

She got up, moving to the door to be sure it was locked. "My friends tend to be bargers. Can't have that."

When she got close, he picked her up, surprising her, but not for long. She wrapped her legs around his waist and held on. Her fingers tunneled through his hair, holding him in place as she kissed him.

He held her easily, taking a few steps until her back met the hallway arch. He pressed against her just enough to send a wild thrill through her. He sucked her tongue, sliding his along it in a way surprisingly close to the way he ate her pussy.

Like a switch he pressed, just a look or a touch from this man and her libido went from simmering to roaring inferno. She wanted. So much. Wanted him to fuck her. Touch her. Whatever. She wanted to leave scratches on his back. Wanted to be just a little sore when she woke up from their nap.

And she knew he'd make it happen.

He bit her neck and she made a needy sound. Her hands made their way around his arms to grab at the hem of his shirt so she could get it off.

"Can't wait," he murmured and went to his knees, keeping her in his arms so her butt came down on his thighs instead of the floor.

"Damn, you're good."

He ripped the shirt she wore up over her head. Her bra followed and she got her belt and jeans open and off as he managed to get his jeans open. She grabbed his cock and he nearly snarled.

"Now."

"You're not ready."

She took his hand, guiding it to her pussy, and proved him wrong.

"Fuck." He dug in his wallet, pulled out a condom, and within a breath she was on her back in her hallway and he was pressing into her.

His jeans were still on and they brushed against the sensitive skin of her inner thighs with each thrust. Hard and fast. She wrapped her thighs around his waist, holding him close, keeping him deep. He felt so good this way. Hell, *she* felt so good this way.

His hands held her ass, keeping her at the perfect angle, dragging his dick over her clit again and again. Outside the sun began to rise and birds sang as he fucked her on her runner.

He got to his knees, thrusting still. The muscles of his abdomen rippled with his movement as his skin gleamed from the sweat of hard work. "Will you make yourself come, Curly? Hm?"

She cupped her breasts, her thumbs sliding back and forth over her nipples. He watched with such naked greed it only emboldened her. He took one of her hands, sucking on her fingers, making them wet. She felt a little woozy just watching, it was so hot. The tug and draw on her fingers echoed in her nipples and clit. Then he guided those fingers to her clit.

Shew. He was so dirty it left her delirious. She stroked over her clit, slow but firm. Drawing the pleasure out, knowing he watched, knowing it fed his pleasure in turn.

And then he reached back to adjust her leg, his fingertips finding that place behind her knee. She blew out a gust of air as her muscles tightened around him.

"Shit." He did it again, this time with a little more pressure, sending ripples of sensation from that spot to her cunt. "This is so fucking hot."

She agreed.

He dug into her pussy in short, deep thrusts. The carpet at her shoulder would most likely leave a mark. And she found she liked that idea.

She was so close. Her body knew it. Her eyes drifted halfway closed as she took him in. The power of his upper body, the hotness of the way he still wore his jeans while she was totally naked. The fullness as he fucked into her body while she fluttered around him. It was nearly too much and then it simply overflowed as she came.

He bent, one hand on the carpet next to her head to brace his weight, and he sped up. Deeper and harder. Over and over until he came as well, dropping that final inch to kiss the last of her wits away.

"Now I think I could really take a nice, long nap." He kissed her once more and then behind her knee before helping her up.

She woke up after a long nap, feeling much better. He was still sleeping so she got up carefully and headed to the bathroom. After a shower she'd check her work messages and make another pot of coffee.

One message from her assistant to let her know the breakfast had ended well. She'd known that already because she'd checked in once she'd arrived in eastern Washington yesterday. A call from Jules, apologizing and asking for a return call. A message from Daisy checking in to see if she'd returned from the Gorge yet. Cal being grumpy because she hadn't called Jules back yet. Her mother. Two calls about possible jobs. She wrote those numbers down as she turned her laptop on and called up her calendar.

Damien came out of the bedroom right as she was dealing with the second call. He moved to her quietly, kissed the top of her head and indicated he was going to shower.

He looked as good going as he did coming.

Once she got that call taken care of she figured she'd best deal with Daisy first.

"I'm back. We got in at nearly four this morning." She discarded the junk in her inbox as she made the call.

"Was it fun?"

She smiled. "Yes. It was an awesome show. Adrian was amazing. Sweet Hollow Ranch was amazing. Gillian should be back today too. Miles starts school on Tuesday."

"I can't believe he's going to be in high school. Our little Miles."

"He's so mature. This trip really changed him. He carries himself differently. With more, I don't know, authority? Gillian positively glows."

"Is he there?"

No use pretending she didn't know Daisy meant Damien. "Yes. In the shower."

"I'm waiting for you to invite us to dinner."

Mary laughed. "All right. Come to dinner. Bring some wine. Let Levi pick. I'm making gumbo. I saw some good-looking shrimp at the market day before yesterday. I'll pick some up with some spicy sausage. Damien gave me some filé powder and I'm anxious to try it."

"Yum. Are you assailing my choice in wine?"

"Your man has excellent taste. In wine and women. If I wanted a painting, I'd definitely ask you."

"You should invite Jules too. She's sad. She didn't mean to upset you."

Mary sighed. "For god's sake, it's not the first time I've had a spat with Jules. I've known her since kindergarten. We've fought about probably every single thing under the sun. Why everyone has to be involved with this is beyond me. He's going to be here two days, then he goes back to his life. I don't want to overshadow this visit with any negativity or drama. I'm done with it. Things will be fine but I'm not going to let anyone make me feel bad or stupid or guilty."

"She's sorry. She loves you. *We* love you. We let that get in the way and ended up making you feel a way we never intended. You know how miserable she is when she's in a fight with anyone. I'm sorry. I want you to be happy. I really do. I like him. I like that you like him. I promise."

"I'll see you guys at seven. But if this comes up, I'm not letting you have any food."

"That's so sneaky."

"I'm a sneaky bitch."

Daisy laughed as she hung up.

11

He came out a few minutes later as she was pouring herself a cup of coffee. He looked tousled with his hair still wet, wearing low-slung lounge pants. Clearly freeballing it. Yum.

His expression lit when he saw the coffee. "Oh, just the thing. Can I have some too?"

She poured him a mug. "There's milk in the fridge."

He sipped with a happy sigh. "What shall we do today then?"

"Daisy called and invited herself to dinner with Levi. You'll have to share the gumbo though."

"Sounds good to me. I like your friends." He sat across from her.

"I'll need to run to the market to grab it and a few other

things. They're bringing wine. As for what to do between now and then?" She checked the clock. "We've got six hours. Can you think of anything?"

"C'mere."

He pushed his chair out and she climbed on his lap. "Now then." He parted her robe and took the sight of her in. From her neck to her pussy. The curve at her waist and the beauty of her breasts. "You're so beautiful, I don't know where to start."

She squirmed and got his attention.

"Stop that."

She laughed and he leaned to kiss her collarbone.

"You don't really want me to stop, do you?" She undulated, stroking herself over his cock.

He grabbed the material of her robe, gathering it at the small of her back to hold her arms in place. Her pupils got very large and her breath hitched as her nipples drew tight.

"Well now. Someone likes it a little rough."

She said nothing, just waited for his next move, which only made him hotter for her. He kept the robe tightly gripped in one hand and slid the other down to tease across her labia.

"You're wet."

"You said you liked me wet."

It was his turn to laugh. He bent to lick over and then bite her nipple. She made a low sort of whimper when he did. The heat of her cunt sat right against his cock, the only barrier the thin material of his pants.

"You're so hot." He spread her open as he looked between them, down at the slick darkness of her cunt. He took those

fingers to his mouth and she gasped. He traced over her lips and
groaned when she licked them.

"I'm going to make you come."

"Yes."

He kept her arms bound as he went back to her pussy, barely
touching her clit with the tip of his middle finger. She arched to
get closer and he moved his finger back. "Be still."

She frowned and he had to kiss her before he got back to
work.

"Your clit is hard." He brushed against it harder and she swallowed. "And slippery." He slid down to circle her gate, just barely
dipping inside and then back up to her clit. The way he held her
arms she was arched toward him, close enough that all he had to
do was move just a bit to lick and bite her nipples.

He held her there for some time. Teasing. Taking. Seducing
her. He wanted her to want him to come back. Wanted to see her
again after he went home to Oregon. Wanted to burn himself
into her skin so she needed him as much as he needed her.

He squeezed her clit gently. Over and over and then back
into her gate, turning his wrist to find her sweet spot. She froze
and groaned, her head falling back. "Ah, there it is."

But when he came up again to touch her clit she arched,
grinding herself against him. It was so close he knew he had to
push her over that last bit so he did, biting her nipple as he
plumped her clit over and over as she came in a hot rush against
his hand.

"I love to watch you come. Goddamn."

"You're certainly good at it," she managed to say.

He picked her up and deposited her on the table, standing between her thighs. He took his cock out, stroking it slowly as she watched, her bottom lip caught between her teeth.

"I don't quite know what to do with you."

He kept stroking, fucking his fist as she watched, lying on the table they'd be eating dinner at in a few hours. *Christ.*

She made him so fucking hot.

"I'm going to jerk off and come all over your belly."

Hey eyes widened and she whimpered. Not a bad whimper. No, Mary Whaley got off on what he just said.

Which was good because he sure as hell did too.

"While I was on the road all I could think about was you. Being in you. That soft little squeal you make when I first get my dick inside you all the way. God, I love that."

"I could help, you know. With that." She tipped her chin to his cock.

"That so?"

She slid off the table to her knees, licking around the head as he fisted down to the root.

He cursed under his breath at how good that felt. She did it again and again before kissing and licking over his balls.

"Fuck yes."

Then she kissed back to the head and slick fingers brushed against his asshole. Slowly, with just the right amount of pressure.

He breathed out slowly, but she made it impossible not to rush toward orgasm. The balls of his feet began to tingle, his scalp, even his teeth. And then she pushed in just a little and he grunted, speeding his pace as she licked over the head and crown, keeping him wet.

Over and over again, dragging him into climax and then tossing him over the edge as he began to come. He pulled back and let go on her tits and down her belly. She gasped, arching into it, which brought a second aftershock round to his orgasm until he had to stumble back to the chair to sit or he'd have lost his ability to stand.

She got up. "I'll be right back."

He watched her sway down her hallway and knew he was a total goner.

After pulling his pants back into place, he drank the rest of his coffee and let himself enjoy the quiet for a bit. After the chaos of the road, he'd learned to appreciate the silence. And that he also had a pleasant, post-orgasm buzz was icing.

Some minutes later, he heard the shower turn off and stood, stretching before heading for his phone. While he still had a quiet moment he figured he'd check in back home to be sure everyone got in safely the night before.

He called the main house and his mother answered.

"Hey, Momma. Everyone get back okay last night?"

"Hello, darlin'. I haven't seen either one of your brothers but I know they got in all right. Vaughan's car is in his driveway and Paddy came to collect his mail while we were still asleep. How are you? You're with your Mary?"

He smiled. He'd talked some with his mother about Mary. About how she felt different than the other women.

"I'll be here for another day or so. I'll come home this weekend."

"Take your time. Bring her if you like so we can meet her."

"She's got a business. A successful one, remember? She even

worked yesterday morning before coming out to the Gorge. She's got today off but she runs a supper club thing and I'll go to that tomorrow night. Her friends are a little wary, I think."

His mother sighed. "Well, sweetie pie, you have a reputation. I'll refrain from telling you I told you so. You'll just have to prove them wrong. Put in the time."

"I know. It's all right. Give everyone my love. I'll see you this weekend."

"Love you too."

There was a knock at the door but Mary was still in the bathroom, so he went to look. It was the blonde, Jules, so he let her in, pulling on a T-shirt as he did.

"Mary's in the bathroom. Come in."

She looked him over. "What are your intentions with Mary?" Jules demanded.

"Um. What do you mean?"

"She's not some skank groupie, you know."

"I know. What makes you think I'd believe otherwise?"

"Oh, I don't know. Let's say, fourteen pages of Google results with you with your face in one floozy after another's cleavage. Usually holding a glass of something alcoholic. I know about you."

Mary came out, starting when she caught sight of Jules.

"What's going on?"

"Nothing. Jules here just came over and I let her in." Whatever her friend's deal, he wouldn't solve it by involving Mary.

But Mary wasn't a dummy.

"Jules, I need to get dressed. You can come with me." She pointed to the bedroom, a storm brewing in her beautiful features. Jules skirted past him and into the bedroom.

"I'll be out in a few minutes. If my brother comes to the door, don't answer it."

He took her hands. "Is everything all right?"

She smiled. "Yes. Yes. Small town. Nosy friends. It's fine. She didn't say anything offensive, did she?"

He shrugged. "It's fine. She's concerned for you, and I do have a reputation."

She cursed under her breath.

"I'll be back out in a bit. There's coffee. I have cable. Music is over there." She tiptoed up and he bent down, meeting her mouth in a kiss.

She stomped off and he didn't envy Jules one bit.

"Why are you here?"

"You didn't call me back."

"So you came here to insult him? What the fuck is wrong with you?"

"Before he came around you never said the F-word very often."

"Yes, well, my friends were sane then. You are out of line, Juliet. This is none of your business. You've been really rude, not only to Damien, who is my guest, but to me. I expected better of you." Mary quickly got dressed, catching her hair back from her face.

"I came over to apologize."

When you had been friends with someone since kindergarten, you knew how they did most things. Jules knew when Mary was sad and trying to hide it. Mary knew when Jules was upset too. But they also knew how the other fought. She fought with Jules right then knowing that no matter what, they'd be friends when it was over. But that didn't mean she wasn't going to give her friend a piece of her mind.

Mary put her hands on her hips. "Well then, A-plus effort. You are a total dookiehead, Juliet Lamprey. I like him. He likes me. What the hell is your deal? I helped you when you were struggling with the whole Gideon and Cal thing. I never, ever tried to make you feel guilty or bad. I accepted what you wanted and I helped you make it happen. I don't think it's too much to ask that you stop acting like a self-centered dumbass and realize I'm not stupid."

"I never said you were stupid." Jules slumped, sitting on the bed. "I worry about you. Have you searched this guy online? He's got quite the reputation. I want to protect you from that."

"I know what he is. I know what he's done and I know what he is to me. Last I checked Cal had a reputation too. Also, in case it's escaped your notice, I'm a grown woman. I am absolutely capable of making my own decisions, so step back. What he has done with other women before me doesn't matter as long as it was consensual and all that. Otherwise it's not my business as long as he's not treating *me* that way. And he isn't. He's respectful of me. Of my job and my life. We're having a good time, not planning a wedding. Back. Off."

"Is that so wrong? Am I bad because I care?" Out came the eyes and Mary's anger wisped away into amusement.

"You look like a Precious Moments figurine. I've known you too long to be swayed by your game. You're wrong. Admit it. Really be sorry. Apologize to him for being rude and we can move on. Otherwise, you need to leave. He's a guest in my home and I'm not going to let you make him feel bad. He's a nice guy, Jules. You should give him a chance."

Jules sighed. "I want him to be perfect."

Mary laughed; she couldn't help it. "Oh Jules, what man is perfect? Huh? He makes me happy. I like him. He likes me. That's really it. There's nothing more complicated here than that. Be a big girl and own your shit or get the hell out of my house."

"You're mean."

Mary put on some moisturizer, waiting Jules out. Jules wouldn't leave without doing the right thing. That's why she'd come over to start with. She was a good person and in the end, she'd do what she knew she should.

Heaven knew she'd been on the other end a time or two. That's what friendship was. Give and take. And when you messed up, you made it right.

"Fine. But only if we get to come to dinner tonight."

"I should disinvite all of you for this petty bullshit. In fact, I want to go to dinner. I'm not making anything here."

Jules got up, moving to Mary and taking her hands. "I'm sorry. I was a bitch. I won't make excuses. I called Daisy because I hate it when you're mad at me. Anyone else and I can deal. But you? I just can't. She didn't go around you, I swear. She only told me about dinner because I said I was going to come over here. Please forgive me? I'll be your best friend."

Mary rolled her eyes. "Honestly, you're so full of shit. You owe me. And you owe Damien a real apology. You guys can come to dinner." She held up a hand to silence Jules. "But *only* if you tell my brother that if he so much as gives a mean look

I am really, truly, pinky-swear going to cut him off. This is not all right. I mean it."

Jules hugged her. "I love you. I'm sorry."

"Mm-hm."

"I am. I never, ever wanted to hurt you. I did it all wrong. I told your brothers how smart and awesome you are and how you can manage your own life and sex life and stuff, and then I went and did this and undermined everything I said. I don't think you're stupid. Not by a long shot. And I know you can handle your own life."

Mary opened the door and jerked her chin. "Go on. You have an apology to give."

True to her word, Jules went out to the living room where Damien had settled in on her couch, listening to music and reading a magazine. "I was pretty rude to you just now. I'm sorry. I promise I'm not normally like this. I'd really like if it you could forgive me."

Damien worked hard to keep a straight face. Which only amused Mary more. "Apology accepted. You wanted to protect your friend. As it happens, I like Mary a whole lot too. So I get it. We can hit the reset button."

12

He wasn't one of her kitchen assistants, he'd been told. So she sat him down at the table always reserved for friends and family—which he did like—and marched away back to her kitchen.

Tart, the place she held her twice-weekly supper club, was small, but not claustrophobic. It was intimate. Pretty lights twinkled and candles flickered in the chandeliers dotting the space. But even they fit the space. They were elegant without being too much. The candles took them away from formality.

"The chandeliers were her idea, weren't they?" Damien asked Daisy.

Daisy grinned, nodding. "Yeah. She found them at a warehouse sale place. They totally work. I want some in my house."

Levi just looked amused.

Gideon came in with Jules and Cal. Gideon tipped his chin in Damien's direction in greeting. He knew they all had reservations. Fueled by all the idiot stuff he'd done and been dumb enough to have been photographed doing. He knew he had to prove himself.

He did like that she'd taken Jules aside and spoken with her. He had no idea what was said, but Jules's apology had been genuine and when they'd had dinner at Mary's the night before, they'd taken some tentative steps toward getting to know one another.

If she hadn't been . . . well, so wonderfully Mary, he wouldn't have made the effort. But she was. He needed to have a long talk with Ezra about it when he got home. Ez would have great advice, would listen without judgment and wouldn't ever let him weasel out of anything.

Gillian and Adrian came in with smiles for everyone.

"Didn't expect to see you guys tonight." Jules waved at them, coming to sit, a drink in her hand.

"Miles is at the movies with his friends. He's a little sad now that they'll be here at the high school and he'll be in Seattle. But they've all pledged to keep hanging out so he's off for pizza and movies." Gillian smiled at Damien as she sat. "Hello, you."

"Evenin', Miz Brown. Hey, Adrian."

"Hey, Damien. What's on the menu tonight?" Adrian picked up the card on the plate. "Fuck yeah, fried chicken. Mary's fried chicken is so good. I hope there's extra because I could eat eight pieces."

Gillian laughed, leaning into his arm. "The crime is that you could and it would never show."

He turned to her, tracing over her bottom lip. "English, you know how much I love your body. Eat as much fried chicken as you want; I'll *keep* loving your body."

She ducked her chin, blushing furiously.

Mary came out with one other server and began to place things on the tables. There were fifteen tables in the room, seating a maximum of four people. And their table, which seated ten. Seventy people maximum, she'd told him. She wanted to keep the feeling intimate and the quality of the food high.

"Smoked salmon dip with vegetable chips." She smiled at him before she looked at anyone else. "And a quick vegetable pickle."

"She'll sit with us once the main course is served. But for now she's going to get the salad course set up," Daisy explained as everyone began helping themselves, passing things up and down the table, pausing to hum their delight.

He wished she was with him right then, but he also liked this chance to watch her at work. She moved surely, confidently. This was her world and she was in charge. Hot.

He broke his gaze away from where she'd just disappeared into the kitchen and turned to Adrian. "Saw the news this morning. Triple platinum. Damn. Congratulations."

Adrian grinned. "Awesome, isn't it?"

"Reg Thorne did an amazing job, but it's the songwriting that really pushed it over. You and Erin are such a solid team."

Gillian made a little hum. "Even though they fight like cats and dogs sometimes."

Adrian laughed. "If you think Erin and I fight, you should see the Hurley boys throw down. Didn't Paddy break your nose once?"

He snorted. "Twice actually. Vaughan sort of stays out of it. My mom says it's because Paddy and I are so close in age, only ten months apart. I say it's because Paddy is a control freak and a dick. But he plays guitar like nobody's business, and he can sing better than the rest of us, so we let him stay."

Gillian laughed, reaching out to pat his hand. "Oh, that's all talk. You three love each other very much. I saw how he reacted when the photographer tried to take that shot of you and Mary."

Cal leaned forward to listen. "What's this?"

Damien hadn't meant to have that brought up. Mary didn't know about Paddy's defense of her and how he'd nearly ended up in jail over it. Damien knew his brother wouldn't want her feeling guilty. "She doesn't need any of that stuff." Paddy had been so enraged that the photographer had invaded their privacy and was threatening Mary that he'd nearly gone to jail over it when the photog called the cops. Luckily, the guy had been trespassing and had made a threat to Paddy first. "Look, Mary doesn't know about it. He'd be embarrassed about it and I don't want her to worry. At the Gorge, the photographer climbed a fence and Paddy caught him with his camera and high-powered lens pointed at Mary while she was backstage. My brother, um, physically removed the guy, who tried to call the cops to press charges. But people saw him threaten Paddy first and he'd been trespassing too. We sign on for that crazy. People like Mary don't."

"Thank you. For, you know, getting her back. Thank your brother too." Cal tipped his chin in Damien's direction.

He shrugged, feeling awkward.

More food came, including the famous fried chicken, and she finally sat at the table, right next to him.

It was indeed so good he could have eaten eight pieces. She seemed to glow when people loved her food and he knew it was because she loved to take care of people. Loved it when what she created made folks happy.

He wanted to help clean up but she refused. He sat around with her friends drinking beer and chatting while she and her crew got things ready for the following day.

Adrian watched Gillian as she laughed with Jules and Daisy. "Hard to break in to a long-term group."

They were letting their guard down around him. He should probably send flowers to Gillian for that story she told about Paddy and the photographer. Until that moment they'd only known him as the guy with a beer in his hand and his face in cleavage.

Damien shrugged. "They don't know me. I get it."

"Doesn't make it any easier while you're dealing with it. They're good people. Close to each other. You're doing fine. Mary is an awesome woman. You have good taste. If it helps, they didn't like me much at first either. I was a dick, handled things wrong. But they want her to be happy and from what I can tell, you make her happy. They'll relax once they get to know you."

"I like her. She makes me smile. How's Miles liking his new school?"

"So far it's just been orientation stuff. He starts for real on Tuesday. But already the Kid's kicking ass. He's not the only son or daughter of a musician there, which makes it a little easier. The school knows how to deal with security in a way his other school wouldn't have. Not that it was bad, just not their norm. I feel better with him there. Safer. After this tour he's thriving in a new way. Making music is now a much larger part of his life and he digs it." Adrian paused. "You were right to suggest it. Right to suggest he get more specialized education."

"Your kid has mad talent. No surprise really, given who his parents are. I'm glad it worked out."

"He'll miss his old school, I know. But I'm thinking this is a good new start for him."

"How's life now that the tour has ended?"

"I'm still getting used to it. I mean, we had the house built, I made a record, we got married, had a short honeymoon and went directly on tour for a few months. It's really only now that it feels real. I've seen a lot. Done a lot. But when I'm with Gillian and Miles, I'm *home*."

Adrian's gaze moved to Gillian again, a smile on his face. Mary came out from the kitchen and they all moved to leave.

They went back to her place and talked until long after midnight. He was going home the following day. She didn't ask him to stay any longer and he wanted her to. She didn't push for any more than he'd already given. But he wanted her to.

He'd thought about it pretty much the entire trip back home. Especially after the conversation he and Adrian had had. He'd known Adrian for a long time. There was a big, soul-deep change in his friend.

Mary had already changed the way he thought. Part of it was that he couldn't figure her out. Which was unusual and maybe part of her appeal. But he doubted it. She didn't have an agenda.

It kept making him nervous. And then he'd realize how fucking nice it was that he didn't have to constantly worry about it.

He'd had a few longer-term relationships before, mainly before they broke big. But women usually wanted to spend time together. Mary had a busy life and when he left that afternoon, she hadn't dug around about when she'd see him again. In fact, he'd been the one to say he'd call her soon.

And then the appeal of moving on to the next city and therefore not having to worry about anyone wanting more from him than a night or two wasn't enough. He wanted more. The tour was over, his life would have some quiet moments, and he realized, quite clearly, that he wanted to spend that time and energy pursuing this thing, this possibility of a thing with Mary Whaley.

He stopped in Portland to grab doughnuts and coffee. His mother was of the opinion that Folgers was just fine and any fancy crap he bought was a waste of money. He never knew any different until they'd started to make some real money and stopping at gas stations for seventy-five-cent burritos and ulcer-creating sludge wasn't their only option.

Now he knew and now, as his mother said, he was a bit of a coffee snob. He had his favorites and was sure to have it when they traveled.

Mary had Kona coffee in her pantry. He smiled. Showed what good taste she had. He should take her to Hawaii. So they could have it fresh.

It was late enough that he didn't catch too much traffic, and by the time he got through Portland, he started coming home.

The road changed, the sights became more familiar. The river glittered.

He'd been all over the globe. But nowhere else made him feel like coming home the way Hood River did.

When he pulled over the last rise and saw the land he let go of his last bit of stress. This was his. He'd run over these hills, chasing things, running from a pissed-off older brother. Later they'd ridden horses and ATVs. There'd be activity at first light in the morning. The pears were close to harvest.

His window was down and the scent of freshly cut grass and alfalfa hung in the air. The lights were on in the main house, he noted as he passed. He'd stop at his place first and wander up to see his parents once he'd cleaned up.

The porch light was on at his house. He smiled. Probably Ezra, who lived closest. Damien's house would be on the way back to Ezra's and he'd have stopped to turn it on because Damien was returning. There was something to be said about your family leaving the porch light on so you could find your way home.

The garage door made that horrible squeal when he opened it though. He sighed, something to look at. The next day or maybe the day after. The house had been aired out, he noted when he came in from the garage. He flipped the lights on. His bags had been dropped in the living room. Paddy had left a note saying his drums had been taken up to the barn.

A shower first. He stopped by the fridge and peeked. He grinned as he grabbed an ice-cold beer and cracked it open. There was milk and butter, yogurt, cheese. He knew there'd be fruit, something never in short supply around there. Bread sat on the counter. His mother, most likely.

After a shower he changed and grabbed his bike. He could have walked. It would have taken him about fifteen minutes, but he preferred to ride his ages-old Schwinn over instead.

Ezra and his dad sat on the front porch drinking iced tea.

"Thought I heard a car earlier." His dad gave him a hug when he came up the front steps. Ezra followed.

"Just got back. Took a shower, had a beer, looked at the mail, put the mail back in the pile and came over here. What's up?"

"Nothing much. Just talking about tomorrow. Just need to check the fruit. Looking pretty clean this year. Probably have another week or so before we need to harvest."

"I'll be around to help."

His father nodded. That's what you did when you lived on a family farm. He and his brothers would go away and do their thing, but when they were home, they helped. It was hard work, but it was honest work. It built character, and his father liked to say it kept them out of too much trouble.

Ezra sat again, stretching his legs out. His big brother topped six and a half feet. Because he worked the way he did, he was solid muscle, a lot like their father. He'd let his mustache and beard grow back, and when he was out on the back of a horse with a cowboy hat on, he looked like a cigarette ad from the 1970s. Right then though, he looked like a guy who'd most likely been up since five.

He wanted to talk with Ezra about Mary, but now wasn't the time. He still needed to think on it himself.

"I'm going in to check on Mom. I'll be back."

"She's in a good mood. The babies are here."

Vaughan had two kids that had resulted from a very short marriage three years ago. She'd crumpled under the weight of being married to a musician and had divorced him about two months after Kensey, their youngest, had been born.

But to her credit, she'd agreed to settle in Gresham so they could share custody. She had a part-time job while she finished school. Vaughan paid her support and all her bills. Mostly out of guilt, but he had a lot to be guilty over. And he loved his kids without a doubt.

His support enabled her to be home with the girls and it kept her reasonable about how much time the girls spent with them. It didn't erase the fact that he wasn't there every day for his kids, but he was trying.

Damien grinned at the thought of the little dynamos. Vaughan wasn't the only one who loved those kids. His nieces were awesome little girls.

Inside the house, the sound of giggles drew him toward the huge kitchen where his mother was standing at the island while the girls sat nearby coloring as their daddy looked on.

"I thought I heard there was a monkey infestation. I see there is. I'd better run."

The girls saw him and jumped down, running to him. He scooped them both up into a hug, kissing their faces.

They laughed and so did he.

"When did you get back?" his mother asked once he put the girls down and they scampered back to their dad and their crayons.

His mother had not been pleased when Vaughan and Kelly

had decided to split, but it was clear she approved of how he'd handled the situation since. It wasn't perfect. But the girls would always know they were loved. Both sides of their family lived within an hour of them. His parents regularly had them for weeks at a time through the year, even when Vaughan was on the road.

He kissed his mom's cheek and grabbed a piece of the cinnamon bread she'd been slicing. "About an hour ago. I'm sure you'll thank me for the shower I took first. Speaking of thanks, glad I've got breakfast in my fridge."

"I figured you'd come back with that coffee you like, but you'd forget milk and then come up here looking for it."

"Appreciate it." The bread hit the spot. He hadn't eaten since the lunch Mary had made him before he left Bainbridge.

"There's leftovers. Want some?" His mother tipped her chin toward the fridge.

He got it himself, still wanting the memories of Mary making him food to be the main ones in his head.

He listened to his nieces chatter away, Kensey more actually just chattering, as she was only three and didn't have all her words yet. Vaughan helped them color and his mother supervised.

Paddy wandered in just as he'd finished up.

"Thanks for dropping my stuff off."

"No big. How's Mary?"

His mother didn't try to hide her naked interest in that subject.

"She's fine. Went to that supper club of hers last night. I know why it's so popular now. We went for a hike yesterday."

"She outdoorsy?"

His mother hadn't liked Kelly. Mainly because Kelly was, as his mother saw it, too soft for the type of life they led. Not just the ranching aspect, but the Hurleys were rough-and-tumble. They rode horses and dirt bikes. They toured and lived hard on the road. Kelly hadn't much been up for that sort of thing and while Damien couldn't argue that she was incredibly beautiful, she just couldn't keep up. She had been jealous of it, saw it as something that took Vaughan away from her.

And he supposed, she'd been right.

"She's one of those people who is rarely still. She gets up early and goes and goes."

"'Course she is. Girl has her own business. Who else does it for you?" His mother sniffed.

"Promised we'd go kayaking the next time I made it up to visit."

His mother handed Kensey a crayon that had dropped before she looked back to Damien. "Did you invite her here? Have her come down harvest time."

That would be . . . interesting. The ranch would be alive with activity. The pears would be harvested by hand and then cooled to spur ripening before they were shipped. There was even a harvest festival in town that she'd probably love. Even though they were celebrities, they were hometown boys and people rarely bugged them.

He wasn't sure if Mary was ready for a full dose of Sharon Hurley. Then again, who ever was?

"I'll talk to her about her schedule. Weekends are hard. That's when the bulk of her jobs are. She's very business-minded."

His mother nodded as if that satisfied her.

"You'll like her." Vaughan spoke from the table. "You should see how hard he chases her. She's got her own stuff to do. It hasn't even occurred to her that she's far more than some . . . um, friend he met on the road."

His mother turned to him, one brow rising. "That so?"

"I think so, yeah. It's early days. I've only known her three months."

"You'll need to show her she's not the same." She left it there for the time being. He knew his mother though; she'd seen for herself that he wanted Mary. Once she was sure he deserved her, his mother would turn into his greatest—albeit probably most annoying—ally.

13

He woke up. Alone. Normally he'd have been fine with that, but really, he missed turning over to find a tiny, dark-haired woman burrowed down into the blankets next to him.

He frowned at his inability to get used to life without her in it. It wasn't like she was with him on tour or anything. So why now?

He gave up, looking at his phone to see it was already nine. She'd be awake.

He dialed her number.

"Why hello."

He smiled. "What's up, Curly?"

"I'm chopping carrots for a salad. Luncheon thingy for one of Levi's mom's charity gigs."

"Nice."

"Seriously. His mother is sort of scary, but her friends and all their foundations and stuff keep me pretty busy lately. Can't complain about that. What's up with you?"

"Kensey and Maddie, Vaughan's daughters, are here. We're doing a cookout and hanging by his pool. You should come down." He said it so suddenly he surprised himself. "Have you ever seen a pear harvest? It's set for the day after tomorrow. Stay for a few days. Maybe we'll go windsurfing down on the river. ATV a little. Ride horses. Have lots and lots of dirty and inventive sex."

She laughed. "I don't know if I can."

"It's during the week. I'd have you back home for your supper club on Friday. I have a small plane if you can meet me. Then I can get you door-to-door a lot quicker."

She sighed, but he heard that she wavered. "It does sound fun, but I have jobs every day this week. And the supper club is Wednesday night, Friday night and Sunday night. This is the one week a month it's on Wednesday too. I can't be gone for that long right now."

He frowned. What was he going to say, blow off your job you've worked so hard for? "After harvest, how about if I come up? Then you don't have to worry about not doing jobs. I can even help. And then, you know, the hot-sex part can occur around your schedule."

"All right. If that works for you. I feel bad that it's always you who has to do the traveling."

That did make him feel better. "It's okay. Right now it's my schedule that allows for it. It's worth it to see you."

"That's a very nice thing to say."

"I have a secret."

"Uh-oh."

He laughed. "I like to say nice things to you. Mostly because they're true, but also because I hope it keeps you sweet on me and all."

"You're so full of it. My goodness. It's quite a lucky thing for you that I am, indeed, sweet on you and that you happen to look as good as you do."

He blushed, filled with pleasure at her compliment.

They chatted a little while longer before hanging up; he didn't stop smiling for hours.

"She doesn't seem bothered that we don't see each other more. Isn't that weird?" Damien kept an eye on the girls, who were in the pool with Vaughan and their grandparents. Paddy and Ezra's dogs were involved as well.

Ezra turned the steaks. "Maybe she's not into you?"

"That's not it. I'd know. It's not that she's disinterested in me. It's that, well, other women would have pushed to see me more. She seems content with it. When we're together it's smoking hot. We're both into each other. We laugh. Things are easy. She makes me laugh, Ezra."

Ezra laughed. "Well, good. But if you're expecting her to be like other women, and your previous other women had not been the type you'd want to be with, then maybe you need to readjust your expectations."

"Some of her friends think I'm a drunken man-whore." There. He said it.

"You *are* a drunken man-whore."

"You're supposed to be on my side, Ezra."

His brother looked up and into his eyes. Very few people saw to the heart of him like Ezra did. "I am on your side. But you tell me, you go search the Internet for yourself right now. Tell me what the first images are. Go on. I'll be here."

Damien snorted. "I know what they are."

"No. I mean it. My laptop is on the kitchen table. Go. Look."

He did, annoyed at his brother. But when he did the search he cringed. Hell, he was in those pictures, he couldn't deny it. They weren't a lie. But that's not who he was. Not totally and certainly not anymore. The problem with the media, and with Google searches, is that they only seemed to catch moments of your whole life. They weren't getting shots of him playing Barbies with his nieces. Or helping out in the orchards or fields.

Was this what she thought he did? He scrubbed his hands over his face before returning to the back deck some minutes later.

"Look, I know what it is to be a drunken man-whore, okay?" Ezra spoke before he did. "It's fun and all. For a while. But the hangover is a motherfucker. You can fix this, but it's going to take some energy. This woman isn't a groupie. She's not with you for a backstage pass. She's a real person with real feelings. She's got a business and a life. She's not going to want any of that stuff in her life. Can you blame her?"

"She should know me enough to know I'm not that. Not anymore anyway. I've always treated her with respect. She's different."

Ezra grabbed a pull or two from his cream soda. "Sure. Which is why it suddenly matters. And probably also why she lets you keep coming around. But you're going to have to work it to get her to see you're more than a Google search."

"Like what?"

"Court her. Woo her. Whatever you want to call it. She's got brothers and a father and family, and they're all around her. They're not going to let some pretty boy come in and hurt her. You'll have to introduce them to the real Damien Hurley."

He slumped. "This sucks."

Ezra shrugged. "Not really. You just have to work hard. And you hate working hard. You're used to getting by on how good you look and your fame. Oh sure, you know what it is to work in the fields all day, and to play one shitty little club after the next until you finally made it. But with women? Well, you're a lazy fuck because you're handsome. You gotta work now. If she's worth it, you will. If not, well, you already know the road is full of chicks who don't give a fuck who you are other than the pretty-boy rock star with more money and booze than sense."

Mary looked up from loading things into the back of her car to see Damien's car pulling up her drive.

Unexpected.

She didn't bother to hide the flush of delight at the sight of him. She really did have a lot of work to do when he invited her down to his family's ranch. And she was sorry to have had to say no.

No matter how hard she tried to maintain her distance, she couldn't deny she liked him. Liked being around him too. Didn't so much like that she'd received a call from a *reporter*—though she was doubtful of such a claim—after a picture of her at the Gorge with Damien had hit the Internet. She said, "No, thanks," and hung up. But it made her wary.

He got out and she took him in and the wariness faded. Damn, he was pretty.

"So glad I caught you."

He approached and pulled her into a hug. She hugged him right back, tipping her face up to receive a kiss. He settled in until her knees were rubbery.

"You're here."

"I am. Harvest is done so I decided to get away for a few days to come see you. What are you up to?"

"I'm on my way to Tart. I have a job. A dinner party. You're welcome to hang out here until I get back. Should be ten or so. Or Adrian is around. I know because I just spoke to Gillian about twenty minutes ago."

"I can see Adrian any time. Can I hang out with you for a while? I promise not to get in your way. Obviously not at the party, I get that. But at Tart while you prep?"

She eyed him carefully and shrugged. "Sure. Come on then."

She drove the quick two miles to Tart and led him through the back doors, locking up behind them.

"Don't you keep supplies here? Must be a pain to haul stuff

here and back home." He placed the boxes of supplies on the worktable.

"Thanks. Yes, I do keep supplies here." Her hair was already tied back, but she put on an apron to keep her clothes clean. "But a girl has to grocery shop." She washed her hands and indicated he do the same. If he was there, she may as well put him to work. "I went to the farmer's market today and found a few things. I snuck off to Seattle and did a little supply shopping over there too."

"You're going to let me help? I'm coming up in the world."

She handed him a colander, a bundle of carrots and a peeler. "Baby steps, Damien." She grinned and he kissed her hard and fast. "I'm glad to see you."

He started peeling carrots as she laid out all the components to the salad. Sometimes she prepared things in the kitchen of the house where the dinner party was hosted. But that night's party she'd only be taking the completed food and helping arrange it.

"You are? Glad to see me, I mean."

She cocked her head as she julienned jicama for the shrimp salad. "I rarely say things I don't mean. It's unnecessary."

"Sometimes you get sort of like a schoolteacher. I feel sort of pervy admitting it, but it's hot."

She laughed.

"So . . ." He trailed off and she kept chopping. Working in the kitchen always helped her gather her thoughts, so she gave him time to do the same.

"What's been up with you since I saw you last?"

"Lots of work. So much now that I have to actually say no.

Imagine that. Someone asked me last week if I'd consider being a personal chef. It's not something I'd considered before. I said no. But Daisy brought up that I could prepackage enough meals for a week and have them delivered to certain clients. There'd be instructions on how to combine to make the food. Heating in some cases. That sort of thing."

"Daisy's pretty smart." He held up his hands. "Done with carrots."

She examined them and must have found his work to be acceptable. Though she took them to her work area. He clearly wasn't up to snuff yet enough to slice them.

"I'll let my mom know you found my carrot peeling skills acceptable. She made us help in the kitchen from a pretty early age. She's teaching my nieces now. Why don't you want to spend more time with me?"

She tipped the jicama into a nearby bowl before turning to him again. "Say what?"

"God, this isn't coming out right. Probably because I suck at this stuff. You're a hard woman, Mary Whaley."

"I'm what?"

He took a deep breath. "I like being around you. A lot. I want to, you know, investigate to see if this thing could be more than a few days here and there until we get bored. But you're resistant. Is it the tabloids? Is it me?"

"Get started on that celery. It works better if you leave it together to cut off the bottoms and the tops. Don't get wild with the peeling, I just don't need the threads in the salad."

She pulled out the shrimp and moved to the sink to clean them before she put them in the marinade.

"I like being around you too. I'm not being resistant. I have a job and a life that is here. I can't just up and go down to Oregon whenever I get invited. And, to be totally honest, this is a fun thing, but I'm not looking for anything permanent."

"Bullshit. You're not a one-night-stand woman."

She burst out laughing. "Hello, I fucked you the second time I ever saw you. How is that not me being a one-night-stand woman? I don't normally do that. The having sex the second time I clap eyes on a person." She frowned.

"If you did, I probably wouldn't have been so excited to see you again." He paused. "Look, I dig you. I texted you all those times because I wanted to know you. I still want to know you. You can expect more from me. I wanted you to know that."

She blew out a breath as she worked. He was so unexpected. She wasn't sure what the hell to do with this man. The sex part was easy. They had that connection in such a major way it wasn't anything she worried about. It just worked.

But the rest?

"Last week I got a call from a guy claiming to be a reporter at XYZ. He wanted details about me. A picture of us at the Gorge had made your fan site, I guess, and people were clamoring to know who I was."

"Ah. I'm sorry. Did you say?"

"No. I mean he knows who I am enough to have my number and call me for a quote. So. Anyway, I told him to fuck off and hung up. I'm not interested in that life, Damien. I like you. A lot. But I don't like reporters in trees across the street from my house like Gillian had to deal with. They have a fence and a gate around their home because of fans. People come to Tart now looking for him. I've watched her try to deal with it for the last year and it's been crazy. I don't want it. I don't want hateful letters from women who tell me in detail how many times they've fucked you, or what you're like with two girls at once." The thought of it actually made her sick to her stomach.

"That happened to Gillian?"

"Yes. It's very hard. I have enough to deal with. You're a great guy. You make me laugh. We have some pretty stellar sexual chemistry. But I don't even really follow the celebrity news and I've seen you in it. I just don't want that. So we keep things chill and casual and I'm no target in the media, and when you move on, no one gets hurt."

"Are you so convinced I'll move on? I'm . . . This is different. What we have. I want to see what it can be. I've never wanted that before."

"Maybe you only think you want it because unlike all those other women, I'm not begging for you to marry me and buy me diamonds."

He snorted.

She created a quick marinade, and after drying the shrimp, she put them in it and closed the lid.

"Okay, so the deal is, I think you not begging for me to marry you is different and it does catch my attention. But not because it's a challenge or whatever. Because it's part of you. Because you don't want me because I'm a millionaire. You don't want to toss aside your life and be in mine. You're your own person. It makes you more beautiful. Interesting. I think you should give me a chance."

"I'm letting you peel my celery, aren't I?"

She was scared. She liked him. A lot. It could be more if she let herself envision it. But what she could envision a lot easier were those pictures she'd seen, and those letters to Gillian that Adrian's people dealt with now.

She wasn't tough like that. A man like this could break her heart and it would be monumentally stupid to let him get close enough to have that power. What they had right then was nice. It made her happy but she didn't depend on it. If he stopped calling, it would be sad for a bit. A week or two. But she'd get over it and keep on with her life.

"How about this? Just give me a chance to prove to you that I am more than Damien Hurley, pretty-boy drummer with a bottle of Jack in his hand. That's all I'm asking."

She turned. "I already know that. Dumbass." She went back to work, but didn't say more and he didn't press.

He insisted on driving her to the home where the dinner was being held and even helped her unload the food. But he went back to wait in the car while she did her thing. And when she was done, he drove her back to Tart where he helped her clean up all her equipment.

"Would you like to go look at the moon?"

He looked up, surprised. "Yeah."

"Let's go back to my house."

Once there she grabbed some snacks, a blanket and a flashlight, and they went out through her yard. She pointed. "There's a rise just through that stand of trees. There's even a path; just watch your step."

She wasn't sure why she was taking him to her thinking spot, but she wanted to look at the moon and be with him, and he was there and the moon hung high and full on a very clear September night, so why not?

"Smells so good."

"It was a pretty day. The bark got warm. I love this smell. And the pine needles. The water off in the distance." It was dark out there on her side of the island. Dark enough that the stars above were bright and clear.

"It's a good thing I work out. This is your idea of an easy walk?"

"Pfft. This is a totally easy walk. It's just a little steep this last bit. Don't cry about it."

He laughed then. "You're tough."

"I have two older brothers. If I wasn't tough, I'd be in trouble. Plus my dad is a retired ironworker. Do you know what an ironworker thinks about weak people who sit on the couch all day?"

"Ha! My dad is a rancher, so I bet I heard the same thing growing up. We were only allowed to watch television or play video games on weekends, and only for very restricted hours. I think now, looking back on it, that they did it when they wanted to lock their bedroom door to get it on. We were too dumb then. But my mom is pretty crafty."

He laid out the blanket once they'd arrived and they settled. She opened the cooler and popped a stuffed mushroom into her mouth. She passed one his way and he scarfed it down.

"Damn, it's beautiful up here. You can see everything."

"This is my parents' land. I've been coming up here since I was, I don't know, eight or nine? Ryan and I discovered it. I come up here when I need to be reminded of the beauty of the moon and stars." She laid back on the blanket and marveled at the world just above. "Over the years people have tried to buy it. But my dad loves the wildness all around. My mom would be grumpy too. She likes to do little improvements. Their yard has gotten bigger over the years." She snorted a laugh.

"Why do you laugh?"

"She's hilarious. She gets a bug to do something. Build a little water feature, or some decking, whatever. And she starts leaving little articles about it, pictures, how-to guides, that sort of thing around until my father finally relents and does it. It's a little game between them. They have a zing. It was good to have that example growing up." It was why she had the attitude that she'd wait as long as she had to to find it for herself. That zing was worth the wait.

"They sound a lot like my parents. My dad is a third-generation rancher. We started in Kentucky and moved out to Oregon when I was six. They'd scrimped and saved and got up enough to buy a good, solid plot of land. Then we all built the house while we lived in a shitty little trailer. That first winter I'm surprised we didn't kill each other. But when you're a kid you don't really know. Anyway. He decided on alfalfa and that's what he did. We took in the first harvest as we finished the house. That got us through the next year and so on. My mom directed us; he set the course. They both have this intensity of connection. When I was a kid I remember going to other peoples' houses and wondering why their parents didn't kiss each other or talk to each other all the time the way my parents did." He paused for a bit as they watched the sky.

"How did they react—your parents, I mean—when Cal told them about Jules and Gideon?"

"I was there when he showed up to tell them. My dad was downstairs dealing with his computer. Ryan and I have to go over there once a week or so to run a virus check and to get rid of eleventy billion cookies and stuff. Anyway, my mom made us shut the door and get her emergency kit down."

"Emergency kit? God, I'm starting to wonder if our mothers being together in the same place might rip a hole in the space-time continuum."

Mary started to giggle and it took a bit to get back under control. "It's a pack of cigarettes, some whiskey and a few twenties. I can proudly tell you she's never had to get the emergency kit down for me. My brothers, god, they were so wild. You'd never know it to look at them now, all successful and stuff. But holy cow, they were hard to handle growing up.

"Anyway, she took two shots, lit the cigarette, cross-examined Cal, who likes to think he's smooth but my mother could have been a code breaker in the war. No one can withstand her. Anyway, in the end she said she supported him and would handle my dad. They always took his being bi pretty easily, but you know a threesome is a whole different matter. But they love Jules and that he does too worked out. Gideon is impossible not to love as well. I'm lucky. I know some people don't have parents like mine. I'm spoiled to live in this little world where I'm supported and loved the way I am."

"My brothers and I weren't easy. Ezra and Paddy were the worst. But my mom should have had a parking space with her name on it at our schools, she was down there so much. She used to threaten to homeschool us. Ezra got in fights a lot and later he drank and carried on. I remember my dad having to haul him home by the back of his shirt a few times. But it's always been my mother who kept us in line. I mean, we got into a shit-ton of trouble, but without her and her very strong hand in our upbringing, it would have been way worse. Ezra was a handful but she kept him out of jail with music. He loved to play music. He was the first of us who learned an instrument."

"He used to be the lead guitarist for Sweet Hollow Ranch, right?"

"Yeah. He still song writes with Paddy. Ezra got out of high school and flirted with going into the military, and I think my parents would have supported that idea. But then he started on at the ranch and we started Sweet Hollow Ranch. Then Paddy graduated and he worked at the granary part time too. We started getting gigs in places none of us were legally able to go into were we not playing there. By the time Vaughan was done with school we were ready to make that move to L.A. She came with us as I said. Kept us fed, beat off the worst of the people who'd have bled us dry."

"There's a big *but* there."

"I assumed you knew."

"I have been a fan of your music a long time. I know there was trouble, but to be totally honest, ever since Adrian came into our lives I try not to look at the tabloids. It's a self-defense mechanism too, now that you're around."

She reached out to take his hand in hers as they watched the sky.

"He partied hard. Harder and harder as things went on. Lots

of alcohol. Then drugs. After a while they affected his game. He started to show up late for shows. A really scuzzy element started hanging around backstage. He kept borrowing money. It just . . ." He had to stop to swallow back the emotion.

"He was my hero. The big brother who always had my back, and suddenly he was the guy who I caught stealing shit from my wallet. The guy who left used needles all over the fucking place. He lost a huge amount of weight. He stopped taking care of himself. I knew he had a problem with heroin but we kept hoping he'd turn it around. We gave him ultimatums and he'd stop. For a while anyway. Finally, he and Paddy threw down after a show when Ezra literally fell asleep on stage. Just nodded out while he was playing. We had to cancel the rest of the tour. He took off. We tracked him down. He was in bad, bad shape. He refused to go to rehab."

God, he'd never felt so fucking helpless. They'd had to watch Ezra; worried he'd take off again to get more drugs. Ezra had said all sorts of mean shit to hurt them, push them away. Damien had worried about the band, about their tour, all that money riding on the extra dates. Felt guilty that he'd worried over those things.

"Anyway, my mom showed up. She went in the room with him, locked the door and stayed in there for two hours. Afterward, she came out, told my dad to get the car, we drove him to the rehab facility. He stayed for four months. Did another six in aftercare and he's been clean ever since. He threw himself into the ranch, taking over the majority of the day-to-day operations from my dad. He quit the band, which he needed to do, but he still writes with Paddy. He produces our records now too.

He's my big brother again. He's changed a lot in many ways, but for the better."

"Wow. I'm glad he's okay now. Sorry you all had to go through it. It must have been so hard to see him that way."

He sucked in a breath. "Yeah. But he's strong. Seeing him come through it changed us all."

"I imagine so."

"Not that we don't get wild when we're on the road. But it was so much less controlled then. It could have been any of us really. My family came together, which is what counts. I don't know what my mom said to him that day, but whatever it was, it scared him into dealing, facing it and really committing to rehab. She's a strong woman. 'Course she blames herself."

"That's what mothers do."

She got him. And that should have scared him. But it didn't.

"Thanks for sharing all that with me." She squeezed his hand and he pulled her onto him.

"Thanks for listening. Now, I have some other ideas for how to spend this lovely evening."

14

What do you want to do today after your morning job?" He kissed her shoulder as they still lounged in her bed.

"Hm. I was thinking of going to Seattle later. There's a warehouse where I get some of my supplies. This is all quite boring to you, I'm sure, but I need some new dishes for my small plates menu."

"That doesn't sound boring. Why don't we have lunch over there too? I need to buy a birthday present for Ezra so maybe we can do that too."

"All right. That sounds like fun."

"I have a few other ideas. You know, for before you leave this morning." He rolled on top and she smiled up at him.

"Yeah?"

"Oh. Yes."

He bent to lick across her nipples. Back and forth as she seemed to warm and melt against him. This was perfect. The time neither of them had to worry about what they did or how they did it.

She wrapped her legs around him and held him to her as she arched into his mouth. Her nails dug into his shoulders and he knew she'd leave marks. He hoped so. He loved it when she left marks.

"I don't want to wait," she murmured as he kissed down her ribs. "I want you in me."

He warred with his desire to taste her, to drive her up with his mouth, and to comply with her request, sliding deep into her body. It wasn't as if either plan had any drawbacks.

He groaned as she slid her hands up his sides, scoring her nails over his ribs, sending shivers through him. "Now." Demanding. She reached down, grabbing his cock. "In me."

"Once you scratch the surface you're a horny, demanding, cock-hungry woman."

She laughed. "Don't tell anyone. You'll blow my cover."

He fumbled until he got suited up and lined his cock at her gate, pressing in so slow, beads of sweat popped out on his forehead. He had to rein it in before he thrust. He wanted to take it slow. Wanted to tease.

"You're like the best all-you-can-eat buffet ever. I want to gorge and gorge. So I have to make myself taste slowly. Here." He kissed her mouth and she sighed into his. "And here." He made his way to her throat. She arched, giving him the line of her neck, offering herself to him, and he didn't try to stop. He tasted the softness of her skin. The salt of her warmth. Her scent was strong at the hollow of her throat and he breathed deep. Wanting to hold her there inside himself.

She was physically small, but against him she was strong. Vibrant. Her muscles flexed as she moved to meet his thrusts. He kissed over her freckles. Across her cheeks, over her shoulder.

Outside it had begun to rain and the sound seemed to make music in between the gasps and groans. There were no words just then. Just sensation and the sound of the rain on the roof.

Her hands landed on his ass as she dug her fingers in, holding on. She hitched her thighs higher and he shifted, grabbing her thighs and sliding his hands back to her knees.

Her eyes rolled up as she groaned as his fingertips stroked the skin at the back of her knee. She was flexible enough that once he levered up a little he could shift her, turning his head to lick where his fingers were.

She moaned rather loudly and his cock throbbed in response. Throbbed in time with the frantic beat of his heart.

He grabbed her hand, moving it to her pussy. She kept his gaze as she slowly began to circle her clit with her middle finger.

She tightened around him. Each time he thrust deep, she squeezed. He wanted more. Wanted this to never ever end. But it would. Sooner rather than later. He began to hurtle down that one-way street. Climax dug into his flesh, into his heart and body with sharp claws.

He knew she wasn't far either. Her cunt superheated, slicked up as little earthquakes of her inner muscles began to echo through her pussy. He bit her thigh just to the side of her knee and she cried out, clamping down around his cock until he nearly saw stars.

With a gust of breath, her name a tortured sound on his lips, he joined her, thrusting until he had to fall to the side, her legs still tangled with his body.

"I think I might last until after lunch now."

She laughed, sliding her fingers through his hair.

"Hey, you finally fixed this back door. It's about time." Daisy strolled in and tossed herself onto Mary's couch.

"Why, good evening to you too."

"I'm hungry. Take pity on me."

Mary rolled her eyes. "Don't you have a boyfriend? Also I just brought you a huge bag of food yesterday."

Daisy laughed. "I know and it was all very good. But said boyfriend took a lot of it to work for his lunch. He gave me a very sad story about how nowhere in town makes food as good as yours and how it helps him get through the afternoon. He even gave me the eyes and then he made me come and I forgot why I should even say no. He's got a magic penis. I'm powerless against it."

Mary choked out a laugh and couldn't stop. Soon she had to sit down next to Daisy, who'd begun laughing along with her. This went on for some time until she could finally breathe again.

"Wonder if there's a twelve-step for that. My name is Daisy Huerta and I'm a Levi-holic. Hi, Daisy."

"Ha! But then I'd have to want to be cured and I don't. But he did eat all your food and I could make a peanut butter sand-

wich or some soup. But you live right here and you have delicious food and I haven't seen you in a few days, so really, look
at all those birds I killed with that one stone. Also, ew, I don't
like that saying. I don't want to throw rocks at birds. See what
being hungry does to me?"

"Good lord, you're a mess." She kissed Daisy's cheek and
stood. "Yes, my door is fixed. Damien fixed it and the window
too. I've got *carnitas*. Want some with rice and beans?"

"I'm sure that was a rhetorical question as the answer would
never be anything but yes."

As much as she teased, she did love it when her friends and
family showed up wanting to be fed. It was her way of taking
care of them. Their way of letting her do it.

"There's tea, juice, beer, milk. There might be more; you'll
have to check the fridge."

She got to work putting together a plate.

"Have you eaten yet?"

"I ate earlier. I just got home from a job about twenty minutes ago."

"When did Damien go back to Oregon?" Daisy poured them
both a glass of red wine and she clinked her glass to Mary's
once she handed it over. "Cheers."

"He left this morning." It had been a good visit. She'd learned
a lot about him. He'd listened to her stories, asked questions.
Helped her when she'd needed it and backed off when she didn't.

"When do you see him again?"

"He wants me to come down to visit him there. He said he
wanted me to cater an event so if he hired me, I could spare the
time."

Daisy laughed. "Well, certainly that job would be way more fun than most. I'm just guessing, by the way, that you aren't nailing all your other clients after you make them dinner."

"I'll never tell." She slid the plate into the oven to heat. "Be ready in a few."

"So . . . how are things? I mean, this is more than a fling, obviously. He totally digs you. That much is clear for anyone with eyes. He also did repair work, hello. That's a true sign."

She sighed and took a gulp of her wine. She told Daisy about the conversation she and Damien had had. About how he wanted to move things into relationship territory but that she was concerned.

"I admit, I was worried for a bit. At first when it was just a one-off I was like, *whoo*, get some, girl! And then later it was more than that and I didn't know if he was good enough for you. I certainly knew from what I'd seen online that he had a reputation. But I've gotten to know him a little and I gotta say, I like him. I like how he treats you. I like how he looks at you. I like that he fixed your broken stuff. I don't like that he lives in another state. What would I do without you if you moved? But that's selfish. I know I've spent more time with Levi lately and less with you. I miss you a lot. But I want you to be happy. I want you to find something real, and if that means you live four hours away, that means I'll drive down to see you all the time."

"Don't go getting ahead of yourself. I don't know. I really don't. I hate his lifestyle. Not all of it of course. He's close with his family. He works hard. He values the same things I do. But, you know I look at Gillian and all the stuff she has to deal with, and I already got a call about a single picture someone took.

I don't want that. I don't want to hear from women who fucked him before me. I'm not cut out for that stuff. I'm not thick-skinned enough for that."

"So end it."

"He brought me salt. As a present. Flower of Bali and Fleur de Sel." That had sent her reeling.

"This is a good thing?"

"Yes. Don't you see? He didn't buy me diamonds. He bought me salt that's sort of hard to find. Salt I'd love to use because I cook things. He thought about me, knew me enough to understand I'd find this incredibly moving. I could have resisted jewelry. And it's not the first time. He brought the filé I made the gumbo with before that too. He's clever. And really, really good in bed. My god. He's . . . Anyway. He's good. We're good. I don't want to end it."

Daisy grinned. "So don't. Let him prove himself to you. And if he does, the other stuff won't matter as much. You'll find a way to deal with the distance and the media. Like Gillian does. Like I deal with Levi's dumb society stuff. Like Jules deals with bossy Cal and bossy Gideon. I'm giving up my house. Levi asked me to move in with him."

Genuine happiness filled Mary to near bursting as she hugged Daisy. "When?"

"Two hours ago. He came home after court. Well, came to my home and we—well, we *visited*. Anyway, after the visit he said he thought it was silly that we were apart when we liked being together. He said he wanted me with him every night. He said he had spoken with one of his brothers, the architect, to convert one of the guest rooms into a dressing room. Like I have in my house. Only bigger because, well, you've seen his house. Anyway. He wants his house to be our house."

"And you said?"

"Hello, do you think I'm dumb? I said yes."

Mary grinned so hard her face hurt. "I'm so excited for you!"

"Me too. Scared a little, but mainly excited. I'll keep my studio space where it is. No sense in moving that. I love the light and the size is perfect. Plus I get to work with my grandmother around and that's the best part. I'm in love. So much love my life is overflowing with it. I'm really, really happy right now and I'm so glad you're happy too. You're the first person I told. There was more visiting in a carnal sense to celebrate the answer, and then he had to go back to work and I came over here."

"This totally calls for something more exciting than leftover *carnitas*! I have champagne."

"Yay!"

"Shall we call over the troops?" Mary got up and began to rustle through her kitchen. "I'm making a feast. We need a feast of celebration."

Daisy laughed, moving to hug her again. "You're the best person in the world. I knew if I told you, you'd make me feel even better, and you totally did. Thank you for being my best friend."

Mary sniffled. "What else could I be?"

She called Gillian and Jules and told them to get over to her place to celebrate some news. Both women said they were on it.

Damien called just after everyone had arrived and the champagne had been poured and toasts had been made. She was giddy and slightly drunk.

"Sounds like I'm missing something good." She heard the smile in his voice when he said it and realized she missed him already.

"Celebrating with my friends. Daisy's had some good news. You got home all right?"

"Yes. I miss you already though."

She took a chance. Later, if it didn't work out, she could blame the champagne. "I was just thinking that."

"Come down. Spend some time here with me. Two days at a time isn't enough. Spend a week. Stay in my house. Meet my family."

"I can't take a week off. I have supper club and various jobs I've already booked."

"How about if you come down here first thing on a Monday? Your Sunday Supper Club will be finished and then I can fly you back whenever your next job is. If it's just a day later or whatever I can even fly you home, even for a few hours, and then we can come back. Whatever. I wasn't joking when I said I wanted to hire you to cater for me. I want to do a big dinner for my family and I can't cook worth a damn. You can though."

He was so charming, so earnestly wanting to be with her. How could she not relent? "Are you sure? That seems like an awful lot of work to fly me up and back. Twice even."

"Am I not being clear about how much I want to spend time with you? I like flying. It's fun for me, gets me hours in the air and it means it cuts the travel time down enough to make it doable."

"Let me look at my schedule to see when I've got a stretch of time without jobs. I think it's not going to happen until October though." She paused. "But I can probably swing a day or two. If we left on a Sunday night after supper club and came back Wednesday morning."

"Yeah?" She pictured his smile and it warmed her.

"Yeah. And I'll make the feast. You will not pay me for it."

"Your time—"

She cut him off. "There are things I do freely because I care about the people I do them for. Trying to pay me for them would make me feel bad."

He paused. "All right. That's fair. Also a compliment, if I'm not mistaken. Also, if I fly up to get you, that means I have more time with you and you have more time being here instead of traveling."

"You like getting your way."

He laughed. "You've found me out."

"All right. Let me get back to you on dates. I've got to run. I'm glad you're home safe."

"I'll talk to you soon then. Night."

15

·····················

They stood in a coffee shop and she had to rein in her impulse to punch the woman currently gushing all over Damien. A good solid jab to the throat might cure this bitch of her manners problem.

He was flirty, but in a general way. It was his nature, Mary had realized some time ago. But it was clear the woman took his nature as an excuse to keep it up.

Damien stepped away and the woman stepped closer. Mary watched, her head cocked, white noise in her head. She didn't like being jealous. It sucked. It was ugly, and yet she totally *was* jealous.

To his credit though, Damien kept trying to find nice ways

to tell this woman to back off and go away. Finally he stepped back, grabbed Mary's shoulders and put her between them. Then Mary felt like she'd been given permission to step in.

"What Damien is trying very hard to say and you're trying very hard not to hear is that he's here with someone. That's me." She waggled her fingers in greeting. "If you walk away now, you can keep some dignity."

He pulled her back into his body, encircling her shoulders in his arms. His heart beat so steadily she calmed a little. He kissed her temple.

The gusher looked a little surprised, her gaze going back to Damien.

"This is Mary. She's my girlfriend. I'm here with her. I'm with her," he repeated, and finally the gusher shrugged and wandered away.

Girlfriend? She thought to protest and realized she didn't want to. Even if it wasn't true. Was it? Oh man, now was not the time to have this internal panic attack.

"Thank you for saving me," he murmured in her ear. "I'm sorry, that was so rude."

Well, he'd learned from the time in New York. He'd dealt with it quicker. It wouldn't be the last time either. She had to decide if she could find a way to deal with it.

"I wanted to punch her in the throat."

He turned her, tipping her chin up. He didn't care who was looking. In fact he hoped everyone was, because he wanted the world to know this was his woman. "It's hot when you get this way." He brushed a kiss over her mouth.

"Mm hm. I'm told this is part of the whole deal. I know

enough at this point to be certain I don't enjoy it. The private plane part is a thumbs-up, though."

He laughed, tucking her against his side. Their coffee order would be up soon and then they could be on their way.

"Mainly that sort of thing doesn't happen here. In town most people leave me alone. We grew up here. We're locals. I go grocery shopping and that sort of thing and people are mostly respectful. I see old schoolteachers and that sort of thing. I'm sorry. I really am."

She sniffed but said no more. In all the times they'd been together she'd never really shown any jealousy. Other women he'd been with had been jealous when they had no right to be. That had been annoying. This one though? He wanted to pump his fist in victory.

Their coffees came up and he grabbed them.

"Sometimes people do this sort of thing to Adrian at Tart. Jules kicks people out. I guess they do it sometimes at Erin's café as well. Once, Jules actually jumped the counter to haul out some skank who flashed her boobs at Adrian. Unbelievable that some people have no self-respect at all."

"Clearly you need to be with me to protect me at all times."

She laughed. "Mmm hmm."

"Come on. You ready for Sweet Hollow Ranch?"

"Bring it on."

He got her back into the car as she sipped her coffee. He'd warned everyone to back off until he slowly brought her around. The last thing he needed was to have his family scaring her off. He'd gotten her this far, he wanted to be sure he got everything right. He wanted her to be in his life regularly.

He took her in the back way so that when they came around the last bend she'd see the river off in the distance along with his house. He wanted to preen and show off for her.

"Wow, this is so beautiful." She looked around as they got out of the car. "Smells good too. So quiet."

"It's nice to be up here. You can see what's happening elsewhere, but it's quiet and off the beaten path. Come on in. We'll drop your stuff off and decide what to do. You can look at the groceries I picked up as well to see if I need anything."

She took his free hand and he calmed.

"Horses?"

"Yeah. They're mainly Ezra's thing. He loves them. My dad uses the ATVs, but Ezra rides out to check the orchards and fields. He's got dogs too. Chickens. Pigs." He opened up and ushered her in, her bags in the hand not in hers.

She stopped, her mouth dropping open. "Damien, this entry is stunning." Letting go of his hand, she turned in a circle, checking the place out.

Flagstones and slate covered the floors. The entry was open to the second floor. Huge windows let the light rush in

"Thank you. Come in and see the rest." He drew her upstairs. "Let's drop your bags off in the bedroom."

The floors up there were hardwood. Honey maple. He loved the warmth it lent the space. His bedroom took up half of the entire second floor. She went in first.

"I remember seeing a sitting room in some movie when I was a kid. I've always wanted one in my bedroom ever since."

She motioned toward the two love seats and the floor-to-ceiling bookcases bracketing the large windows. "More than a sitting room. How you even manage to make it outside is beyond me. I'd be curled up on that couch all day long reading books."

He made a mental note to be sure to keep a throw out there so she'd be warm while she did.

"The main room is through here." A fireplace open to both the sitting room and the main bedroom served as a divider. His bed was custom, as was the mattress. He liked a very large bed, and this one fit the bill. It dominated the space.

She looked back at him over her shoulder. "This is a rock-star bed."

He laughed. "Totally. What's the point of being one if you can't have a giant bed and a house you designed?"

She went to the windows to check the view. He came up behind her, one arm sliding around her waist. "That over there is Ezra's house. His horse pasture. His is the house closest to mine. Orchards over that way. On the other side is where we grow the alfalfa. The main house is around that bend. You can see the roof from the guest room. Paddy is over that way and Vaughan on the other side. He's got a pool. The girls love it as does Ezra's damned Lab."

"This is huge."

"It is. When we first came here it was about a third this size. We had the alfalfa first. Then my dad picked up some more acreage a few years later and then when we broke, me and my brothers all kicked in and grabbed up the surrounding land when it came up for sale. It made sense to live here in the off-season. Close to family but not on top of one another. Then of course Vaughan got married and they lived here for a few years. I think he'd be pretty happy if he could get his ex to move back to Hood River so he could see the girls more often."

"It's nice that you like being around your family. By the way, I heard Paddy tossed some photographer out when he tried to take our picture. Why didn't you tell me?"

"I didn't want you to panic and not want to come see me play anymore."

She paused and leaned into him again. "I appreciate the gesture. Seems to come with the territory. I know I don't like it. But I appreciate your trying to protect me from it anyway."

He wanted to get into it a little more, wanted to pursue this discussion about taking their relationship to the next level. But he sensed she wasn't ready yet.

It was hard to be on someone else's schedule. But if she was worth it—and he thought she was—it was what he needed to do.

"Want to see the rest of the house?"

"Yeah."

He drew her into the bathroom where she stared, openmouthed. "Holy crapdoodle. Damien, this bathroom is a temple to hedonism. Oh my god."

"In a good way?"

"Yes. Yes, definitely." She peeked in the huge soaking tub and he noted her smile.

"See the benches? I'm going to have you sit there while I eat your cunt until you scream."

She blushed.

"The shower has six showerheads. Two are removable. I'm going to use those to make you come too. The floors are heated so you won't have to be cold walking around naked. The windows are treated so you can't see in."

"You're a deviant, Damien."

He caught her up, laughing as she did. "I am. You make me that way. All I can do is note all the places I want to fuck you. I don't see any place like I did before you."

He kissed her, tasting her mouth, loving that he knew it and yet craved more.

Forehead to forehead, he let himself enjoy the very essential pleasure of being with her. "Kitchen?"

"Yes, please."

He led her past the guest rooms and down the back stairs. "Screening room."

She poked her head in. "I've had such media-room envy since I met Adrian and saw his. This one though? This beats his hands down. Wow."

"I love to watch movies. It's hard for me now." He shrugged. Getting recognized was fun. At first. Now it just stood in the way of doing normal stuff like going to the movies. He could go in town, and he did from time to time. But generally, he was sent movies all the time and he liked holing up and watching them all day.

"I imagine." She tucked her hand in his and he marveled, just for a moment, at how it made him feel. Calm.

"We'll watch movies later then. Come on." He tugged her down the hall and into the kitchen.

She didn't say a word. He leaned against the doorjamb and

watched as she slowly moved through the huge room. She poked open doors and peeked in his pantry. Covetous fingers slid over his countertops and the knobs on the stove and grill.

He noted the way her eyes had glittered as she opened the fridge drawers built into the center island. He hadn't really cared one way or the other when they'd suggested them to him. But now he got it. He looked at his kitchen through her eyes and appreciated it on a whole new level.

"Even if you didn't have a massive cock and a private plane, this kitchen would totally get you lucky."

He laughed, pleased to his toes.

"I'm glad you like it. So you think you can cook in here then?"

She turned to face him, so much pleasure on her features. Her cheeks were flushed, eyes bright. "I'm not sure if I could leave this kitchen. This kitchen is like a wet dream. I want to make something right now. Oh my god, you have refrigerated racks for dough? How is this even a thing?"

"Am I going to have to get jealous of my kitchen?"

"It might be close. But for now you're in the lead."

He laughed, hugging her. "You up for a walk? Or some ATV'ing? Or horseback riding? Swimming? Fucking? I should qualify this with the fact that my family wants to meet you. Fucking is always at the top of my list where you're concerned, but I don't know how long they'll leave us alone."

"I want to ATV, absolutely. I love it. But I'll be dirty and stuff after. Not really the way I want to look when I meet your family. So how about we walk?"

"I think that's a fine idea." He took her hand and led her out the front. She paused to look at the big swing.

"I like that. You know what I saw the other day? We went to the home and landscape show; don't ask. The things I do for Jules. Anyway, they had beds for porches. Like on swings. It was the awesomest thing. Just to nap on the porch. Not very applicable in Seattle though."

Boy, once you got her away from Bainbridge she turned into a chatterbox. He liked it.

"I think I could warm up to that. You and me out here on a lazy Sunday. Drinking coffee and reading the paper in bed. 'Course if we did it inside, I could have sex with you as well."

"You do have a point."

They started to walk up the road toward his parents' place. In the distance he heard a bellow and a string of curse words. It was Ezra, and if Damien heard right, the demon pig was on the loose again.

"Um." He looked to Mary, who clearly had no idea what was happening. "There's a pig on the loose." He shrugged.

"A pig?"

"Ezra has pigs too. Anyway, he just took on a new one, a baby that had been abandoned, and he's hoping the others will help this baby calm down a little. It's, the pig I mean, a little, um, vicious."

The pig came up and over the rise, trotting in their direction. Ezra came shortly after.

"Aww!" She knelt and the pig ran to her. "Aren't you just a teeny tiny wee piggy baby?"

Damien had been poised to snatch her away from the demon pig's jaws. But it turned out to be unnecessary.

Instead, the damned pig looked up at her and made a few squeaky grunts. She reached out and Ezra hissed, but instead of a bite, the pig got closer when she petted its head.

Ezra looked at Damien, surprise on his face. Mary sat down right there in the dirt and the pig got into her lap.

"Well, we now know Pork Chop isn't always a demon pig from hell."

"You named this sweet baby Pork Chop?" Mary's tone was scandalized.

"That sweet baby bites! And poops." Ezra saw that she didn't believe it. "And is not nice," he added.

"If you named me after meat, I'd bite too. I think her name should be Violet." She got close to Pork Chop's face and the pig gave her a few soft grunts. "She approves of the new name."

Ezra sat down across from them. "I've been trying to get that pig to be nice for the last two months. You're clearly magic with pigs, and drummers too." He held his hand out and she took it with a grin. "I'm Ezra. You must be Mary."

"I am. It's very nice to meet you, Ezra. Damien talks about you all the time."

"He does? Well, I hope you know Damien is full of crap a lot."

She laughed and Damien just watched, sort of stunned, as she sat in the dirt, a pig on her lap and his gruff older brother seemingly just as charmed as the demon pig.

"It's all been nice. I promise. What have you been doing to this sweet piglet that she's been mad at you?"

"Existing, apparently." He sighed. "Maybe it's because she was mad that I called her Pork Chop. I'm afraid to be left alone with her to see if she reverts."

Damien snorted. "The people at the shelter know Ezra is a soft touch. The pig was abandoned and they knew he'd taken in others, so they called him and he brought P—Violet to live here with the other pigs he's got."

"Aw. Violet, he gave you a home. This is your daddy. You need to be nice to him."

Violet looked back to Ezra, not entirely sure that anything Mary was saying had any truth.

"I think you should give him a chance. There are other pigs here too. Better than being left alone with no one to care for you, don't you think? Plus all these Hurley boys are awfully pretty to look at."

Mary stood with Ezra's help. The pig still cradled in the crook of her arm, she dusted off her ass with her free hand and Damien had to work not to hum his satisfaction. Damn, she had a nice booty.

"All I'm saying is that you should give Ezra a second chance."

The pig looked to Ezra and grunted, clearly not convinced. Mary laughed and put the newly named Violet down. The pig trotted next to her happily. Ezra sent him a raised brow and Damien just shrugged. Hell, of course she was good with animals. He shouldn't be surprised.

"Let's go up to the house. See if she has similar powers with Mom."

"Damien tells me you have horses?"

"I do. Do you ride?"

"I haven't in many years. I used to when I was a kid, though. I love horses. So smart and strong."

Loopy, Ezra's dopey Lab, came loping up the lane toward them.

He yipped at Violet, who grunted but didn't seem afraid. But when he saw Mary, the dog danced around her, barking happily.

She scratched him behind his ears. "Hello to you too."

"That's Loopy." Ezra snorted a laugh. "Hey, Loop, this is Mary."

Loopy, tongue out, head butted her a few times until she bent to grab a stick.

Loopy's eyes lit and she barked several times. Mary threw the stick and Loopy ran after it, Violet in her wake as well.

"Jesus. You're like Dr. Doolittle." Ezra looked her up and down.

"I like animals."

Which seemed an understatement.

"But you don't have any at home," Damien said.

"My mom has really severe allergies, and even when I moved out I was working all the time and it didn't really seem fair to have them if I couldn't give them the time they needed. Miles"— she looked to Ezra—"that's my friend's son, he's sort of like my godson. Anyway, he has a menagerie and I do a lot of pet sitting when they're gone."

"Well, Ezra has plenty of animals you can love all over when you're here." Damien put an arm around her shoulders.

The dog came back several times and she threw the stick for her each time. Violet stopped chasing after a bit, content to trot along as they went up to the main house.

She'd never been nervous to meet someone's parents before. His brothers had all been pretty nice. But she'd heard about his mother and wow, Sharon Hurley sounded formidable.

Mary saw the woman on the front porch and knew instantly it was Damien's mom. He raised a hand to wave, but kept his arm around Mary's shoulders, which made her feel a little better.

Sharon Hurley was long and lean like her sons. Her hair a deep brown, again like her boys. Her eyes flicked up and down Mary's body, judging. She didn't know if Damien had brought girls around before. She got the feeling that he didn't.

"You're Mary." Sharon came down the steps and gave her a closer once-over. "Walk with me."

Panic swept over Damien's features, and instead of panicking *her* further, it only made Mary laugh. She patted his arm and held her hand out to Sharon. "Yes, I'm Mary Whaley. It's nice to meet you."

Sharon shook her hand and neatly pivoted them to walk in the other direction. Violet trotted along with them and Mary figured if Sharon got violent, she could sic the pig on her.

"You're the first woman Damien has brought to meet me in five years. The last one was a twit. Lord above, you put some knockers in front of a man and he thinks he's seen God. She had 'em. Even I was impressed."

They kept walking. "This was where we lived in a tiny little trailer while we built the house. My husband is good at most things, including carpentry; that's why it's still standing today. What do you do? For a living, I mean."

"I have a catering business and a supper club two nights a week."

"What's that? A supper club? I know what a caterer does."

"People pay a subscriber's fee to get a certain number of meals each year. I make dinner for them. They come eat and pay me for it. It works for me. I like to try new menu ideas." She shrugged.

"How's that working out?"

"I'm booked nearly a year into the future. I have a Wednesday dinner once a month that's open to reservations so people can check me out to see if they like me enough to subscribe. Those are also reserved eight months in advance. Catering is good too. Helps when you have lots of friends who love your food."

"And when they're famous like my son and Adrian Brown."

Mary turned, giving the other woman a hard look. "Certainly when your best friend's husband can throw label party-type business your way, it's helpful. But I had a business long before I met Adrian Brown. And long before I met Damien. I don't need your son's success to run my business, and any implication that I would is uncalled for."

"You should be mad at me. That *was* rude. I wanted to see what you're made of." She indicated a bench under a big oak tree. "Sit. Please." She glanced at the pig. "Is that the demon pig?"

"Violet's just misunderstood. She's going to be giving Ezra a second chance."

Sharon laughed. "The music business has done a lot for my children. Far as the eye can see, other than the original piece of land, is because of their success. They've been able to travel all over the world. Makes them happy too. Mostly. But it's also brought a lot of pain. Ezra, well, he's had his struggles. Vaughan's babies being raised in a home apart from their daddy. Paddy, well, he's Paddy so he'll go his own way. And Damien. I won't let anyone hurt them if I can help it. I can't always help it, which is the worst part of being a mother, let me tell you. Damien is the one who always wore his heart on his sleeve. And then after a few years in the business he sort of, well, he hardened up. Got himself a tough outer shell. Need one really to survive of course. But then he stopped bringing anyone around. Stopped dating. He just had flings."

Mary stared out over the land. Violet rooted in the dirt nearby.

"You're not a fling."

"I started off that way. I want to be honest with Damien because I like him. I respect him. I did not intend to meet his parents and hang out with his pig." She shrugged. "I don't like some very pervasive aspects of his life. I don't like cameras on my every move. I don't like tabloids. I don't like stumbling over one woman after the next that he's been with either."

"What made you change your mind?"

"He's persuasive. He makes me laugh. He loves his family in much the same way that I love mine. He respects my life and my business. I tried to resist. Even when he first started to push for more. But he's irresistible."

Sharon laughed. "Of them all, he really is. When they were growing up their dad and I had to go down to the school at least once or twice a month. When you have four sons it's sort of expected that you'll have to deal with it at least once or twice. But my boys got an extra helping in the trouble department. We couldn't keep sitters. Oh, all the teenage girls would be charmed, but by the time we got back from dinner they'd be weeping and swear to never set foot on our land again.

"Damien actually convinced a few to come back more than once. One of them even came back three times. So I can see why you'd be unable to resist his charms. He talks about you a lot. I like that you have your own life. I like that you've made yourself a success on your own. Would you sign a prenup?"

Mary started laughing. "Prenup? I've known Damien since June. That's like three and a half months. We're nowhere near marriage."

Sharon nodded. "Come on down and meet my husband. I made him promise to stay in the house long enough for me to have a private conversation with you. I expect all the boys are worried I'll chase you off. But you're not that easy to chase away, I wager."

She stood and Mary followed.

"I've got some freshly brewed tea. Want some?"

And just like that, Mary passed the Sharon Hurley test.

16

"You sure you know how to do this?" Paddy tried to keep his expression grim, but Damien noted the smile at the corner of his lips.

"I know how to ATV. How to ride a dirt bike too." She was so small Damien understood why Paddy was being so careful. But she was strong. So much stronger than he'd suspected when he first met her.

Damien handed her a helmet and some goggles. "She's a tough cookie, Paddy."

Vaughan loped up. "Been a while since we did this. Seems like a good day for it." He took the helmet down and put it on, strapping the goggles on as well.

Paddy took the lead, Vaughan followed, then Mary. Damien

brought up the rear. He wanted to keep an eye on her anyway. Ezra met them at his place, and once they cleared all the houses, they opened up and hit the sort of course they'd created over the last several years.

She was fearless. A few times he'd nearly swallowed his tongue at how fearless she was. Once she got the lay of the land, she took hills quickly, bumping down the other side without hesitation. She liked it fast, which made him grin. Inwardly of course; he didn't want bugs in his teeth after all.

It was rare that outsiders could keep up with the Hurley brothers. But she did. She kept at it, never complaining that she got muddy or that it was hot. She didn't fall behind or signal for a break. And when Paddy finally rolled to a stop at the overlook, Damien pulled out the lunch she'd made earlier and they all dusted themselves off enough to sit.

Of course, despite her game attitude with ATV'ing, she also was clever. She'd brought some wet wipes to clean up with.

"What? I'm going to be touching food. Can't do that with dirty hands." She handed the container to Ezra, who'd been staring, but he took it with a nod.

"I like a woman who thinks ahead."

"My ass is going to hurt big-time tomorrow though. It's been a while since I've done this."

Paddy laughed. "You'll have to come down more often so you can keep in practice."

She handed around the food and everyone was quiet for long minutes as they scarfed it up.

"It's really a good thing I'm such a nice guy or I'd be trying so hard to steal her from you." Paddy winked at her before looking back to Damien. "She can cook. She can handle Mom. Dad thinks she's awesome. The animals love her. And she's not afraid of getting dirty."

Mary sent him a look from under her lashes and a bolt of heat shot through him. No, Mary was not afraid of getting dirty.

Oh, he'd been with women. Lots of women who did lots of sex things. But she truly enjoyed sex in a way he'd never really experienced in a partner before. She didn't just do stuff because he liked it, or because she thought it seemed sexy. She was a dirty girl who loved to fuck. She wanted to make him hot, wanted to make him come, but she wanted to come too. She wasn't shy about it, didn't pretend she didn't want to get off. So totally sexy.

"I find it hilarious that you even think you could steal her from me."

"I'm older and wiser, Damien. The ladies like that."

Mary laughed, leaning back into Damien. "We do. But I'm pretty happy with what I've got. He's a year younger than I am. I suppose there's something to be said for younger men too."

Vaughan laughed then. "Well, if you ever get tired of Damien, keep in mind that I'm younger than he is."

"Boy oh boy. You four are going to ruin me forever."

Damien pulled a leaf from her hair, blowing it away with a puff of breath.

It was a good day. One of the best he'd had in a very long time. Funny how all his good days of late were because of her.

Ezra stood, stretching. "When you're all ready, I think we should take her by the stream. It's pretty down that way. Plus I want to check the fence. We did a fix a few weeks ago but I want to be sure it's still holding."

Lauren Dane

"We have a problem?" Damien stood, brushing his ass off.

"I don't think so. But I'd prefer to keep Haley's cattle away from our stream." Haley was the cattle rancher who lived several miles away. But the farthest edge of their land abutted the farthest edge of Sweet Hollow Ranch, and their water could be devastated if the cattle got into it. Vigilance was a good thing because clean water was a necessity for their crops.

"I'm ready when you are."

He held a hand out and pulled her to her feet, pausing to brush a kiss over her lips. She smiled up at him.

"You having a good time?"

"I really am. Thanks for inviting me."

"I wish it could be for longer. Gonna suck when you go back home."

"There's time. I'm not going anywhere just now."

He took her hand, squeezing it. "Good thing."

She handled things in Vaughan's kitchen like a boss. She currently wore a bathing suit cover-up as she moved efficiently around the room. Damien was her appointed assistant that day. His mother had checked in, edged into the kitchen, but she'd been pretty respectful. He was glad Vaughan had suggested she cook there instead of their parents' place or even Damien's.

Paddy and their dad were in the pool. Ezra sunned himself and Vaughan split his time between the kitchen and his backyard.

He'd wanted this for his family. A gesture to say thank you for the way they always supported him. He was out on tour for months at a time, but when he got back his parents had dealt with his mail and his mom kept his place aired out. They'd loved him through a lot of fuckups, a lot of changes. That support had meant everything to him. And now Mary was making them a feast and it meant even more than having a random caterer do it, or to take them to a restaurant.

"This kitchen is pretty fabulous too." She checked on the chicken, apparently satisfied. "I could have made something way more complicated than fried chicken, you know."

"I do know. But your fried chicken is ridiculously good and I wanted my family to know that too." And his mother would approve of something simple versus something really complicated. Oh sure, she'd appreciate the skill, but a good fried chicken would be something she could admire. Practical as well as tasty.

"Oooh, potato salad too?"

She grinned at him. "Vaughan mentioned that he loved it."

His mother liked that answer; he could tell by the way she stood up a little straighter.

"You need another root beer?" she asked Mary.

"That'd hit the spot. Thank you."

It wasn't that no one ever drank around Ezra. They did from time to time. But drinking in the middle of the day wasn't something he engaged in usually. Maybe at lunch he'd have some wine or whatever. But this was family time and root beer would be just fine with fried chicken.

"Damien, can you take the tomatoes out of the fridge please?"

He did, placing the platter next to her. He watched as she cut mozzarella into discs and slid them between the tomato slices. "Now I can use that balsamic you gave me."

The smile she gave him shot straight to his toes. Weird that a gift of some old vinegar would do that, but when he'd given it to her she'd teared up a little. And that had meant he needed to kiss her a few times. And that had led to a fast, hard fuck on his kitchen table.

He caught her eye and knew she'd been thinking of that too.

She drizzled the balsamic and olive oil over the tomatoes and cheese. "Thanks for the tomatoes, Sharon. They're really lovely. Perfect for this cheese."

"Glad they could be of use. I've canned a million of them this year it seems. But this last crop I figured could be put to good use."

Mary dished some up. "Damien, can you hand this to your mom?"

His mother took a few bites. "I admit to you now that I was not convinced such a thing would taste good. I figured I'd take a bite and then find a way to dump the rest. But damn if I wasn't wrong. This is delicious."

Mary beamed at his mom. "Thank you. That's a wonderful compliment. When the tomatoes are fresh it's a million times better. I don't make this during the rest of the year, only when I can get local tomatoes that are fresh off the vine. Once you taste them this way, you're spoiled for life."

Mary checked on the corn. "Nearly done. The salad is ready too." She peeked in the oven. "Give the biscuits another two minutes. We're nearly finished."

"I'll get everyone out of the pool and have Ezra and Vaughan set the table as they're dry anyway." His mother headed out.

Damien got close enough to risk a kiss. "Thank you for doing this. By the way, I think you've totally won my family over. They like you better than me."

She laughed, her eyes dancing. "Yeah? I like them a lot too."

"Let's eat, Curly."

"Sounds good."

She paused in the doorway of his practice room at his house. He went inside, a sweet pride on his face. "Just a place to play. I have a studio space where we practice as a band up in the barn."

Ha, the *barn*. The barn was a sophisticated, fully kitted-out studio and rehearsal space. The barn had been filled with Hurleys. Here? Well it was just the two of them. At last.

All day they'd been out with his brothers, riding ATVs. Visiting the orchards and the horses. They'd even taken a dip in Vaughan's pool and had a barbecue. She'd wanted him a little bit more with each passing moment.

He was so . . . hot. He stood there in low slung jeans and a T-shirt, his tats showing. No shoes. Every inch the rock star. It made her sweat.

"I think you should play for me."

He turned back, startled. "Me?"

"Yes. Just because I'm not a groupie doesn't mean it doesn't make me wet to watch you play."

He gaped for a moment and then smiled slow and sexy. "Yeah?"

She nodded. "Oh. Yeah. When I told you I wanted to lick you I wasn't lying. I would have if it hadn't been in front of tens of thousands of people."

He pulled his shirt off and she sighed happily.

"You're going to give me a swelled head."

She laughed. "I hope so. Come on. Show off for me."

She settled on a pillow she tossed in a corner.

He grabbed his sticks and sat. And a change came over him, over his face. He was more than the guy who'd taken her out on the ATV earlier in the day. He was Damien Hurley. *The* Damien Hurley. She swallowed hard and watched.

He started out slow. Setting an easy beat. And then he added something. And another something. She recognized a few songs. It was so clear to anyone with eyes just how much he loved music. He lost himself in it, in all the different movements. His gaze sort of blurred as he went away while he played.

He got sweaty as he played and she got wet, just as she said she would. He was so . . . God, she wanted him right then and there. She stood, tossing her shirt to the side, and his sticks clattered as he dropped them, moving to her, his face still intent, only on her.

He grabbed her to him, skin to skin. The heat from his body enveloped her. He smelled good. Like hard work and exertion. She licked up his pecs, pausing to flick her tongue over the bar in his nipple. He groaned, pressing into her kiss.

Humming, he tunneled his fingers through her hair and tugged, exposing her throat. He kissed, breathing her in. She surged back, sliding a hand down the front of his pants to grab his cock.

"Goddamn." He snarled, taking her to the floor.

She forgot that she had planned to take him once he'd started taking her first. His hands were everywhere as her clothes seemed to disappear right and left, leaving them both naked as the sun poured in through the high windows.

Bent over her body, he pressed a kiss to her chest, right between her breasts. His hair fell forward, brushing over her skin. She traced over his tattoos and down to tweak his nipples. Sensitive. He mimicked her movements and it was her turn to moan as he tugged and then pinched just right.

"I want to suck your cock," she whispered in his ear, pushing him back, scrambling to her knees.

"Fuck," he murmured as she kissed over his chest and made her way south. His cock was in her fist, his pulse throbbing against her palm.

She took her time. Wanting to taste him in her own way. He was greedy, she knew. As greedy as she was.

"Yes. Yes. Yes." She licked over the head and crown, tasting the salt of his pre-come on his skin.

She liked this power, his cock in her hand, in her mouth. He watched her, his gaze on her like a caress. She took him as deeply as she could. Over and over. She ran her nails over his balls and just behind. He liked a little ass play, she knew, so she slid her middle finger back and forth across his asshole as she sucked and licked his cock.

He often liked to come inside her. But she wanted this. Wanted to finish this way. She held tight, continuing to flutter her tongue just beneath the head where he liked it as he tried to move her.

"I want to fuck you."

"Time for that later. I want you to come in my mouth."

He cursed, a snarl of a sound. She knew that got to him. His pupils seemed to swallow the color of his eyes as he watched. His fingers found her hair again and she moaned when his hold tightened.

He guided her. Clearly holding back.

"It's okay," she whispered against his cock. "I know you want to. I'll let you know if it's too much."

He groaned again, but his grip tightened so that tears sprang to her eyes. But it wasn't from pain. It was so good when he let go, his hands pushing and pulling as he fucked her mouth.

Delicious. Dirty. He fucked her mouth and didn't apologize. Didn't hold back. He took exactly what he needed. That she could satisfy that need did something to her. Set off little brush fires of desire over her skin.

She loved pleasing him. Loved making him groan and snarl.

He kept going. Over and over. She breathed through her nose, not wanting to pull back. She knew he was close. His balls drew tight against his body and finally he exploded, arching his back, his hands holding her still as he thrust.

And then she was on her back and he was kissing her hard.

"Where do you come from?" He kissed her ear, nibbling down the outer edge.

"Bainbridge Island," she managed to stutter as he sucked her earlobe.

His laugh sent little puffs of air over her neck and ear, and shivers of delight outward from there.

"You do something to me, Curly. Leave me breathless."

She smiled, holding his head.

He had this thing he did at the back of her jaw that sent liquid heat through her body. Made her rubbery and languid.

He did that for a while until she nearly came unhinged and he moved on. He paused, kissing each rib. Up one side and down the other. He kissed and nibbled underneath her breasts, teasing until she was ready to beg before he got to her nipples.

"Your mouth is—oh my god—perfect."

He looked up her body and into her face, pausing. "No. *You're* what's perfect." He kissed one nipple and then the other. "Every part of you."

"Again with the perfect mouth." She knew she blushed, but he made her so deliciously giddy.

He kissed down her belly, licking a line from her belly button to her clit before he rolled onto his back. "On me, Curly. I want you on my face."

She managed to fire her brain cells enough to move. To sit astride his body and move up as he moved down. The rug under her knees dug in, but in a good way.

This position was raw. There was no hiding this way. She had no time to be self-conscious. There was just the two of them. Damien and Mary in the late afternoon sunlight. His hands on her hips, holding her steady, his mouth on her pussy.

No shame. No hesitation or fear. Just want.

His hair was cool and smooth against the skin of her hands as she slid her fingers through it, tugging.

He moaned and it echoed through her.

She knew he'd leave marks where his fingertips dug into the muscles of her hips and ass. She knew it and it got her off. Knew she'd look at the bruises when she was back home and remember this exact moment when pleasure raced through her, hot and savage.

He edged her closer and closer, his mouth on her, all over her, his tongue and teeth sliding over the most sensitive parts of her until she began to unravel, unable to hold orgasm back another moment.

She came hard and fast, slumping over until he finally laid her back on the carpet where she could catch her breath.

And then he moved close, his fingers clasping hers, and the emotion welled up so great that she was glad she didn't have to speak.

17
·············

Now was your visit with Damien?" Jules bustled about their shared kitchen space, cleaning up from her morning as Mary arrived to get ready for that evening's supper club.

"It was really good. I hung out with his family a fair bit. They're all very nice. Rode ATVs, got dusty. Rode horses too. His eldest brother has all sorts of animals. Pigs, horses, chickens, goats. He's got a fabulous Lab. Dude, you should see Damien's kitchen. It's like heaven, only in Oregon."

Jules laughed, pausing to put her head on Mary's shoulder. "I'm glad."

"Of course we seem to have to run a gauntlet of pussy everywhere we go. He brought me home first thing this morning and he got recognized at the airfield. At the coffee shop near his house. At the damned gas station."

"How does he handle it?"

Mary continued to stir the sauce. "He has that thing that Adrian has. They're charming, compelling. You want to be around them. He's always appropriate. At least in front of me. Women just, gah, I don't know how to handle it. They grab at him, show him their boobs, totally bald-faced come on to him right in front of me."

"That you care tells me this is more than a fling. Also the way you carve out time for him and the little smile you get when he's mentioned."

Mary sighed. "It's more than a fling. Yes. He wants more, he says. I wanted it to stay casual, but the longer I know him the less casual it feels."

"Cal, looking the way he does and all, has women coming on to him a lot. Sometimes in my presence. Men too." Jules hopped up on a nearby stool. "It's hard. Being jealous, I mean. I used to be envious before Cal was mine. I hated that he was with other people and not me. But now that he's mine it's different. If that makes me petty, so be it. But he's my man. He's always so appropriate, though you know your brother is a ridiculous flirt. It helps that he's always got eyes for me, or Gideon, when he comes into a room."

"I don't think I've ever really been jealous before. It's unpleasant. But there you go. Also, my brother flat-out adores you, so you're not going to have to worry about him like that."

Jules waved a hand. "Oh I know. I was just commiserating. And saying, I guess, that I've seen him with you around and he watches you like you're the only person he's interested in. The fame thing is hard; we know that from Gillian. But Damien digs you, stupid tabloid pictures or not."

Mary huffed a breath. "Oh man, those pictures. I made myself a promise, a pact I suppose, not to look at them. It drives me crazy to see. Because that's not the Damien I know. It's scary, and then I start doubting myself and him and what I feel and maybe he doesn't feel it and this is only so hot because I'm not like the others and I don't just fall at his feet."

"I know a little bit about that. I mean, about feeling like perhaps it's the novelty and not the reality that is getting the dude all hot for you. You know I was worried at first about Cal not wanting me, not really. I'm not sure words or reassurances can make it totally go away. It's going to take time and example. He's going to have to show you, and you're going to have to believe it's real. And there's really no way around the fact that he is that Damien too. At least in some part. He's got a persona. His band has a persona. So where that Damien stops and the real one begins is something you have to accept."

"I know."

And she did. It scared the hell out of her, but she realized the stuff in the tabloids and on the Internet would always be there. It was up to her to deal with it and up to him to not be a womanizing dick.

If she meant to let this go further. Which, she guessed, she did.

His mother caught up to him as he got back from a ride with Ezra. Having taken Mary home just that morning, he knew his mother would want to debrief.

Ezra gave him a face, but Damien shrugged.

She sat on his porch, rocking back and forth in the porch swing. "Nice day to have a sit for a while outside. This is a good spot for the swing. Come up to the house and I'll make you and your brothers lunch."

"Brothers?"

"Vaughan and Paddy are up at the house helping your dad finish the enclosure for the back fence. There's a ham in the oven."

Score.

He and Ezra took up on either side of her as they began the walk back to the main house.

"Mary get back all right?"

"Yep. She left her car at the airfield. She left a message for me when she got back home safely." He'd liked that she had. It made him feel better. Next time he'd stay, drive her back home. That way there'd be more time with her.

"What do you think of the girl, Ezra?"

"She charmed the demon pig."

"That's a good point. Your dumb dog loves everyone, so that's not a big deal. But the demon pig, well, that's another story."

"Violet misses Mary already. I hope she doesn't revert to her evil ways in Mary's absence. Elsewise we'll have to make the girl live here to keep us all safe. Once the beast gets bigger she'll be a killer if she gets mean. She's pretty. Mary, not the pig."

Damien laughed.

"And she cooks like a boss. Christ, if you stay with her, you'll have to exercise a lot more or you'll have to roll around everywhere."

"I went for a run on the treadmill earlier for that very reason." And the sex was also a good workout.

"I asked her if she'd sign a prenup."

Damien halted, his mouth open. "You did what? Mom, I've been trying to get this woman to give me a chance and you go and do that?"

"Close your mouth. Of course I did. You know what Kelly did to Vaughan. She's got her monthly check, it's all she wanted. Do you think I want that for you too?"

"She's not in it for the money. If she were, I wouldn't have to fight her so hard to be with me. God."

"Don't you take that tone with me. And no, she isn't in it for the money. She told me she'd only known you three and a half months and you were nowhere near marriage. I like that she told me to back off but with manners."

"Kelly was too young. Like Vaughan was too young. I don't think she did it for money. I think she felt like if she had Vaughan's babies he'd stay home. He'd make a commitment and love her." Damien knew his family hated Vaughan's ex. But he mainly felt sorry for her. Vaughan was twenty-five years old when he'd married Kelly. She'd been six months pregnant. Kelly had been even younger at twenty-three. Neither of them had been ready. It fell apart because of that. Another baby to try to keep Vaughan home where he should have been. But that never worked.

"He pays her so she'll stick close. She could up and move to San Francisco, you know. She stays close so the girls can see him." Ezra kept walking. "He's gone four months a year. She's the one who parents them every day. Give her a break."

Their mother loved them all fiercely and, at times, with a blindness only a mother can pull off. Vaughan was not blameless in the mess, and while he was a great dad and he loved his daughters, Kelly wasn't the mercenary bitch their mother believed she was at times.

Their mother sighed. "I love you boys. The problem is that you're all talented and handsome. Women see that and sometimes you get blinded by what's under their skirts. And they're blinded to that by all your charm. It's my job as your mother to watch over you. Yes, yes, you're all adults, but I'll always be your mother. Anyway, I like Mary."

Well, that was lucky.

"She didn't run out the door when I called her my girlfriend. That's a step in the right direction. It's an issue that I get recognized a lot. But I can't help it. It's part of this gig."

His mother laughed as they went up the porch steps. "She's far enough away that it's going to cause her worry. You have to understand it."

"I know. She's worried about the life. Worried I'll stray. Worried I live too hard."

"You do live too hard." His mother paused at the door.

"I did. I'm trying not to. I'm trying to be worth it to her."

His mother looked back over her shoulder at him. "Good. That's what I like to hear."

"The two-states thing is odd. How you gonna handle that?" Ezra held the door open for their mother as he spoke to Damien.

"Well, it sucks that I can't see her as often as I'd like. But travel is part of my job too. So it's not actually as big a hassle as it would be if I didn't tour and all that."

"I've been working with Paddy on some new stuff." Ezra spoke once their mother had moved into the kitchen. "I've blocked out time in November."

They would start work on their next album in two months. Recording was grueling. They spent a lot of time in the barn working. Reworking. Working some more. Paddy was a perfectionist. He insisted on fifty takes if that's what it took to get it just right. He and Vaughan were at each others' throats a lot. Damien had to do his level best to ignore most of what Paddy said and did while they were in the studio or they ended up bloodying each other far too often.

One thing was that Ezra was the leader of the band again while they recorded. It saved them from breaking up over and over. He did the guitar work on all their records, wrote nearly all the songs with Paddy and kept things as chill as possible with all the hotheaded Hurley brothers.

"You should ask Mary to come down and personal chef it. You know, while we work on the record."

Damien paused. That wasn't an entirely bad idea. He'd considered asking if she'd be their tour chef. He knew she had the supper club, though. But the tour was a year out anyway.

But if she was there while they recorded they'd probably be healthier. They spent a lot of time eating crap and takeout. She'd be a calming influence. Most likely they'd be better behaved and she'd get to see him work.

"I want her to respect what I do. I mean, I think she does. She loves live music and she was a fan before she met me. The questions she asks about the work seem to show she's interested and not in that fangirl way. I don't know. I'm . . ."

Ezra squeezed his shoulder. "She's good for you. I'd totally vote for her to come down here to cook for us. God knows we'd probably work better with real meals instead of potato chips and frozen burritos."

"I'll bring it up. Thanks."

His brother tipped his chin. "Any time. Plus she's gorgeous. Not like it's a hardship to look at her."

He flipped Ezra off as he walked past. But he smiled.

18

S he missed him.

She didn't want to. Didn't plan to. But she did anyway. Missed the way he said her name. Missed the feel of him next to her in bed in the mornings. Missed the sex most assuredly. Mainly though, she missed talking with him about the flotsam and jetsam of her daily life.

Of course her daily life was menus and catering jobs and his was winning awards and making records. He was probably bored with her stuff. Maybe.

This was dumb. She stood up decisively. For something to do she uploaded the pictures from her camera to her computer. Of course there were hundreds of shots and 90 percent of them were of him or the ranch. They were good, she thought. Even if she did say so herself. The gleam of the chrome on his drums catching in the sunlight at the Gorge. The steam rising from the fields in the early morning. Ezra on a horse, or dealing with his animals. Paddy and Vaughan, heads bent close sharing some trouble of one kind or another. Violet.

She needed to frame some of these.

She was going to get mopey if this kept up. He had a life. She had hers. They had just seen one another a week and a half before so it wasn't like months had passed or anything. She had work every single day so she couldn't have taken a break anyway.

She called Daisy. "We should go dancing."

Daisy gasped. "We totally should. Like tonight? Are you busy?"

"I had a lunch thing but I'm free now."

"I'll be at your house in an hour. I'll call Jules and you try Gillian?"

"Got it."

Gillian was delighted by the idea and everyone would be meeting at Mary's house in an hour.

Mary rushed off to take a shower. Dancing would keep her mind off how she wasn't with Damien.

"You're totally not going to wear that." Daisy gave Mary a critical eye as she got dressed. "You have a gorgeous body; why are you wearing a potato sack? You're usually way better at this."

Jules laughed. "Better you than me."

Daisy was sort of the fashion police of Delicious. She had excellent taste and quite often little gifts would show up in Mary's house. A blouse or a dress. Something she may have never chosen for herself but Daisy, as always, had a strong sense about it.

Daisy moved to go through Mary's closet and tossed out a few things. "The blue one I think."

She held up the minidress. "It's October. This is an August dress."

"We'll be in a club. It'll be a million degrees. You can wear a wrap until we get inside."

She sighed and obeyed. Daisy wouldn't quit until she did anyway.

Daisy grinned once Mary had finished.

"Perfect. You look hot. We need to take a picture of all of us and text it to our respective boys. It'll do them all good to know what they've got. Also, Gillian, baby, are you okay to be out tonight?"

"I'll have to forgo the tequila shots of course, and the wild sex with random passersby. But I can dance and visit with my friends. It's been ages since we've done this."

It had. They'd all been falling in love over the last two years. Each one, bit by bit, and things had changed. Mary was still adjusting, but it was overwhelmingly good.

"Since we're headed to Seattle, I think we should invite Erin, Elise and Ella. I bet Ella would love a night out." Daisy grabbed a wrap and tossed it Mary's way. "That one."

"She may not want to leave the baby for very long, but we should definitely invite her." Their friend Ella had a two-month-old and a gorgeous husband, so Mary wouldn't blame her one bit if she said no, thank you.

"I'll call while we're on the way." Gillian said. "I've got

Adrian's SUV. The windows are smoked so you can't see much out the back. Or we could take the bridge and go around." Gillian looked to Jules casually. Jules had a horrible fear of water. The ferry was not her favorite thing. She rarely said a word, but they all tried to spare her when they could.

"I'll stay in the back between these hot mommas. Gillian, let Mary drive."

"I'm pregnant, not unable to drive, for goodness sake."

Jules laughed. "I know. Humor me."

It had been far too long since she'd shaken her ass until she was red in the face and sweaty. Well, she thought of Damien for a moment, in a nonsexual fashion. Ella and Gillian hung out at the table, laughing and chatting. Jules alternated between the group dancing and the table.

Daisy was ridiculous. No one danced like her so Mary had gotten used to it. But she had her own groove and she worked it in her own way. Elise, also a dancer, was graceful and sexy, her pale hair whipping around as she moved. Every once in a while Erin would take a picture on her phone and send it god knew where, most likely to her men. Daisy took a few of herself and Mary, most likely sending to Twitter or one of her other social network addictions.

Every few minutes a dude would dance up and try to grind. If he kept his distance and didn't touch her with his cock, she danced with him a while. If he touched her in any way, she sent him packing. Even without Damien she'd have sent them away. She didn't go out dancing to have men buy her drinks or rub all over her. She could buy her own damn drinks. She liked being with her girlfriends, laughing, getting a good workout and hearing some great music.

"I need a drink. This round is on me." Daisy tugged on her arm and they left the dance floor, heading toward the big bar at the far end of the room.

While they waited they danced and laughed. "I've missed this."

"I'm sorry!" Daisy hugged her. "I feel like I've abandoned you."

Mary tipped her head back and laughed. "Baby, you're in love. That's amazing and wonderful and I'm thrilled. You haven't abandoned me at all. You just made room in your life for Levi. Like you should. Everyone's lives are going in such a great direction. It's all good."

The bartender gave her a tip of his chin, his gaze sliding over her breasts. It made her smile. A girl needed to feel desired, and this night was all those things in spades.

He poured their drinks quite liberally and brushed his fingers over hers as she grabbed her glass. She winked and they danced their way back to the table, passing around drinks and the water they'd picked up for Gillian.

"That person over there keeps taking pictures of you guys." Ella nodded toward a far corner.

Erin turned and snarled. "That's the asshole who caused all the drama with Gillian. What is he doing here?"

"That creepy reporter who started that fight outside the club? The one that almost broke Gillian and Adrian up?" Mary could still remember how torn up Gillian was when the reporter had dumped the story of her criminal father on Adrian and his family. All to hurt them and try to create a juicy story. Mary had never seen Gillian cry so hard.

"No, you stay here." Mary took a sip. "I'll handle this." Dude seriously needed some violence in his life if he thought he could hurt her friend ever again.

"I'm coming with you." Daisy rose. "Wheee! Just like the old days."

"Of all of three years ago. Let's go deal with this asshole."

"It's better if you just ignore them." Gillian put a hand on her arm. "You're going to learn this yourself. But if you give him any attention, he'll make it into a story. *What was the pretty wife of Adrian Brown up to that she sent her friends over to silence the press?*"

Mary curled her lip. "He shouldn't be taking pictures without your permission. At the very least, let me track down someone who works here to deal with that."

Gillian thought a moment and then nodded.

"In the meantime, if you adjust and switch places with Jules all he'll be able to see is the back of your head."

"Good idea."

She found a bouncer and whispered in his ear. He nodded, spoke to someone off to the side. A manager came out quickly once Adrian's name had been spoken.

"There's a guy over there by the back bar. He's been taking pictures of Gillian Brown all night long. She's never given her permission. All we want to do is come here to have some fun. It's not much fun if we can't even hang out without this sort of thing."

She cocked her head, adding a little wistful, a little guile and a little sexy. He exhaled and nodded. "We obviously want our patrons to be comfortable." Especially their celebrity ones, she knew. And for once she wasn't hesitant about using that. Gillian deserved some damned privacy.

He was gone and they went back to the table for a few minutes before they headed out to dance again.

"Dude." Paddy peered over his shoulder as he looked at his phone. Mary had forwarded a picture of her and her friends when they'd gone out the night before. "Wow. Your woman is fucking hot."

"Shut up."

She did look hot in a pretty blue minidress that showcased her tits and her legs. He bet she and Daisy tore that place up. And then he frowned. He bet she got hit on too.

"Why are you frowning?"

"She looks hot."

"And that's a problem why? You prefer your women not hot? 'Cause I call bullshit on that."

"Shut up. God."

"Oh, I get it, she's not supposed to be hot when you're not around."

"Well. She probably got hit on. Dudes probably danced with her. She won't commit to me; god only knows what she got up to."

Paddy socked his arm really hard.

"Ow!" He shoved Paddy, who fell back over the arm of the couch. "Dick."

"Fuck you, crybaby. You're a dick." And he socked Damien again, dancing out of the way of any retaliation. "You really gonna tell me you think she gave a guy a BJ in the bathroom? I'm not even dating her and I can tell you that's bullshit. She's not like that, which is why you dig her so much. But she has a life without you, which is why you're so bugged. And you know it's stupid and shitty to be bugged, which bugs you more."

"Why'd she send this picture then?"

"What is wrong with you? It's like you've never dealt with women before. They always send you pictures of times they look great. Duh. She's like, hey, dude, look how foxy I am. Not, hey, dude, I'm going to bang a stranger. She wants you to see what you have. You're dumb. Is she supposed to stay home and wear sackcloth? Because we're headed out the damned door to go party in Portland. That's what Mom would call a double standard."

"I'm not all duded up!"

"You're going to get hit on by dozens of women. They're going to show you their tits and buy you drinks." Paddy shrugged. "Are you going to bang a stranger in the bathroom?"

"No! I told you, I'm with Mary."

"So why would you expect that she would do that to you? She's a nice girl. A. Nice. Girl. Sure you're not used to that, but that's what Mary Whaley is. You? You're not so much a nice boy, but you're not going to fuck around on her. So I think you should afford her the same trust you'd expect her to give you."

"When did you get so fuckin' wise?"

"I was born wise. One of us has to be smart since the rest of you are dumbasses who lead with your dicks."

"Oh, the irony. I'm surprised you didn't get struck by lightning right now."

"Let's go get our drink on." Paddy slapped his shoulder. "I told Vaughan we'd grab him on the way out."

It wasn't that Ezra couldn't deal with the sight of them drinking. He was far enough down his road to recovery that he wasn't bothered by people drinking around him. But they did it out of respect and also, Portland had great clubs and hot women. Well, for Vaughan and Paddy anyway.

"You drive. I'm gonna call Mary." Damien settled in the backseat and dialed her number.

"Hello there, Damien."

He smiled at the sound of her voice. There was enough noise in the background that he knew she was with her friends. It was supper club night.

He missed her.

"Hello there, Mary. What are you up to?"

"Wrapping up supper club and then we're headed to Adrian and Gillian's for a movie marathon. What are you up to?"

"Going out with Paddy and Vaughan. Thanks for the pictures you sent last night. You looked hot."

Her laugh made him miss her even more.

"Thank you. There was some jerk photographer there taking pictures of Gillian. We got him removed."

So ferocious in the defense of those she loved.

"Did you punch him in the throat? I seem to recall you have a penchant for that."

Again she laughed. "No, I batted my eyes and got wistful with the management. But I think it was probably more the fact that she's a sort of celebrity in his club and they didn't want to lose her business more than my eyelashes."

He doubted it. She had great eyelashes.

"How's my pig?"

"Ha! So far she hasn't reverted to her former ways. But Ezra says she misses you. You should come down again to visit her. Keep her on the straight and narrow. Me too."

"Are you in danger of straying from the path of righteousness, young man?"

"Only if you'll discipline me after."

Her laugh had changed, lowered. Shivers slid through his system.

"And no, I have no plans to stray. You know that, right?" Flirting and joking aside, it was important she understood that.

"I should hope so."

"When can I see you again?" He hadn't planned to ask, but he didn't plan lots of things about the way he felt for her. It simply was. He needed her in his life, damn it.

"Going into some busy times. Over the next three weeks I've got jobs every day of the week. Some days I have two. Nice to be able to pay for Christmas presents."

"We're going into the studio in November. Would you consider being our personal chef?" He'd broached the idea with Vaughan, who was fine. Ezra had brought it up first anyway. He didn't care what Paddy thought by that point. Damien wasn't above admitting he wanted her with him and it would only be fair to have her work there. She was good at what she did. He knew that. She'd be a calming influence. "We work all day and

---

into the night. It'd be good to have real meals and snacks. If you were here to do it for us, we'd probably get a lot more done."

Paddy gave him a look in the rearview, but held his tongue.

"We can talk about this the next time we see each other."

"Fine, fine. I've got to run. I just wanted to check in with you because I wanted to hear your voice."

"I'm glad you did. I miss you."

Pride roared through him. She rarely gave him little bits of praise like this when they were apart. It made him unbearably happy.

"Yeah?"

"Yeah."

"I miss you too. Sweet dreams, Mary Whaley, very nice girl. I'll talk to you soon."

"Bye, Damien Hurley, very dirty musician with the very big heart."

She hung up and missing her came right back.

"What'd she say about the personal chef thing?" Vaughan asked.

"She said we'd talk about it when we see each other next." Which would be very soon because he was sick of not being with her.

19

She was still smiling when she pulled up to the garage. It had been an awesome night with her friends, though she was the only uncoupled one now. Adrian had asked her to do an event for Gillian. Just a little gathering with their friends and family to celebrate the pregnancy.

There had been too much food, lots of laughter. Ice cream and scary movies. She'd left full up of laughter and love. Though she did still miss Damien.

She grabbed the totes with all the dishes in them. Adrian, Cal and Miles had done cleanup in exchange for the cooking, so all she had to do was put her stuff away. When she came around the corner to her back door she screamed and jumped three feet when a man stepped away from her stoop.

"Curly, darlin', it's me. It's Damien." He stepped closer his hands up in the air, voice calm the way you use with toddlers and crazy people.

Her heart threatened to beat out of her chest as she tried to catch her breath.

"You scared the hell out of me! I thought you were a prowler."

"I'm so sorry." He approached and she allowed him to hug her. His scent registered and she calmed a little. "I didn't mean to scare you. I didn't want your neighbors to call the cops if they saw me on your front porch so I've been back here. I parked on the side of your garage like I always do. I figured you'd see me. Um. Surprise?"

"I didn't see the car."

"It's a rental. I had them meet me at the airfield. I . . . Is it all right that I'm here?"

She hugged him again. "Yeah. Better than all right. I'm glad to see you. Come on inside."

He took the totes and went in first, making sure no giant zombies or anything were inside. She went to her junk drawer and pulled out a key. "Here. You may as well have a key. That way you don't have to sit on the back porch in the cold. How long have you been here? Why didn't you tell me you were coming?"

He kissed her and she melted into his embrace. Loving his mouth on hers.

"Now then. Thank you for the key. I've only been here about forty-five minutes or so. I didn't call because I wanted it to be a surprise. I knew you had two jobs today so I figured I'd come in later so as not to interrupt. Also, yesterday when I called you and heard your voice I knew I'd rather be here than anywhere else."

"Oh. Well." She grinned and tiptoed up to kiss him again. "Hi. I'm glad to see you."

"Me too."

He looked back over his shoulder. "Door locked?"

Her heart, which had just stopped pounding over being so surprised, started to *thud-thud-thud* again. Desire pulsed through her, slow and heady.

"Yes. Why?"

He smiled. "I have plans for you, Curly. Plans that would send a casual viewer into therapy."

"Only because they'd be sorry you weren't doing it to them instead."

"You always know exactly what to say. How is that?" He unzipped her fleece, peeling it back and then down off her arms.

Her hands went to his belt, getting it unbuckled, and then to his button and zipper. His cock was hot and hard in her hands within several breathless moments.

But he spun her to face the wall, his hands moving to cup her breasts before he peeled the cups of her bra back to tug on her nipples over and over until she nearly cried for him to get on with it.

His cock nearly burned through her pants as he pressed against her. Taunting.

One of his hands left her right breast and slid down into her jeans, down into her panties. He cupped her pussy for long moments, just holding. The heat of him singed her memory.

She'd be unable to forget this moment. Not for a long time and maybe not ever.

No one had ever done this to her. Only Damien with his cocky smile and his clever fingers. With that mouth of his. He drove her crazy.

Her head fell back to his shoulder and he kissed her temple with so much tenderness it brought the prick of tears to her eyes.

"All I could think of over the last two weeks was this. The smell of your skin. The way your hair tickles my lips when I kiss your face or neck. The way your nipples feel against my palm." He tugged and pinched and she squeaked.

She felt the curve of his lips against her neck as he smiled at her reaction. "The way you give over to me, demanding your due. You're the sexiest thing I've ever seen."

She swallowed back the emotion, throwing herself into the sensation instead. The ground was more solid there.

The hand in her panties moved, his fingers spreading her open to pet her clit.

"So hot and wet. Always."

"You could put something far better than your hand in there. Just sayin'."

He laughed. "Oh, darlin', I will. But I like to make you come. It makes me happy. After. Then I'm going to fuck you so hard you stutter. Ah, your cunt just got even hotter."

She closed her eyes, resting her forehead against the wall, her fingers curled into the wallpaper.

That hand slid a little further down, enough that he circled her gate, entering her ever so slightly before moving back to her clit. He knew her so well. Knew just how to touch her. Just how much pressure to use, how fast, how slow to draw it out.

Pleasure rose, slow and steady. Building. Filling her from her pussy outward. Outward until it scorched through her system and there was only the need to climax. It overflowed, sucking her under so hard she barely registered the way he shoved her pants down.

They kept her in place, hemmed her in, much like his body at her back did. A wild thrill spiraled through her as he bent her to angle her body better. His cock brushed against her and then he pushed inside in one hard stroke.

"Goddamn."

He thrust and thrust, wanting more. Wanting everything. And she gave it to him. She always did. Despite her protestations, she was his.

The need to fuck her, to be in her, to possess her, drove him. Need nearly made him blind. Consumed him. He touched every part of her that he could. Slid his palms over the curve of her hips, the weight of her breasts, the strength of her thighs as she got to her tiptoes to meet his strokes better.

Sweat broke over his skin, his muscles burned and when he came it seemed to last forever, echoing through him, making his fucking teeth tingle with it.

He gasped for air, kissing the back of her neck as he pulled out carefully.

"Wow." She turned, her eyes glossy, her lips wet.

He grinned, but his legs were shaky as he got himself back to rights. He was head over heels in love with Mary Whaley. In so deep that if he had any sense at all he'd be scared.

The following morning at Tart he watched her while she worked.
Careful of course to keep out of the way. She could be a bear if
people got into her flow when she cooked. It made her ferocious
and bitchy. Which only rendered her hotter to him.

He played on his tablet, answering e-mail, sending instructions to his manager, declining to participate in a label event in
New York the following week. Paddy loved that stuff so he could
go instead.

Jules wandered in and gave him a raised brow. "Well, hello
there."

"He surprised me last night. Nearly scared the life out of me.
I thought he was a prowler." Mary continued to seed cucumbers
as she spoke, a smile on her lips.

"I'm glad you didn't shoot him." Jules winked at him. He
knew Cal and Jules were protective of her. Knew too that they
didn't trust him at first. But over the last weeks, each time he'd
seen them and interacted with them, things had gotten a little
less tense. "You want a coffee? Something to eat?"

"I'd love you forever if you made me a latte." Mary fluttered
her lashes and went back to her work.

"You already do love me forever on account of me being so
pretty and charming."

Mary barked a laugh. "I'm sorry for your deep self-esteem
issues, Juliet."

Damien liked their interplay. Liked knowing she was surrounded by people who cared about her. It made it easier to be
away from her, though on some levels it also made it harder. He

wanted her to come to him for emotional support, but she didn't need to.

"I'd love an Americano if it's not too much trouble. Thank you."

Jules nodded. "No trouble. Be back in a sec."

She moved to the large espresso machine and began to work.

Mary spoke over the swish and swirl of the espresso machine. "Oh, I have something for your mom if you'd take it back when you go home again."

"Really? Of course I will. What is it?"

"I took a lot of really great pictures when I was down at the ranch. There are a few I thought were pretty spectacular. One of her and your dad. I had an extra frame so I put it in. Nothing big."

He warmed. His mother would dig that. A lot.

"Thank you. Can I see them? The pictures, I mean."

"Yeah." She rattled off a URL and then a password. "They're all there."

He looked, pretty amazed at her eye. "Wow. These are really good."

"I'm no Daisy. She's got so much talent it's not funny. But I like taking pictures and I think there are several in there with some nice composition."

He grinned. "The demon pig even looks sort of sweet in these."

Mary laughed. "She's a sweet animal. Just sort of lost."

"You're pretty special, you know that?"

She looked up from her work, her hands glistening from the vegetables and, God help him, it shot straight to his cock.

"Thank you. They're just pictures."

"Mary has a difficult time taking a compliment." Jules placed a cup at Mary's right hand. "Latte here. Honey and a little chocolate." She handed another cup to Damien. "Americano. Milk, cream, soy, sugar and all that is right over there. I don't know how you take it."

"Hush, both of you." Mary blushed, sipping her latte. "Perfect. Thanks."

Jules kissed Mary's cheek. "Anytime."

"Pictures of food. I should have known."

She looked up again. "Oh, I'd forgotten about those. They're for a cookbook proposal."

"Really? Tell me about it?"

She blushed. "A while ago an agent contacted me. She was at a dinner I catered. Anyway, she suggested I write a cookbook. I put together a proposal. Those are just some shots I took for it."

"Wow."

"I don't know if it's wow-worthy, but it's pretty cool. Anyway, I just sent it to her a week ago. I've been so busy."

"What did she say?"

"She did some sort of whiz-bang formatting for it to make it look better. She said she had a few sources she was going to pitch it to. I haven't heard. I put it out of my mind. Easy enough when I'm busy."

"I think it totally merits a wow. I hope you hear good news soon."

Mary's assistant came in a short time afterward and they

began to put together the luncheon she'd been preparing, packing it up.

"I'll be back in a few hours."

He stopped her, pulling her close for a kiss and not caring who saw it.

And was relieved she accepted it without hassle, even rewarding him with a smile. "Thank you."

"Believe me when I assure you my kisses are available at any time. I'm heading over to Adrian's. Text me when you're done?"

She nodded. "All right. Tell Gillian I said hello."

And she was gone.

Jules cruised back in. "So, I'm going to try to ask you this in a way nicer fashion than I did the first time. Which was totally rude and unfair, I admit."

"I'm in love with her. I want to make something real with Mary. But she's skittish." He knew Jules was going to ask what his intentions were so better to just answer honestly.

"Love?"

"I'm over thirty. I know the difference between infatuation and love. I've known her since June. She's dominated my thoughts every single day since then."

"You have a reputation."

"I do. But that's manufactured by the media."

"Not all of it."

"No. Not all. Look, I don't regret anything I've done. I was a young man with lots of success, lots of money and lots of women. But I never hurt anyone. I never misused anyone. Everything I've done has been with consent. And none of them has been Mary. That's how I know the difference. I'm not going to apologize for what I've done in the past with people before I even met her. But I can tell you that since the moment she came into my life, that Damien has been retired."

"She's special. She works harder than anyone I've ever met. She takes care of the people she loves. She needs a man who is worthy of her." Jules looked him up and down. "You that guy?"

"I sure hope so. I'm trying my best."

"If you hurt her, I'll hunt you down. She's my family."

He nodded. "I'd expect nothing less. But I don't plan to hurt her."

"Which is why I made you an Americano and didn't throw it in your face." She smiled and he laughed. "She has always been there for me. For all the people she loves. I don't blame you for loving her. I don't know how anyone could resist loving her. If you're who she's chosen, you're part of us too. You make her happy. I like that. Keep it up."

She turned and went out to deal with customers.

Mary went home, showered and then headed over to Gillian's place. Miles had just gotten home from school and he chattered nonstop about this or that class, music composition, the song he'd been working on for a project.

When they were alone, Miles told her about something he'd seen on the Internet. She didn't know how to process it, so she'd stew on it a while to figure it out.

Gillian came back into the room, smiling when she saw him still chattering away to Mary. She kissed her son's cheek.

"Enough. You're going to talk Mary's ear off. Go on and do your homework. I made you a sandwich; it's on the counter."

He grinned. "Thanks, Mum!" He sped from the room, cats in his wake.

"Looks like he loves school."

"I have to admit I was wrong about how amazing a choice this school would be for him. I wanted him to be with his friends and to keep his life here. But he's made more there. The kids there are talented like he is. And better than that, he's connected with this huge part of himself. All that art that lives in his soul." She shook her head. "I should have known. My time at Juilliard was incredible because I was surrounded by people who were like me."

"I know you, Gillian. You're feeling guilty for not having him in the school for years."

"How could I have been so blind to it?"

"Hush, you. You thought about his life in terms of his safety, of the stability in the face of all this change. By that I mean you're his mum and you did what you should have. There's enough guilt in this world. Don't let this small thing add to it."

Gillian was an amazing mother. She had no idea how good at it she was. Miles was beyond lucky to have her. Mary squeezed her friend's hand.

"You're good to me."

"I only speak the truth."

Adrian came into the room with Damien. Damien saw her and lit up. She felt it to her toes.

"Miles was just gushing about his composition class."

Adrian grinned. "That kid. Man. So proud of him. He hit the

ground running and he's been kicking ass. Even doing the home-work for his academic courses. Should have seen their faces when Damien showed up with me today when we picked him up. I think they like him better than me."

"Yeah, sucks to be you and all. Triple platinum, sold-out tour, hot wife, baby on the way, great kid. Too bad you're so ugly." Damien snorted and headed straight to Mary. "Hey, you." He kissed her.

"Hi."

"How'd the job go?"

"The client is pretty difficult." Mary sighed. "She was very specific about what she wanted. I advised her that some other choices would work better. She insisted on what she wanted. And of course then she threw a giant tantrum about it. Thank good-ness I had all our e-mails printed out and with me in a file so I could refute her claims. And Cal's card to hand over when she threatened not to pay me."

He frowned. "What a bitch."

Mary shrugged. "Sometimes you have clients like that. Mainly they're pretty nice."

"This isn't going to hurt you, is it? It was Kathy Bonebright, right?" Gillian's concern made Damien's gaze sharpen.

"I think most people who know her know what she's like. I won't be working with her again, even if she hadn't sworn me off as incompetent in front of the entire room."

"She did wha?" Gillian's eyes flashed and Adrian squeezed her shoulder.

Mary laughed, turning to Damien. "You may not have

noticed, but when Gillian gets mad, she loses consonants and her English comes out."

"Who is this woman, Curly?"

"She's no one. Her husband has money and she thinks it makes her important. But I know my food, I know my business, and anyone who's worked with me knows it. I'm fine."

"She said you were incompetent?" Gillian was mainly sweet, but when someone she loved was threatened, she could be a sharp-tongued bitch.

"Yes. In front of half her party. So tacky. Most of them cringed in embarrassment. Several of them asked for my card. She's nothing to me, Gillian. It's all right."

"She'd better watch herself." Gillian sniffed. "Incompetent? I'll show her incompetent with my boot."

Mary hugged her friend. "I love you."

"Of course you do. You have excellent taste."

Damien absently tugged on one of her curls only to watch it spring back into shape. "What's the plan for the evening?"

"We're having dinner with my family."

He raised a brow. "We are?"

"Yes. I'm sorry I didn't tell you before. I bumped into my mother on the way over here just now. She invited me to dinner. I told her you were here and she said she'd set an extra place. Is that all right?"

"Yes. I'm happy to meet them at last."

20

Damien was never nervous. But he sure was now. He gave himself a little pep talk about how he totally could do this. Her mother was a woman after all. He was good with women. But this was Mary's mom and dad. People who were really important to her.

Mary squeezed his hand. "I promise you they're really nice people. She just wants to get a look at you. If she thought you were a bad guy, she wouldn't be inviting you to dinner, I can tell you that much."

"Oh yeah? There's a story to that. Tell me."

"Let's see, um, five years ago? No, six. I went out with a guy for a while. He was nice enough. But I never quite trusted him. Anyway, it got back to her that he had a fiancée of all things.

This woman he'd actually been living with down in Tacoma. I had no idea. He had an apartment here; how on Earth could I have known? But she found out and she tracked him down. She never told me what was said. He never told me what was said. But he confessed about the other woman and moved out of his apartment that same week. She's sort of ruthless. So what I'm saying is she's not one to hide or beat around the bush. If she likes you, she likes you, and she does not have people she dislikes at her kitchen table."

She pulled up the driveway and got out.

"You should let me open your door." He frowned at her and she laughed, holding a hand out.

"I promise next time. Come on."

He noted that she did not bring any food.

They went up the front steps. She tapped on the door and they went in. "It's me!"

"In the kitchen."

She shut the front door and he took her coat, hanging it on the coat rack near the door, along with his own.

"Come on back then. Your father is making what he thinks is a compelling argument as to why we should have ice cream with the pie."

"My dad has really high cholesterol and high blood pressure," Mary told him in an undertone. "He's always trying to sneak his favorite foods, most of which are forbidden now."

The house was nice. Pictures of the kids from babyhood into the present day all over the walls. Nothing fancy. Nothing rundown. It was clear a family had been raised there with love. He liked that a lot.

Jeanne Whaley stood in front of a very tall man wearing a sheepish expression.

"I don't see why a little tiny scoop is a problem."

"Because you have Doritos in your shed. Don't think I don't know."

"Hey, guys." Mary moved to hug her mother and then her father, both of whom turned to face Damien. "Jeanne and Mike Whaley, this is Damien Hurley. Damien, my parents."

Damien smiled and held his hand out. "It's really a pleasure to meet you." Mary and her mother bore a very strong resemblance. The shape of the eyes, the curly hair, the smiles were very similar as well.

Jeannie looked him up and down. "Mary says you're a musician."

"Yes, ma'am." He looked to her father and took his hand in a shake. Not too hard or too long. "Nice to meet you, sir."

"Manners are a good start. There's beer in the fridge. Want one?" Mike tipped his chin.

"That would hit the spot. Thank you."

"Sit. I'll get one for everyone." Mary moved to the fridge as they all sat.

"Company is here. Ice cream is a must for company. Jules sent over the cherry walnut bars. It's a crime not to have ice cream with them."

"Are you sucking in your cheeks? Mary, look at your father pretending to be scrawny to get some ice cream. I hope it hits the spot as it clogs your arteries and kills you. Leave me with three kids. Two of them without enough sense, though Juliet will save Cal from himself. Ryan? Well, goodness knows. You can't die yet because it would be terribly unfair to leave me with these creatures to raise on my own."

"What's for dinner?" Mary interjected smoothly as she put the beers down on the table.

"Meatloaf. Mashed potatoes, corn. Tomatoes and cucumbers. Oh, and bread."

"Yum." Mary sat next to Damien. "She makes the best meatloaf in the whole world. I promise."

"I'm not one to turn down meatloaf. It's one of my favorites."

Jeanne turned her gaze back to him. "Do you play cards?"

Mary snorted. "Watch her. Dad, how's the computer?"

"Slow. This thing keeps coming up telling me I won a laptop. Pretty cool, huh?"

Mary paled and Damien had to work really hard not to laugh as he knew she counted to ten. "Dad, I told you about that. You didn't really win a laptop. No one ever wins the laptop. Did you give them any information?"

"I clicked the pop-up thing. Is that bad?"

Mary looked to him and he bit the inside of his cheek.

"Go on and fix your dad's machine. I'll watch the meatloaf and in the meantime, Damien can play some cards with me."

"Watch your wallet, boy. She's crafty as well as beautiful. The curse of a Whaley female." Mike winked at his wife. "The blessing too. Always got your back in a corner. Vicious."

Jeanne waved a lazy hand at him. "Charmer. Go on and don't worry, Mary, I'll keep him safe." Mary's mother patted his hand with a cheeky grin.

"Lord," Mary muttered as she escorted her father from the room.

"Now then." She pulled out two decks of cards. "I've got a few games I like to play. 'Course they've got special rules, but you're a quick one, I wager."

He liked Jeanne Whaley. Even when she played cards fast and loose, and he wasn't quite sure, but he thought she may have played fast and loose with the rules too.

"You must like her a lot to let me cheat so much." She lifted her beer and tapped it to his.

"I do like her. A lot."

"What's your plan?"

"I'm trying. She's wily, your daughter. We're moving forward into something deeper. I hope, anyway. It's going slow. She wants it that way so I'm doing my best to accommodate her wishes."

"Lots of differences between you." She caught his eye. "You live in another state. Part of your job is to travel around a lot. A fast life. Mike is atrocious with computers. But I'm not. I researched you and your band." She didn't say more. She didn't have to.

"Fame is . . . well, it's not easy, no matter how well adjusted you are. So much is beyond what you can do anything about and you have what seems like an unlimited amount of money. People don't tell you no. In fact there are people around you who make it their business to get you everything you ever dreamed of. We live hard. The road is sort of crazy. But we have a business, it's our band and we know better than to screw that up."

She looked him over carefully. "What does your family think of this thing between you and Mary?"

"They like her. She's a small-town girl in a lot of ways. When we're not on the road we live on a ranch. Work on a ranch. It's grounding. My parents have been married thirty-six years. They're solid people and they see that Mary is solid too. She values the things they value. Family. Hard work. Compassion."

"How do you think this will work with you out there traveling around? Surrounded by women and drugs. You live over four hours away even when you're not on the road. My daughter has a life. She's built something for herself."

"I know that and I respect her business. I respect her life. I don't want her to give it up to be with me. I don't know how we'd handle the living situation. But we have a ways to go before we take that step anyway."

"Fair enough. You plan to get out there and start nailing every female you take a liking to? On the road?"

He shook his head. "No, ma'am. That part of my life is over."

She looked up from her cards and he realized she was the disciplinarian of the family. She caught him in place and held him, the threat in her gaze totally and utterly clear. The only other woman who had that gaze of terror was Sharon Hurley. "You see to it that it is. Because if it isn't, if you hurt her, you'll have me to deal with. I will hunt you down and make you sorry you ever looked twice at my daughter."

A shiver of fear went through him. Man, she and his mother could possibly have been separated at birth.

"Yes, ma'am."

She smiled, the threat relayed. "All right then. I believe you owe me ten dollars. I'm going to get the bread under the broiler." She stood.

"Can I help?"

"The plates are up in that cabinet. It's just the four of us tonight. Silverware is in that drawer." She pointed and went about her work and he set the table like he was supposed to.

"So? You ready to hightail it back to Hood River yet?" Mary asked him, backing down the drive.

"Nah. Your mom is a great cook, though not in your league. Don't tell her I said so though. Your parents are nice people, just like you said. Though your mom is really scary."

She laughed. "What'd she say?"

"Don't worry about it. She's concerned for you. I get it. It's my job to prove her fears are groundless."

"Yeah?"

"Yes." He took her hand. "My job to prove it to you too. I get it. You're wary. My track record isn't the best. But to be fair, I've never really made any attempt to be in a relationship with a woman. I want that with you. I'm willing to wait you out. To prove to you that I'm ready for it."

She didn't say much as they drove back to her place.

When she stopped the car, she turned to him. "I'm really scared."

"What for, Curly? I'm laying it all out on the table for you. I want you. Not for a fling. I don't want to date you. I want there to be an *us*."

"There's a lot of temptation out there. I can't compete with that."

He nodded. "I can't lie and I don't want to. Yes, there is. But you're wrong to think you can't compete with it. You're better than anything out there. There's you. Here. Waiting for me. There's nothing that can beat that, temptation wise. I've done faceless, nameless women in every city. I don't want that anymore. I want you. I want what you make me feel."

She licked her lips and he knew she was deciding on whether or not to share something with him. Finally she sucked in a breath. "My pictures with Daisy were copied from her Twitter account and put on the Internet."

Damn it. "What? When?"

"Today. Miles actually told me. He saw it on some board he visits. I guess it's officially news in some sense that Mary Whaley is dating Damien Hurley."

He scrubbed hands over his face. "I'm sorry. Why didn't you tell me before now?"

"He only told me a few hours ago. I've been processing it. Trying to figure out if it mattered more than being with you."

The pause she took felt about a million years long.

"But it doesn't."

He let out the breath he'd been holding.

"Daisy locked her account. Took all the pictures of me off. She changed the settings on her Facebook account too."

"Do you hate me?"

She shook her head slowly. "No. You didn't do it. And if we're going to do this, I have to get used to it, I guess. I don't like it that my friends have to be affected by it. But I don't like the alternative even more."

"I'm glad to hear that."

"Yeah. So, all right. We can take it slow. But I need to tell you I'm not that woman, you know the one who looks the other way when her man is out on the road. If you betray me, there won't be a next time. I'm not stupid. I'm not desperate. I won't pretend that I don't see it."

He kissed her fingertips. "Of course. I'd expect nothing less. And I told you; I'm only interested in you. Mary and Damien."

She let out a long breath. "All right then."

"Does this mean you'll be our personal chef while we work on the new album? Have you given it any thought?"

"This is serious. This is my business."

"I know it is! I'm serious. I swear."

She got out and he followed her into the house, steering her toward the couch. She kicked her shoes off and allowed him to get close. "It's a real offer. Ezra is the person who suggested it, actually. So it's not all about me having you near, though I can't lie and say that's not attractive."

She gave him a look before snorting and reaching for a nearby pad and pen.

"Here's what I'm willing to do. I'll come down four days a week. I need to be up here on the weekends for supper club anyway. I've decided to hold off on all but weekend catering gigs for a bit of time. But I'm looking into the food-delivery personal chef thing I told you about. I've got two clients already. Anyway, it means I can take off four days a week to be in Hood River."

He tucked the hair back away from her face. "Are you going to be all right? That sounds like an awful lot of work."

She softened, leaning into his touch. "I'm good. Thank you for worrying about me. I'm still trying to figure out what to do with my business. I'm experimenting, and having the income from the personal chef stuff and your job enables me to do it."

"You *are* going to allow us to pay real rates, right? Because we normally eat junk food and takeout and whatever my mom feels sorry enough to make for us. We're sort of wretched when we're recording so she stays away a lot."

"You will pay my standard rates. I'll get free room and board anyway and you'll pay for the food. Fair enough?"

"Good. Yes."

"Particulars? What are your hours? I mean do you work on a set schedule? Or what?"

"We work from about eleven to about, say midnight. Some days it goes much later and starts later the next day. But Ezra and Paddy are super-anal about staying on task. Our last record took three weeks to make. The one before that was six weeks."

She nodded, scratching out notes. "There's a kitchen in the barn right?"

He nodded and she kept writing.

"All right. For my fee, I'll make you guys three meals and two snacks. I'll talk with the others to see what they like and then give you a menu in advance. You have three days to submit changes. After that, if you don't like grapes or whatever, pick them out."

He grinned, leaning in to steal a kiss and then another. "I love it when you're stern."

"Hm. I'm working here, so back off."

He did, but he kept grinning.

"When I come back up here on the weekends, I'll leave you all enough food to last the weekend. If you'd prefer, I can set up a buffet a few times a day and you can graze as you please."

"I'll let you decide after you talk with the rest. What else do you need? Will you be a lady of leisure while you're not making us awesome food? You're welcome to sit in while we work. You may not want to. It gets . . . intense sometimes. You're welcome to ride horses or whatever too."

"I'm going to spend the time when I'm not with you all working on recipes for my book."

"Awesome. In my kitchen? Even better."

"We'll see. I don't know if it'll sell. But it seems to me a great opportunity to work on it while I'm getting paid."

She was practical. It was an attractive quality.

"I'll drive down Sunday night after the supper club and come home Thursday night."

"No, you won't. I'll fly you up and back. No, don't argue. I will worry about you the whole time if you drive. You can leave your car here and use mine when you're at the ranch. Consider it part of your pay."

It would be nice not to have to face a long-ass drive after supper club or on Thursday night up to Bainbridge.

"Okay. If you're sure it won't interrupt your work schedule."

"So we have a deal?"

"Yes."

He took the pad and pen, setting them aside, and then shook her hand. Then he sat back and gave her the look. Oh, that look of his. She was in trouble, but it was the good kind.

"So, I was thinking about how the traditional handshake really seemed boring."

"That so?"

"Yeah. I think sealing the deal in a whole 'nother way would be much more fun."

"Why do I get the feeling your idea involves nakedness?"

"Because you know me really well. I'd like to know you even better. In a carnal sense." He crawled over her as she lay back on her couch.

"I'm perfectly all right with that."

He kissed her lazily because they had time.

He kept from lying totally against her, holding himself away because the lure of her body would have rushed him and he wanted to cruise around the kiss. Wanted it to be a lazy Sunday-afternoon drive instead of a race.

She sighed into his mouth, her palms sliding up his arms, up over his shoulders. It made him hot that she dug his body the way she did. Made him feel invincible to be desired by a woman like her. Not just for his talent and his personality or whatever, but that sort of raw greed for his body.

She opened to him easily, nipping his bottom lip, laving the sting enough to chip away at his resolve.

He managed to hold on until she pushed on his shoulders. When he pulled back, breaking the kiss, she scrambled up, pulling her shirt up and off, bending and tossing her underpants off to the side, leaving her in a skirt and her bra.

Struck dumb, he kept motionless until she tossed the bra over her shoulder. Then he moved to sit and she straddled his lap.

"Are you going to ravish me?"

She nibbled on his earlobe and then down his neck. "Yes, I think so." Then she grabbed his belt and made quick work of getting his jeans open and his cock out.

"I think you should be nice and ready first."

The smile she gave him sent shivers through his system.

"That so?"

She traced his lips and then he sucked her fingers into his mouth. She leaned in close. "Get them wet."

He groaned and she caught her lip between her teeth. Which was hot enough to watch until she flicked her fingertips over her nipples, which hardened under her touch.

One hand slid down her belly and up under her skirt. He couldn't see what she was doing there, but he knew. In his head, he knew her fingers played against her pussy, dipping inside and then back up to her clit.

Imagining it may have been as hot as watching it. And he liked to watch plenty well. The peekaboo nature of her hand, out of sight, and the fingers on her nipple made him so hard he ached.

"Are you wet?"

"Mmm hmm." She hummed, her head falling back, spilling that mass of dark curls all down her shoulders.

He surrounded her fingers on her nipple with his own, and then moved to the other nipple. He tugged the way he knew she liked. Knew she got hotter and wetter.

One of his hands followed the path she'd taken earlier, first suiting up because when she came he planned to get in her cunt as soon as possible. And then he slid up under that skirt and to her pussy. He traced circles around her gate as she worked her clit, slowly easing in and back out. Over and over until she came in a hot rush against his palm, her head dropping on his shoulder as he embraced her.

"Now then."

All her post-climax lethargy wisped away when he pressed

into her in one quick, hard thrust, filling her in a way that was familiar and yet exciting. She knew his shape and size and her body adjusted as it welcomed him.

But he wasn't content to let her set the pace. Instead, he kept controlling hands at her waist, holding tight, guiding her up and down at *his* speed.

Not that she had any complaints. There was something so incredibly hot about the way he did it, about the way he moved her exactly how he wanted. All that laid-back sexuality sort of exploded into something else. Something harder and more raw. And that worked too.

It really, really worked.

What worked even better was the way he walked his fingers over to her pussy and made her come twice more until she was nearly boneless, totally wet and sensitized. Then he began to thrust up as he pulled her down. Harder and harder, sending her breasts to bouncing and a flush working over her skin.

And then he came, her name a snarl, his teeth finding her shoulder, sinking in until she gasped. Not from pain.

"That's what I call sealing the deal." He kissed her chin, then her lips.

21

So starting November fourth I'm going to be in Hood River four days a week. I'll be back for supper club first thing Friday or late Thursday and I'll leave again Sunday night."

Daisy looked over from where she'd been hanging a new piece of art to replace the one she sold the day before. "Wow."

"I told you he asked me to be their personal chef while they worked on their new album."

"You did. And you said you were trying to figure out the catering gig thing too. What about that?"

Daisy didn't word it in an accusatory way at all.

"Local jobs are good. I earn plenty at them. But when I have to go to Seattle it costs me more in time and gas, travel, all that stuff. I've been looking over my numbers and for most of my jobs, like dinner parties and that sort of thing, I'm only barely making more than even. And with traffic and the ferry and all that, it eats up a lot of time. Plus, you know, I'm sort of sick of people like Kathy Bonebright."

"I can't even with that woman. Such a bitch."

"Yes, but your life now means you have to deal with people like her more often. And you soldier on. Because you love Levi."

Daisy blushed. "Honestly, with the exception of a few, mostly people have been nice. It's probably because they're afraid of Levi's mom and Jonah. Levi told me Jonah cut this woman who he overheard talking about me to her knees. Not literally of course, he's way too smooth to need to resort to that. He's got such a way about him. If you think Levi is an alpha male, you just need to spend a few minutes with Jonah Warner to know the true meaning of alpha male."

Jonah Warner was indeed one hunky alpha male. That Levi's older brother had Daisy's back made Mary happy.

"Anyway, so I spoke with those two folks who had approached me about being their personal chef. I'm going to be doing prepared meals for them. They'll come pick them up here on Saturdays. I'll make a week's worth in advance. I'm holding off on non-Bainbridge catering gigs for now. And trying to stick to weekends only."

"So do you foresee this personal chef thing as a long-term goal?"

"I don't know. I love making food. I love the supper club but I don't know if I'd want to do it every day like with a restaurant, you know? And I like catering, but there's not a huge margin of profit for me once I deal with staff and all that stuff. Being a personal chef would be interesting, but I don't know if I'd want it in the long term. But I'm trying it both ways. Down in Hood River with Damien and then up here with the pre-prepared meals. I have the time and the opportunity to try things out. I'm going to take that gift."

Daisy nodded. "All right, that totally makes sense."

"And while I'm not working for Damien, I'll be working on the cookbook."

Daisy's eyes lit. "So exciting!"

"We'll see. I want to do it either way. If my agent can't sell it, I may do some small print runs and sell it here at Tart and via mail order. I have no idea if it'll fly. People may not care a bit about my recipes. But I have the time so I'm going for it. When it's a little more defined I'm going to talk with Gillian about some marketing and logos and stuff."

Gillian was an amazing graphic designer. She'd done the branding for Tart and Mary loved it. She'd done some stuff for Luxe when Mary had run the truck so it was natural she'd go back for the cookbook.

"And this will give you an idea if this thing with Damien can work. I mean if you're down there more. Living with Levi is a new challenge. I mean it's good, don't get me wrong, but seeing him every day is different now that we're living in the same place."

"I get the feeling being around a band while they record an album is stressful. So I'm trying to remember that part. It's exciting, but I'm scared. What if I'm not enough?"

Daisy came over, taking Mary's hands. "You're everything.

The more I'm around Damien, the more I like him. The more I can see he's all about you. Give it a chance. I like how you're using this as a way to explore lots of new avenues in your life. You're smart. You're talented. You're strong. You're beautiful, and of course he digs you. How could anyone look at you and not see what an incredible catch you are?"

"Because he's got access to everything. He's got money. He's got women who literally throw themselves at him. I'm bitchy and peculiar and I'm not willing to give up my whole life to be with him, and so many would."

"He could have had those women but he wants *you*. Don't underestimate yourself. My god. Baby, you're spectacular. Not just to look at, but everything about you. He doesn't want any of that other stuff. He's all about you. Accept that."

That was it really. She needed to really accept it. She was deep in super-duper like with him. She thought about him all the time. He'd never done anything to her but be kind and giving. She had to believe it.

"I'm trying. It's odd, thinking about being away half the week. I'm going to miss this."

Daisy hugged her. "We've all spent time with our dudes, falling in love and all that jazz. It's your turn. And that's good too. I'll still see you three days a week. And that's pretty damned good."

She arrived two days early and set about her work. Damien was busy enough preparing for recording that he didn't have too much time to obsess over her being there in his kitchen. But it made him unbelievably fucking happy every time he came into the house and took a deep breath.

Her cooking smelled so ridiculously good. Garlic and onion, savory and sweet, whatever she made filled the air and made his stomach growl. He'd cruise through, she'd hand him something to taste and he'd oblige.

It was so damned good. Not just the food, but the way it made him feel to have this with her. To know he'd see her every single week. Days of every single week.

He usually went into recording with a lot of stress, but this time was different. That first day when he cruised in to the barn at eleven, he was relaxed from a nearly two-hour-long sex fest with his woman. He'd left her rumpled and sleepy in his bed. He knew her scent would be on his sheets like it was on his hands.

"Someone got some this morning." Paddy looked up from his spot on the floor. He'd been placing his pedals in his own way. His guitar was on his lap as he tested the sound.

"I don't kiss and tell." He pulled his hair back and into a ponytail before wrapping several drumsticks.

Ezra was doing double duty in the booth and would also be doing backup guitar on the tracks. He had a phone to his ear even as he spoke to their producer and sound tech while they fiddled around with the board.

Vaughan strolled in, tipping his chin. "Where's the food? I really only came for that."

"She'll be up in two hours but she wanted me to remind you all there are snacks in the kitchen. She even made juice and withheld her frown when she saw how many sodas I've already had today." Damien grinned as he tested his sound through his headphones.

"You need to lock that shit in and marry her. Otherwise it's back to Doritos and stuff."

"Don't say that around her. She's nervous enough. You go talking marriage and you'll scare her away."

"Don't fuck it up like I did." Vaughan tuned his bass.

"Let's get this show on the road, losers." Paddy stood, ready to go.

"Let's make a record."

She came in quietly through the door to the kitchen. She didn't want to interrupt their work. More than that, she was in her own head space from cooking.

She loved his kitchen so much. It was a total joy to work in that space. It was large and bright, there was more than enough counterspace, double ovens, convection oven, six-burner stove, separate grill.

It was like Disneyland in there.

Smiling, she set up their lunch. Today she was starting them off with a taco bar of sorts. Spiced and marinated tofu and veggies for Paddy; shrimp, whitefish and steak for the others with a variety of toppings.

For dessert she'd made a quick and easy strawberry kiwi granita. Not high in sugar, but would give them something sweet and full of energy for the afternoon.

Once she set up she left as quietly as she'd come in. She'd set up on a schedule and they'd smell it. If they wanted her to break in and tell them, Damien would let her know. She'd come back in an hour to clean up.

The freedom of this new schedule was pretty awesome, she had to admit. She had plans to work on a curry recipe that afternoon. She'd been fiddling with it for the last few days and was very close to being finished.

Sharon had asked her to come up to the main house anytime she wanted. And she would, but for the next few days it would be nice to just settle in to this new routine.

And she couldn't deny how wonderful it had been to reunite with Damien. He'd been in New York on some publicity stuff. Originally it was supposed to be just Paddy but their manager had talked them all into going.

But he'd sent her texts and pictures and had called. It hadn't been too different from when he was in Hood River and she'd been in Bainbridge, but he'd shown her a hearty welcome when he'd picked her up two days before.

She smiled at the sight of Violet trotting toward her.

"Oh, wee baby piggy." She knelt and gave Violet love. "You're such an escape artist. Let's get you back home before the doggies see you."

Not that the dogs would hurt her. Most of them were afraid of the demon pig. But Loopy adored her and got so excited every time he saw her, and it got the other dogs all worked up too.

"We can hang out later. I'm going for a bike ride. I bet you'd fit in the basket."

Violet did a little dance and it made her laugh. "But for now, back home." Dutifully, Violet followed and went back into the enclosure she shared with Mr. Big, Ezra's other pig.

Big gave her a snorty hello before going back to his nap. Violet trotted over and lay herself against him.

She walked back to Damien's house, checking her e-mail. There were several from friends and one from an address she didn't recognize that had an attachment she couldn't open on her phone.

She had also brought her laptop though, so when she got back she fired it up to see what it was.

The name sounded familiar and she realized it was that shithead reporter who'd been taking pictures of Gillian, the one who'd been the cause of Gillian and Adrian nearly breaking up over a year before.

Lip curled, she opened the attachment. A picture of Damien and his brothers at some red carpet thing they'd attended in New York. She leaned closer as she broke into a sweat. Dread crawled through her gut as she blinked.

The woman on his arm was someone Mary recognized. An old fling of his who also happened to be a lingerie model. He leaned in very close to her, a laugh on his features. She held on to him tightly, her lips nearly on his.

There were others attached and she opened them, knowing on some level that she shouldn't. Knowing she was going to see something that would break her heart, and yet she couldn't seem to stop herself.

Another of her hugging him, her hand on his ass. On. His. Ass. Another with her head on his shoulder and a last one, clearly taken after the event, in the lobby of a hotel.

She stood up, sick. Sick at heart. Sick to her stomach. She was so cold. But not cold enough that she wasn't feeling the pain.

Never, ever in her whole life had she felt like this. Felt this horrible shame. This dread and humiliation. Her chest ached and she heard a sound, a rusty sort of laugh, and she realized she was the one who made it as her heart broke.

Why would he do this? How could he do this to her when she'd finally accepted that he wanted to be with her for real?

Damien was a stranger to her. How could the man she'd fallen in love with be so cruel? Surely he must have known he'd be photographed with this woman. And that she would see it. Or maybe he'd been so cocky that when she'd said she avoided celebrity news he thought he'd be safe.

She wanted to go confront him. Wanted to walk into that studio and throw her laptop in his face, and while he was on the ground clutching his perfect nose she wanted to kick him in the junk.

But the thought of his brothers knowing . . . and they must have since they were there. They all knew and no one stopped him. No one told her.

She slammed the laptop shut, grabbing it and heading upstairs.

He found it odd that she hadn't shown up, but they'd been really busy working on the first two songs so he hadn't really noticed until he'd gotten very hungry and realized it was two hours past dinner.

They'd wandered into the kitchen only to find the stuff from lunch still there. Which he found totally odd.

"Weird. She's not the type to blow this off."

"You said she was working on her cookbook. Maybe she forgot because she was super into it. There's still a huge amount of food from the snack she left earlier." Paddy grabbed two sandwiches and some fruit.

He frowned, but maybe.

But when she still hadn't shown up for the late meal, he knew something was wrong. It was nearly midnight. There's no way she would have just not shown up.

"Go check on her." Ezra tipped his chin.

"Yeah. Be back."

"Let's call it a night anyway. It's late and we had a good day. No one drew blood. Win." Paddy stood and stretched.

"Okay."

"Let us know if there's a problem," Vaughan called out as he left.

The house was quiet, though the lights were on in the kitchen. "Mary?" he called out.

Her laptop wasn't on the table though. Maybe she'd taken it upstairs to work and had fallen asleep.

He knew when he got upstairs that there was a problem. His heart thudded in his chest and he was terrified he'd find her passed out or hurt in some way. And when he got into his room he noted her things were gone. He'd given her space in his closet where bare hangers hung now. He rushed into the bathroom, and the counter where she'd left her stuff was empty; her hair stuff wasn't in the shower.

"Mary?" His earlier casual call had turned into a louder demand for her presence, laced with fear as he rushed from room to room. "Damn it, this isn't funny. Where are you?"

His car wasn't in the garage though. He checked his phone and saw a message from a number in town.

"This is Quickie Rental. We're calling to let you know your car is waiting here to be picked up. We close at ten tonight but we'll be open in the morning at six." They left a number.

"What the fuck?"

He ran to Ezra's, pounding on the door. His brother answered moments after.

"What? Is she all right?"

"She's gone. She's . . . I got a call from the rental car agency in town that my car is there. They left it at a little after one. Her stuff is gone. There's no note."

"Did you call her?"

Shit. "No. I'm sure there's an explanation." He dialed her up and was told by a not so cheerful recording that his number had been blocked.

"She blocked me. What the hell?"

"What did you do, Damien?"

"Nothing! I haven't done anything! I swear."

"Woman like Mary doesn't just leave without word and block your number for no reason. Call her house."

"Good idea." She still had a landline.

She'd blocked him on that too.

"Let's go up to Mom and Dad's place. Did you check your e-mail?"

"I looked but there was nothing from her. A shit-ton of other stuff, but there always is."

They got in Ezra's truck and headed to their parents house. His mother came to the door.

"What? Is everyone all right?" The sleep went away, going into crisis-mom mode at the sight of them.

He told her and she yanked him into the house. "What did you do to her? I just saw her this morning. She was fine. She made us enchilada casserole. Your dad and I ate it for dinner. I invited her to lunch tomorrow before she headed back home and she accepted."

"We were together. Right before I went up to the barn to work. Everything was fine. Better than fine." He paced, shoving a hand through his hair. "She brought the snacks and then lunch. She had to have left sometime after that."

"Maybe something happened to a family member?" Ezra's voice attempted to soothe.

"She would have said. She wouldn't have blocked my damned number. She thinks I did something. Someone told her something. Damn."

"Did you do something? Now's the time to come clean. You might be able to salvage it if you just come clean."

"Mom! No. I love her. I wouldn't do that to her. She should know better."

"She does. So that means whatever she heard or saw was pretty convincing. Call Adrian. He might know from his wife. They're close right?"

"It's after midnight. She's pregnant with a kid in school. I can't call him this late."

"All right, why don't you e-mail her and then you can check in tomorrow morning? There's nothing you can do right now."

"I can go to her house right now."

"No, you can't. You've been drinking with your brothers and you're tired out. I don't want you driving or flying up there in the dark. It's not safe."

"Mom, I can't not go. What if she's upset?"

"She's upset. Of course she is! But she's going to have to deal with it until it's daylight and you can get to her safely."

He left the house and Ezra came after him. "She's right, you know."

"I know she is. This is killing me, Ezra. She thinks I've done something and she's hurting and I can't stop it."

"I expect you're hurting too. Never been in love before and now you are, and now you know what it means." He paused. "Is there anything? Maybe something that could have been misinterpreted? Let's go in and check the Internet. You e-mail her and I'll search to see what's out there. All right?"

"I can't lose her. She's everything to me. My god. I've never felt so helpless. Not even when . . ." He looked away from his brother. "I'm sorry."

Ezra blew out a breath. "Don't be sorry. You helped me then. I'll help you now. Come on. If I can kick heroin, you can get your woman back."

22

She got just south of Tacoma and it hit her so hard she had to pull off the road. Up to that point she'd been so involved in just leaving, in getting the hell away from Sweet Hollow Ranch and out of Oregon, that she'd held the tears off.

In the parking lot of a suburban mini mall in front of a chain Italian restaurant she cried so hard she thought she might throw up.

Five hours ago she'd never been happier. She could envision this man and his family in her life. She was loved.

Had been loved.

Maybe.

Never.

She didn't know what to do. She sat there in her rental car

in the bleak, gray northwest November weather and stared for so long she wasn't sure how much time had passed.

Her first instinct had been to call in the cavalry. To tell Daisy about all this. And then she hesitated because the last thing she could endure at that moment was to have an I-told-you-so moment. Especially when it was deserved.

She'd walked out on a job. Even if he had been a cheating bastard, she'd taken money and didn't deliver her promised services. She'd send the money back when she got home.

First thing though, she blocked Damien from her cell. If he came back and found she'd gone, he might try to call, and if she heard his voice she'd lose it. No, it was better to ice him out so hard he got the point right away.

She didn't look at her screen because his picture was there with his number. Once that was done she took a deep breath and got back on the freeway.

Though she felt guilty for slinking back home without telling anyone, she needed to be alone for a while. She grabbed her camp chair and a blanket and headed out, up to her spot.

Cal had been on his way back from his parents' place when he noticed a strange car in Mary's driveway. She was in Oregon until the following day.

Suspicious, he pulled in behind the rental and got out. The car was empty so he went to the house, taking a walk around the outside and finding nothing out of the ordinary.

He knocked on her back door but no one answered. Alarm began to rise so he let himself in.

"Mary?"

Her bags were in the kitchen, tossed, nearly haphazardly, which was not like her at all. After a quick check, she wasn't in the house.

Her cell was off.

He called Jules, who said she hadn't heard from Mary since the day before. Same with Daisy.

He knew of one other place she might be, so he headed out the back door.

He found her in her thinking spot, burrowed in a blanket, staring off into space.

"Hey, I thought you were in Oregon?"

She turned to face him, startled. That's when he noted how red and puffy her eyes were. He moved quickly, kneeling before her.

"What is it?"

She went into his arms, shaking as she cried. And he was helpless. His sister was strong. Scrappy. When they were growing up he saw her cry maybe a handful of times. But when she did, it was really bad.

He loved her fiercely. She was always there when he needed her. Defended him, protected him, got on his case when he needed it. No one had ever loved him as unconditionally as his sister had. It broke him into little pieces to see her cry.

"Tell me. I'm freaking out here."

"Damien cheated on me."

He froze. "What? Baby, are you sure?" He hadn't liked Damien at first, but over the months as the guy had come around, he'd more than proven himself to Cal. The guy was so crazy-gone for Mary, it was written all over him.

"While he was in New York last week. With the lingerie model he was with before me. Her head was on his shoulder. In another picture her hand was on his ass! Oh, and the last one was them in a hotel lobby. After the event."

"What did he say about them?"

"Say? Like I needed to ask? I saw the situation with my own eyes. I packed my shit up, drove his car to town, rented a car and came back here. He's probably still working and hasn't noticed I'm gone yet."

He sighed, holding her and rocking just a little. If this was true, Damien Hurley was in for a healthy dose of fist meeting face. He just hoped for her sake that it wasn't true. Because he knew how much his sister loved the guy.

"Why don't we go back to your house?" He kissed her forehead. "You're cold. Let me make you some tea. I'll liberally dose it with whiskey. We'll get drunk and you can call the others."

"I can't face anyone, Cal. They were right. I told them they were wrong and they were right."

He held her back at arm's length. "No. I don't want you to even think that. Do you truly believe any of us wanted this to fail? Or that any of us would say I told you so? He loves you. If he doesn't, he deserves an Academy Award because I sure as hell believe he does."

He stood, pulling her to her feet. He held her with one arm while he managed to get her chair collapsed. "Come on."

She sighed but let him boss her around, which worried him. She wasn't one to allow such behavior.

Daisy stood on Mary's back porch and she moved quickly once she caught sight of the two of them.

"What? Oh my god, what is it?"

"She tells me Damien cheated on her."

He handed Mary over to Daisy as he got them all inside.

Daisy ushered Mary into the living room and onto the couch.

"Why are you here? God, Cal, when did you have the time to call everyone? I can't take all this nice. Please just go and leave me alone."

Daisy looked to Cal and then back to Mary. "Tough shit. I seem to remember you bursting into my house, yanking my blankets off, taking away my pint of Chunky Monkey and making me shower when Levi broke my heart."

"I'm opening your mail. I want to see these pictures myself." Cal dropped another kiss on the top of her head. "Water's on for tea."

Jules burst through the back door and it only made Mary cry harder.

"Shhh. Oh baby, honey, stop. Stop crying." Daisy hugged her tight, and Jules landed on the other side, hugging her as well.

"I need to be alone." Mary pulled her knees to her chest and buried her face. She hadn't thought she had any more tears left but there they were.

"Bullshit." Jules brushed the hair from her eyes.

Daisy pressed tissues into her hand and a shot glass into the other.

Gillian came through the back door moments later. "What is that prat on about?"

Mary laughed through her tears. "You all should go home. Gillian, you don't need any upset. Jules, you have to work tomorrow and, Daisy, you have Levi waiting for you. You all tried to tell me and I thought I knew better. This is what I get."

"This is most assuredly *not* what you get! He loves you. I know it. I don't know what the hell happened in New York but I know what I know. I know what I saw every time he looked at you." Gillian sat next to her on the couch, kissing her temple.

"What does he say?"

"Nothing. I left. I didn't . . . I couldn't. I just left. I saw enough. What can he say? I blocked his number from my cell."

Cal cleared his throat. "These are some pretty damning pictures. But . . . I think you should see what he says."

They all got up to look, clucking and arguing amongst themselves. Mary lay on the couch pulling the blanket up and over her head.

Gillian simply moved her over and pulled the blanket back. "Baby, remember the night that whole business with Adrian went down? You and Jules picked me up at the ferry? I cried and cried until I nearly threw up. You said to me that you knew Adrian loved me and you asked if we couldn't work it out. I'm asking you the same right now."

Jules snorted. "Why should she? Gillian, he cheated on her with a panty model. My god!"

"We don't know that. I'm saying, Juliet, I know from experience now that the paparazzi sometimes makes things look like they aren't. They catch a certain angle or a moment that is completely innocent but it doesn't look it. I know Damien. I spent a lot of time with him on the tour and I just—Mary loves him.

You know it. I know it. What's the harm in hearing his side of the story?"

"The pictures came from that dude who threw you under the bus."

Gillian exploded with a string of curses as she rose to her feet. Her accent got so thick Mary couldn't understand more than a word or two in every sentence. "You can't trust this man. Or his motives. Mary, he's an awful, petty, destructive little worm. He probably saw you that night at the club and wants to mess with you. I wouldn't put it past him. He's a terrible human being and I bet his mother cries herself to sleep every night."

There followed much drinking of heavy-handed whiskey with a little tea in it. Cal went to return her rental car. Jules made dinner and they all stared at her until she managed to eat a few bites. Mary forced Gillian to leave at ten to go home and rest. Daisy refused to go until Mary retreated into her bedroom. Cal had been very stubborn but he and Jules left with a promise that they'd return first thing in the morning.

Daisy got in bed with her. "You're going to get through this. I know it doesn't feel like it right now. I know your heart is broken and you're sadder than you've ever been. I love you. We all do, and we're here for you. No matter what happens, you will get through this."

"Go home. I want to be by myself to cry and go to sleep. Thank you for being here for me today; I mean that."

Daisy kissed her forehead. "All right. But I'm coming back tomorrow. You will call me if you need anything. Even just a shoulder while you cry. If you don't, I will be very mad at you. As you can tell, this is about me so don't hate America, Mary."

She managed a snort.

"I'll be back. I love you."

At least someone did.

She lay there in the dark, listening to the sound of the rain, feeling totally and utterly exhausted and empty.

23

D ude, we can hold off until this is all settled. Get your girl." Paddy handed him a cup of coffee.

"I'm going to call Adrian shortly. They're up, but he takes Miles to school early so I don't want to catch him until after that."

"Have you tried calling her from someone else's phone?"

He looked up. "Why didn't I think of that?"

"Because you're the pretty one." Paddy handed him his cell phone.

"I'm going to let you get away with that one as a gift." He dialed her number and she answered. Her voice was thick and hoarse, like she'd been crying and his stomach clenched.

"Curly, what is going on?"

She sucked in a breath and disconnected. He called back but it went straight to voice mail.

"She'd been crying. Sounded like shit." He opened his laptop and the mail client.

She hadn't replied to him. He poked around as he'd planned to last night. Most of it was crap. Until he opened one and noticed it was also cc'd to her e-mail address.

"Well, I think I might know why your lovely Mary did a runner on you." Paddy looked at the screen over his shoulder. "What the hell, Damien?"

Nausea rolled over him. "What do you mean, what the hell? Nothing happened! You assholes were there with me."

This reporter had sent these pictures to Mary precisely to fuck with her and make her think something had happened. After he dealt with this mess with Mary, he would be sure that reporter got payback. No one could be allowed to do this to her again.

"Well, you've got to explain. Get up there right now. We'll come with you. I was there that night. Nothing happened. Though the lobby picture?"

"She tripped going up the steps; I reached out to steady her."

"By putting her hand on your ass and her head on your shoulder?" Vaughan shook his head. "This angle does you no favors."

She had put her head on his shoulder. At the time it had felt like an affectionate gesture, but in an *old times* sort of way. He'd just stopped her from falling after all.

Looking at her face now in this photograph, in all the photographs and he saw she may have felt differently. And if he could see it, Mary could.

He scrubbed his hands over his face. "I don't even remember her hand on my ass. I swear!"

Vaughan moved him out of the way and enlarged the photo several times more, peering at it from several angles. "She may not actually be touching you here. I can't tell for sure. But while her hand is over your ass, I don't know if it's on your ass."

"Even so, what are you two doing in the lobby of the same hotel after the event? Can you not see how this would look to Mary?" Ezra was infuriatingly calm and reasonable.

"I saw her in the lobby for like a minute. Lots of people stay in that hotel. I saw her, paused long enough to say hey and then I went up to my room—alone—and called my girlfriend! She should know I'd never do this. And if I did it sure as hell wouldn't be on camera. What about my feelings?"

"Should she know? You know you have a reputation. You can see these pictures. You're with an ex in a situation that even to me looks hinky. What about you, Damien? This woman loves you or she wouldn't have run the way she did. Seems to me this isn't going to be the only time she sees this stuff. Though this reporter guy is totally trying to fuck you over." Ezra shrugged.

He called Adrian's place but it was Gillian who answered.

"*You!*"

"I take it you've spoken to Mary."

"And I've seen the pictures of you with a panty model whose hand is on your bum! What have you done? She loves you. She trusted you."

"Trusted? She ran away the minute trouble came up."

"Did you see those pictures? Ask yourself how you'd feel if the situation were reversed? I can tell you from my perspective,

I'm married to a man I know adores me and I see things sometimes that make me sick to my stomach. And you, old son, have some nerve to get cheeky with me. I'm on your side. You have no idea what it feels like to be on the other side of the country *knowing* what sort of buffet of temptation presents itself to your partner every moment they're away from you. To have to trust, despite appearances, despite the gossip news, despite perhaps even a many-year-long history of that exact behavior being accused of, with photographic evidence. If you were her, if she had been a hard-drinking, hard-living woman who had men in every city, and you had seen these photographs, how would you feel?"

He blew out a breath. A shaky breath, because she was so right and he was sick, all over again, imagining how upset Mary must have been right then.

"I didn't do anything wrong. I wouldn't. I love her. I want to tell her that but she blocked my number and now she's not answering her phone when I call from anyone else's phone."

"If it makes a difference, she loves you. I shouldn't be telling you any of this. But she's my friend and she has relentlessly supported me over the years I've known her and I want her to be happy. But If I were you, I'd come up. I know you're making a record right now—"

"That doesn't matter. That can wait. She's my priority. I'm coming up right now. And Gillian, thank you."

"Don't bollock this up and make me regret helping you."

"I promise."

He hung up and looked to his brothers. "I think I need Mom's help."

Mary looked at her phone and put it back on the nightstand. He sounded clueless. Maybe he had no idea she'd even seen those pictures so he thought his secret was still safe.

Damn him for making her miss him so much, even when she knew what he'd done.

She tried to go back to sleep and ended up going over and over it again in her head. Starting to doubt. Then getting down on herself for trying to talk herself away from the truth. She couldn't allow herself to become one of those women who ignored the truth to keep from admitting her man was a cheater.

But what if it was something innocent and she had jumped to conclusions?

"Damn it." She looked to her clock. An hour and a half had passed since his call.

She rolled from bed and headed into the shower. Avoiding looking at herself in the mirror, she made the water as hot as she could stand and stood in it until it started to go cold before dragging herself back out.

But when she walked out to her kitchen, Daisy stood at her counter, making coffee. "I know I'm not as good at this as you and Jules are. But living with Levi has improved my coffee-making skills. Jules sent along that bag there. Eat or I'm going to tell on you and she'll have to leave Tart to come over here and browbeat you until you do."

"You're not nice." Mary poked the bag open. Lemon tartlets, savory and sweet scones and cinnamon bread.

"I'm very nice."

Mary grunted and pulled out some cinnamon bread and let the scent of brewing coffee wake her up.

"You look like you've been hit by a truck."

"I drank too much last night. I've got a crying headache. My eyes are killing me. I *feel* like I've been hit by a truck."

"I brought *Terms of Endearment* over if you want to watch it."

"God, you really do love me." *Terms of Endearment* was her favorite weeper. But she'd cried enough. "I'm done crying."

"You're a liar. I heard you crying in the shower."

She sighed. "Okay, so I'm trying to be done crying."

The phone rang with a 206 area code showing. So it wasn't Damien. She picked it up.

"Mary Whaley?"

"I'm not interested in buying anything."

"No, this isn't a sales call. I just wanted to get your comment on the story circulating about your boyfriend Damien Hurley reigniting his old flame with Elisa Jovavich?"

She slammed the phone down.

"What?" Daisy looked shocked.

"It was a reporter asking for my comments about Damien and his old flame."

"Oh no, he did not! Next time that phone rings *I'm* going to answer it. Assholes! They're the ones who started this rift between you and Damien and they have the nerve to call you about it?"

"I'm losing my sense of humor."

Daisy looked at her, shock on her face, and then they both started to laugh. For Mary it was more of a hysteria-edged type of sound, but the situation was so absurd and she'd already cried herself into dehydration, so there was nothing left but a killing spree or crazy laughter. So she opted for the one that wouldn't result in prison time.

"All right. So here's a cup of coffee"—Daisy slid the mug her way—"and we can talk about next steps. What is it you want to do?"

"I want to have this coffee while I fantasize about shoving the panty model off a building."

Daisy grinned. "Okay, let's do that."

And that's when her mother showed up on her doorstep.

"I just got a phone call from some asshole reporter asking me about Damien cheating on you with a model. Mind telling me what is going on and where he is so I can kick his ass?"

Her mother barged in, slamming the door behind herself.

"Hey, Mom." Daisy kissed Jeanne's cheek.

"Morning, sweetie." She turned back to Mary and narrowed her gaze. "You've been crying. So it's true?"

Mary got herself some more coffee and a mug for her mother too. "I don't know. I mean, I thought so yesterday. I saw the pictures. They're pretty damning. I can't . . . . I don't know."

Her mother's anger softened and she frowned, tucking an errant curl behind Mary's ear. "I hate to see you cry. You barely even cried when you were an infant."

"I can't seem to stop. Even when I imagine driving a truck over that bitch."

Her mother hugged her. "You're my daughter, that's for sure. Do you need me to fly to New York to do it for you?"

Mary laughed and it was a little easier that time.

She sat Mary down at the table. "I'm going to make you some

breakfast and you're going to eat it and drink that coffee and tell me the whole story."

After she heard the story, she sat back down with a sigh and looked at the pictures.

"This boy sat at my dinner table and told me he loved you. I believed him. I don't like being lied to."

"Me either." Mary traced a pattern on the tabletop.

"You're sure he's lying? I mean, I'm looking here and it's pretty damning. But I hate being wrong about people. I have a very good sense for liars. I didn't get that from him."

She started to cry. "Damn it. I am so sick of crying! I hate him for turning me into this." She pounded the table with her fist. "I don't know. I'm afraid to believe. Afraid he's lying. Afraid he's telling the truth. Afraid if I believe him, I'm fooling myself."

"If something is worth having, my sweet Mary Elizabeth, it often comes with some struggle. You're a brave girl. A smart woman who loves with all her heart. Only you can decide if he's worth your heart. I'm here to listen. I'll protect you the best I can. I'll cut anyone who hurts you. But I can't protect your heart. I can't and it hurts me more than you'll know until the time you sit across a table from your little girl and she's being torn to shreds and you can't save her from it."

Her mother took her hands. "I love you so much. I wish I could make this better."

"You are. You did."

"He's here." Daisy came into the room.

Mary stood and her mother did too. "Damien? Now?"

"He and an older woman just parked."

"Shit, his mother? I'm not . . . I don't . . . ."

Her mother pushed her down into her chair. "I'll handle this."

There was a knock on the door.

"No. I'll deal with it."

"I'll get it." Daisy marched out.

Mary sighed and followed.

She pushed around Daisy and went to the door, opening it up. "Why are you here?"

He was so beautiful there she knew the tears would come. Blinked them back hard.

"Can I talk to you? Please."

"No. Please, just go. This is hard enough." Tears came and she hated them. Hated that weakness.

Sharon touched her arm. "I know what you think. Can we come in? Please, honey?"

"You need to take your boy out of here. He's done enough damage."

"You must be Mary's mom. I'm Sharon. I'm sure you want the kids to work this out."

Jeanne did a head whip and Mary knew they were in for trouble. She stepped between the two women.

But her mother was made of far sterner stuff and her baby was being threatened.

"Get the hell out of here. Take that skirt chaser with you."

In the background she heard Daisy curse under her breath.

"What did you just say?" Sharon's eyes narrowed.

"Mrs. Hurley, please go."

"My son didn't do anything with that girl. You know it. Deep down in your heart you know it. He loves you so much, Mary.

Please, just hear him out. I know you're hurting and embarrassed. But this reporter, he's got—"

"Mom, let me." Damien looked at her, really looked at her, so fucking beautiful she couldn't bear it. "Will you give me a few minutes? Please let me explain?" He held his hands out, empty. Hands that had touched her so many times, never with anything but kindness. With love.

The fingers pressed over her lips couldn't stop the sob from escaping.

"Mary. Please?"

Daisy touched her back and she turned. "What do you think I should do?"

"What do you want to do? When Levi came to me that day I . . . I swallowed my pride and I heard him out. And I'm with him. You love him. I think you should listen to what he has to say. If he's lying, you'll listen to your gut and you'll know. But if he's not." Daisy hugged her. "Do you want to risk walking away from this love you have? You already have doubts. I can see it. I can hear it. Let him explain and if he's full of shit, kick him in the dick and be done with it."

Her mother stepped out onto the porch and Sharon took another step closer.

"Christ."

"Go. I'll handle them. I'll turn the hose on them if they start to rumble."

"Only you could make me laugh today."

She turned to her mother. "Please don't make the neighbors call the cops." Mary kissed her mom's cheek.

She walked down to where Damien was. "Start talking."

He fell into step beside her as they walked. "Do you think they'll be all right together?" He looked back over his shoulder toward their mothers.

"Daisy is going to watch them."

"All right." He walked at her side, reaching out to take her hand. "Can I touch you?"

She needed to hear what he was going to say. And maybe she'd need her hand to punch him with. If he touched her, she'd lose that last little bit of her composure.

"No."

He breathed out. "I want to."

"Hm. I want lots of things. Tell me your story."

"I saw the pictures. You know who she is, obviously. But that's past tense."

"Didn't look past tense to me with her hand on your ass and her head on your shoulder. Oh, and that cozy little moment in the hotel after the event."

"Okay, so I get that. But that was . . . we were on the red carpet. *All* of us. Vaughan and Paddy were right there too. She had on these really high heels and nearly tripped. I stopped her from falling. That's all. She didn't touch my ass. It just looks that way from the angle."

She sighed.

"Mary, I love you. You. Not Elisa. If I wanted her, I could have been with her three years ago. Or a week ago in New York. There's one woman I want in my bed. One. You. Mary Whaley, curly-haired goddess of the kitchen. Dirty talking, horny, cock hungry, beautiful, beautiful woman. Mine."

He turned to her and she sucked in a breath. They stood

face-to-face in her yard. He was close enough that she could smell his cologne. That she could see the dark circles under his eyes, the curve of his bottom lip.

"After the event we all went out to dinner and then back to the hotel. She was in the lobby as I passed through. Right before I went straight upstairs to call you. Alone. I did not cheat on you. I would not cheat on you. If I wanted to be with another woman, I'd break up with you. I have flaws, but I'm not an asshole. I respect you and I am not so shallow that I think with my dick.

"People will try to hurt me through you. I'm sorry about that. I'm sorry if what I was before gives you reason to not trust me now. I've never been someone to look back with regret. But that anything I did before you, anything that makes you cry this way . . . " He shook his head, at a loss for words for long moments. "I'm so fucking sorry. It kills me to see you like this."

She kept looking at him. Panicked. Desperate. So in love she didn't know what to do, so she just froze.

"Say something."

She was so sad it broke his heart. He was the reason for it. He itched to touch her but he wasn't sure if he should. Wasn't sure if she was open to it.

"I don't know what to say." Her voice was hoarse. Anger and fear threaded it, and that need to touch her, to comfort, roared through him.

"Say you love me."

"I love you."

He took a step closer and she didn't move away.

"Say you believe me."

"I don't know."

He took a risk, reaching out to touch her hair. "You don't? Since the first time I met you have I lied to you? About anything? I wanted more from you first, remember? Then I took it at your pace. I respected that you didn't trust me. I proved myself to you, Mary. I respected what you wanted. I gave you what you needed and I have never swayed from that. I wanted to be your man and I've been your man. Sometimes I have to travel but I can take you with me if that's what it takes. I will keep you at my side every moment because I want you there. Tell me what it is you need and I'll give it to you."

He took her shoulders gently, pulling her closer. "I. Love. You. I want to make you happy. Let me. Don't let this bullshit rip us apart. My brothers were there; they'll talk to you. Hell, lots of people were there if you want to talk to them."

"We can't be together if I can't trust you. I can't be with you every minute of the day. I can't travel with you on every trip. I'm not your dick's babysitter. I don't want to be. I have a life. You're part of it, but you're not all of it. I want to live with the man I love, not through him or for him. How can you want that either? How can you want to have to be with me every second? I'd hate it if you didn't trust me."

"I want to be with you, goddamnit. I'll take you however I can get you."

"I would never do that to you. If we're together, I have to be able to know, in my bones, that you would not betray me. Don't you want to believe that about me?"

He thought about that picture of her and Daisy from that night they'd gone out. About the panic he'd felt at how beautiful she'd looked. How he'd known she'd have been hit on.

"You sent me pictures. Remember? From the night you went dancing."

She nodded.

"I looked at them and the first thing I thought was, *Holy shit, my woman is fucking hot*. And then I thought, *Holy shit, my woman is fucking hot! Men will know this. They will want her*. I panicked for a moment. It sucked. I never felt like that before."

"I don't recommend jealousy as an emotion."

He couldn't help it. She was so cranky when she said it, he had to smile. "I've felt it about record deals. I've felt it over cars. Houses. But I've never felt it over a woman until you. I never worried about losing a woman. Until you. You are it for me. Please believe me."

Since the first moment he'd laid eyes on her he'd considered her strong. But he had felled her. He could see it. Had heard it in her voice. He'd made her vulnerable and that had sent her reeling.

Pride warred with fear. Oh, his Mary, she was self-assured. As self-assured as he was in so many ways, which is why they fit so well. But love was different. He hadn't known it either.

"Love makes you strong." He leaned in, brushing a kiss against her temple, breathing her in. His panic at losing her began to edge back so his hands had stopped shaking. "But it makes you weak too. Not in the way you think when you're not in it, of course. But you know what I mean. Now you do, am I right? Because you make me weak. In the knees. You make my heart beat faster. You make my head hurt with the very idea of having to leave here today without you."

She drew in a shaky breath and then reached out, hooking a finger through his belt loop and holding on.

"From now on, when you have a fear, or a question, even if things *look* really bad, please let me explain." He hugged her to his body, slowly, to give her a chance to back away—and he'd never done anything harder. She sighed, going soft in his arms and their connection, which had gone thin and pale, snapped back into place.

"No more pictures with hot panty models."

"I didn't take them on purpose."

She growled.

"You want me to let her fall next time?"

"Yes! Did you not see her facial expression? That was way more than 'thanks for helping me.' God!"

He hugged tighter before she got wound up again. "Ezra said the same thing."

"Hm."

"I'm sorry I hurt you. No matter how inadvertent. I never wanted my job to hurt you this way." Tears crept into his voice and she hugged him tighter right back.

"I'm sorry I hurt you too."

"Damn, how'd I get so lucky?"

"I don't know."

He snorted, pivoting to tuck her against his side, where she fit perfectly and always had. Always would.

Their mothers had some intense back-and-forth going on. Daisy stood on the porch watching both them and Mary and Damien. She blew Mary a kiss.

"You think they'll be all right?"

"Sharon and Jeanne?"

"Yeah. They're both pretty much the same woman. Protecting her child."

"No one is bloody. That's a good sign."

"Will you come back to Hood River with me?"

"I have supper club tomorrow night. I'm sorry I left the job. I've never done that before."

He laughed. "Leave it to you to be that responsible."

"But it's not responsible! I'm mortified."

"You're forgiven. Just say you'll be back on Monday."

"I will."

"Say I can stay with you until Monday. Now that I'm here, I don't want to go again."

"You can stay with me until Monday. But you need to fly your mom back."

"Shit. Yes, I do."

"Come inside. I'll make lunch for everyone. You can take her back and return tomorrow."

"I'll come inside and eat your lunch, and then I'll take her back and return tonight. I want to be with you. I've been insane without you. I couldn't sleep. I couldn't eat. I want to be at your side."

24

Mary moved around her kitchen, stirring, tasting, adjusting. The scent of lunch rose and it made her happy. Happy to be making this food for her family. Happy to watch Sharon and Jeanne, who'd nearly come to blows, laughing together at her table.

Happy to see Cal, one arm around Jules's shoulder as he talked to Damien. Smiling.

Gillian, one hand on her belly, the other being held by Adrian, listened to some story Miles was telling. Love written all over her features.

This was her life.

"You look a hell of a lot better than you did about twenty-four hours ago."

She turned to Daisy, who grinned at her. "I feel a hell of a lot better than I did about twenty-four hours ago." She blew out a breath. "I hope to never feel that way again."

Daisy looked past her to where Levi sat, chilling with Gideon. "I know what you're feeling right now. Levi and I fight because he's insufferably bossy at times and if I don't push back, he'd steamroll right over my life. But since the time he and I broke up, those fights have been doable. We've been able to manage. You and Damien will fight again. He's all chill and you are most definitely not a chill sort of lady. But things will be different now, because the panic that nearly drowned you? You survived it. You went with the current and at the end, he was the shoreline and all you had to do was put your foot down and realize you could stand."

Mary cocked her head. "Holy tamale. Do you have to be good at everything? Jeez. You're a poet too?"

Daisy laughed and their men looked over to them both. Damien's gaze moved over her head to toe and she smiled his way.

She ladled up soup and Daisy put the croutons on top as Mary put the sandwiches on the side.

"You made my favorite." Damien spooned up some soup, blowing on it.

She shrugged. "Not a big deal. I told you it's easy to make."

He took her hand and kissed her fingertips. "You made my favorite because you know it'd make me happy. Thank you."

Six hours later he'd flown back home. Delivered his mother, who talked of little else but Sharon Whaley, back to her place, reassured his brothers that things were okay and he'd be back to start recording again on Monday. With Mary.

He'd grabbed some clothes, his toothbrush, his music and notepads and had flown back to her. Always to her.

He used his key to unlock the door, only to pause when he entered the house and noted the candles everywhere. Music played, Frank Ocean.

And then he turned the corner to her room and she sat on her bed, naked. Her hair, unbound, gleamed against the pale cream of her skin. She had a penchant for incense, he'd discovered some time back. He'd come to associate it with her.

"Wow."

She smiled. "You should be naked so I can say wow too."

He obliged as quickly as possible without injuring himself. The music changed.

"Who knew you'd have a sexy-times slow-jam mix?"

She got to her knees and met him as he moved to the bed. Skin to skin, the breath seemed to leave him, like he'd been hit in the gut. The glory of her, of him and her, that Mary-and-Damien thing filled him.

"I made it while you were gone. It's a Damien sexy-times mix. This is Robin Thicke. Every time I hear this song I think about you." She pushed him back to the mattress and scrambled on top. "Because I would be lost without you. I *was* lost without you."

She kissed him. Slowly. It started sweetly but didn't stay there for long. Her mouth cruised over his cheeks, his closed eyelids, over the ridge of his brow and the sensitive skin of his temples. She didn't just kiss him; she paid homage to him.

Tears pricked his eyes. He'd held them back. Needing to keep a straight head to get through the thing that had pushed them apart. But the fear of losing her, of losing this, choked him.

She pulled back, cradling his face. "Don't cry. I'm sorry I doubted you. I'm sorry I ran away. I just . . . I was humiliated. You made me feel so beautiful and special and then suddenly it felt like a lie and it was *unbearable* to think you didn't believe it."

The tears fell and she kissed them away. "I couldn't stop thinking about you being upset. Being so far away and not knowing what it was. Not being able to help. And then when I saw you today? My beautiful, strong-willed woman with shadows in her gaze, her bottom lip wobbling. And I was the reason. I was fucking petrified that I was going to lose you."

"You brought your mother. If you'd have brought Ezra or Paddy, I might have resisted. But you brought your mother."

She bent again, raining kisses over his face. His neck. The hollow of his throat. Over his heart. Tracing his tattoos. Her tongue flicking over his nipples, teeth scoring as her nails skidded over his sides, sending shivers through him.

She took his hand and kissed it. The heart of his palm. The heel. Each fingertip. Over his wrist and then up to the hollow at his elbow. Over his biceps.

Each touch was her way of telling him how she felt. That humbled him. Wrecked him to his foundations.

"Neko Case? I had to buy this CD three times because I wore it out." She loved music as much as he did, in her own way. "You're so fucking perfect."

He shifted, flipping her on her back, looming over her body.

"I wasn't done."

"I hope you never are, Curly. But for the time being, I need to kiss you." He took her mouth, devouring it, taking her taste into his body. Her nails in his shoulders. God, how he'd missed this, and it had only been a day.

Her hands cruised over his back. His weight rested against her. Perfect. Just enough to hold her down.

She wrapped her legs around his waist and held on. Never wanting to let go.

She made him cry. She'd spend the rest of her life making that up to him. Knowing he'd do the same.

He moved down, licking his way to her nipples, the pleasure of it slicing through her. He was strong, solid. There was no doubt.

"I want your cock in my mouth."

He'd been kissing his way to her pussy but she wanted him first.

He got to his knees, moving to kneel near her head. He slid the head of his cock over her nipples. She arched to get more. He slapped her pussy and sensation rippled outward as she gasped. He watched her face. And did it again.

She swallowed hard and then he tapped her mouth with the head of his cock. Dominant. Self-assured.

Totally hot.

"Suck me."

She opened up and he slid inside. She licked around the head and he pressed in deeper, retreating. And then he started again.

He played with her nipples until she was wet and on the verge of coming just from that. And all the while he fucked her mouth, slow and easy.

She took the weight of his balls in her hand, pressing her fingertips just behind them, sliding them back a little to brush against his asshole. He groaned and thrust a little harder.

"You're so fucking hot." His voice had gone low and hoarse.

She moaned against his cock and he moaned right back.

Lykke Li's "Get Some" came on and she smiled. He made her feel that way. She could be anything with him. Dirty. Wanton. He accepted her. Gloried in what they had in bed as well as out of it.

Another one of those slaps against her pussy and she spread her legs wider.

"Do you know what it does to me to see you do that? Open your thighs for me? Damn. Your cunt is hot and wet and I want more."

Two of his fingers slid up and into her as his thumb pressed over her clit. She sucked in air even as she kept licking and sucking his cock.

He made her come so hard, fingers fucking her, thumb playing against her clit. She managed to not drown in it, but it was a close thing and it made her want him to come just as hard.

She licked down the stalk of him, down over his balls and then back up. Over and over. She knew he was close, and the closer he got, the more she wanted him to come.

He pulled back with a groan. "Not yet. On your belly."

She rolled over. He kissed down her spine. Bit and nibbled the cheeks of her ass. Gooseflesh rolled through her as he kept going, kissing down the backs of her thighs to her knees.

He licked and laved the dimples at the back as she helplessly writhed to get more. He left a sweet ache, but she couldn't get relief.

He spread her thighs, his fingers tiptoeing up her legs until he got to her pussy. "Wet." He circled her clit with his fingertip and she pushed back.

"Fuck me."

"Oh, I will."

She may have sobbed, but he caught her clit between the pads of his fingers and squeezed. Not hard. But with enough pressure to send a wave of pleasure through her so intense a flush heated her from head to toe in seconds.

His cock brushed against the back of her thigh. Wet at the head. She licked her lips, remembering his taste.

And then he moved, brushing against her with the head of his cock, not quite entering her.

She groaned.

"You're hungry for it?"

"Yes!"

He chuckled, and it only made her hotter. Only made her want it more. He kneaded her ass with his free hand, and every once in a while he'd brush his fingertips over her asshole. Just a little.

"Ass up. Keep your head down."

She managed to get her knees beneath her to comply. She was open this way, she knew what she must have looked like all spread open and she didn't care. No, it wasn't that she didn't care. She *liked* it. Knew he was looking.

And he was inside, right as he flicked her clit over and over so she came right as he got in all the way.

She writhed back on a near shout as she came all around his cock. He had to close his eyes and count to fifty before he moved again.

He sucked in a breath like a drowning man, sliding his palms over every part of her skin he could reach. She was good and right. Strong. Gone was the woman on the verge of splintering apart that had nearly broken his heart earlier that day.

His Mary was back. The connection between them stronger and deeper, and need, as always with her, raced over his skin as he fucked her hard and deep.

"This feels so good I never want to leave."

She moaned her agreement, her fingers gripping the blankets for purchase.

"Think you've got another one in you, Mary Elizabeth?"

"Only if you come with me."

Which worked out, because he was close.

He bent around her, embracing her for long moments, soaking it in, the way she felt there, receiving him, open to him. Wanting more.

"No one has ever made me feel this. Ever. It's only you. Always you."

He brushed his fingertips over her thighs and found her cunt wet and inferno hot. He touched her clit gently, knowing she'd be sensitive. Slowly, he built her up as she squeezed his cock, getting closer and closer.

"I love you," she said softly, and it was too much. Everything.

"I love you too." He bit her shoulder and picked up his speed. Thrusting deep, so, so deep and hard as she rolled her hips to meet him. As she made a sound, a tortured gasp of a moan, and came.

Yes.

He followed, coming so hard he had to roll to the mattress even as aftershocks rolled through him or he'd have fallen off.

He held her. Held on tight and she snuggled back.

25

S he stood to the left of the stage and watched him. Watched her man play drums and sing, a huge grin on his face.

Raven was next to her, along with Erin and Daisy. "Kinda cool to know the drummer's girlfriend so she can get us backstage."

"Ha! Not like you're already besties with Erin, who I'm sure has plenty of backstage-pass connections."

"Seems so odd that it's been a year since we did this before." Gillian and Adrian had become parents to a beautiful baby girl they called Poppy. Poppy was already an honorary member of Delicious and Mary often shipped freshly made baby food from Sweet Hollow Ranch.

Where she'd been living for three months.

She'd given up her life in Bainbridge and had come to Oregon. It had been more and more difficult to manage the supper club once it had become more well-known that she was with Damien. Gawkers had tried to crash, especially if Damien had been there. And that was often because he liked to spend the weekends with her in Bainbridge.

So he'd offered her his home and his kitchen to do whatever she wanted with. Which, at that point, meant working on a second cookbook since the first had hit the bookstores and the bestseller lists.

Her life was not where she imagined it would be the August before as they stood on this same stage in the Columbia River Gorge, listening to a man she had only known a few months play his drums.

But it was better. Full of love and laughter. A new family to go with the one she already had. The Hurleys, who loved her like their own.

Sweet Hollow Ranch's new CD, *Revolutionary*, had come out three weeks before and was enjoying the success it deserved. For the next three months she'd go on tour with them, being at his side as they went from city to city.

Eating the best the country had to offer. She already had the kernel of an idea for the new cookbook. Regional recipes she'd create as they traveled. And then they'd head to South America and Australia.

Daisy squeezed her hand. Levi stood behind her friend, his arms around her. She wore the engagement ring he'd given her over the holidays and of course Mary would do the food for the wedding. And Jules would do the cake. Because that's what Delicious did.

They took a pause and Damien turned her way with a huge smile before speaking to the audience.

"Thank you all for coming out here tonight. A year ago this month we were here opening up for Adrian Brown. He and his family are here tonight and he's graciously agreed to come out and do a song with us."

Adrian came out on stage. The crowd went wild and Mary just kept smiling. Gillian had left the baby back in the trailer with Miles, who guarded his baby sister like a lion.

"Look at our men, Mary. You and I have rock stars in our beds. Who'd have ever thought?"

"Without you and Adrian I'd never have met him. So thanks for finding your rock star and marrying him so I could find one of my own."

Damien drummed a little to get everyone's attention. "So *Revolutionary* is a record about personal change. Revolution in your life and heart that changes you to the bone. During the time we wrote and recorded, I had my own revolution. Her name is Mary, and I would very much like it if she'd agree to marry me."

She wasn't the only one who gasped. All around her, her friends sucked in surprised breaths and then laughed.

"What do you say, Curly? Will you marry me?" He got out from behind the drums and moved in her direction, pulling her out on stage and then getting to one knee, pulling a ring box from his pocket.

"Holy cow. You're so sneaky! What if I said no?"

"But you won't. I've got you hooked. Part of my plan, you

see. First taste is free and then you're mine forever. So what do you say? Huh? Be my missus. Have my babies. Protect us all from demon pigs and crappy road food."

Tears came in a way only he seemed to be able to evoke. She nodded. "I guess I'd better."

He slid the ring on her finger and stood, pulling her into an embrace as the entire Gorge cheered them on.

"I guess I should tell you now that the thing I've kept bandaged for the last week that you thought was from my doctor's visit is really a tattoo. I'll show it to you later. In private."

It was on her hip. His initials, curled with hers in the shape of a four-leaf clover. Erin's brother Brody had done it when she'd gone to visit Seattle the week before.

"Hot damn. I sure do love you."

"I love you too. Now go play me some music and let those girls out there know whose bed you sleep in every night."

He kissed her hard and fast and thrilled her. As he always did.